THE AUTHOR

Angela Thirkell was born in London in 1890. She was a member of a distinguished family – her father, J.W. Mackail, was to become Professor of Poetry at Oxford, her grandfather was the artist Edward Burne-Jones, and her cousins included Stanley Baldwin and Rudyard Kipling. J. M. Barrie was her godfather.

In 1911, against the wishes of her parents, she married James Campbell McInnes, a singer. The marriage was to end in divorce in 1917. By then Angela had had two sons, Graham McInnes and Colin MacInnes (both of whose works are published by The Hogarth Press).

Her second marriage, in 1918, was to George Thirkell, an Australian. Early in 1920 they embarked for Australia on a troop ship, an experience which Angela was to describe in her pseudonymous novel *Trooper to the Southern Cross* (1934). They settled in Melbourne, but this marriage too was not a happy one. Angela desperately missed England, to which she return-ed in 1929 with her third son, Lance.

By this time she had written several magazine articles, and her first book, *Three Houses*, a memoir of her childhood, was published in 1931, with modest success. It was followed in 1933 by two novels, *Ankle Deep* and *High Rising*, and by a further three in 1934. Such a prolific output could scarcely be maintained, but for the rest of her life Angela Thirkell was to produce at least one novel a year, many of them set in Trollope's imaginary county of Barsetshire. They were to win her a devoted worldwide following and a reputation as the supreme exponent of English high comedy, in the tradition of Jane Austen, Mrs Gaskell and, of course, Trollope.

Angela Thirkell died in 1960. She wrote thirty novels in all, a number of which are to be reissued by The Hogarth Press.

SUMMER HALF

Angela Thirkell

New Foreword by
Arthur Marshall

THE HOGARTH PRESS
LONDON

It seems to me extremely improbable that
any such school, masters, or boys
could ever have existed

Published in 1988 by
The Hogarth Press
30 Bedford Square, London WC1B 3RP

First published by Hamish Hamilton 1937
Copyright © Angela Thirkell 1937
Introduction copyright © Arthur Marshall 1988

A CIP catalogue record for this book
is available from the British Library

ISBN 0 7012 0814 7

Printed in Great Britain by
Cox & Wyman Ltd
Reading, Berkshire

INTRODUCTION

Accustomed as many of us have been from childhood to singing hymns in church and school chapel without paying much attention to their words or the messages they contain, the well-worn Number 573 in *Hymns Ancient and Modern* has usually slipped by unexamined.

It repays study. It is that rather jolly one (jolly for some, that is) which begins strongly with 'All things bright and beautiful' and goes on to praise God in a general and comprehensive way for His creation before detailing various attractive individual items – birds, flowers, the sun, ripe fruits, trees, etc. etc. All is indeed as bright and beautiful as one could wish for, until a different note is struck in verse 3:

> The rich man in his castle,
> The poor man at his gate,
> God made them, high or lowly
> And order'd their estate.

Was there ever a clearer message? Resignation to one's lot, however unattractive, was expected in the face of the Divine Will. No use struggling. Did the knowledge that the class system was apparently invented by God help the impoverished to grin and bear it? I dare say. A century ago people grinned and bore more readily than they do now.

The authoress of the hymn is given as 'Mrs Alexander'. This distinguished lady, who also wrote 'There is a Green Hill Far Away' and 'Once in Royal David's City' was the wife of the Bishop of Armagh. Hers was the day when many of the clergy were fairly affluent youngest sons living in prosperous circumstances and a huge rectory, with servants galore and a minimal number of duties to perform. There was a good bit of hunting and shooting thrown in and rectors were on easy terms with the local bigwigs. Large, God-fearing congregations filled the churches.

The hymn is listed in the 'For The Young' section, and in the mind's eye one can see among the children in church a small girl singing away vigorously at Number 573 and, perhaps, old for her years, nodding sagely in agreement with its sentiments. She is Angela Mackail, daughter of Professor J.W. Mackail, O.M., and grand-daughter of Sir Edward Burne-Jones, the painter. Stanley Baldwin and Rudyard Kipling are her cousins. She is being reared in very comfortable circumstances and among persons of considerable distinction, and in due course she will become famous as the successful novelist Angela Thirkell. Furthermore, and despite her vast sales, literary critics will acclaim her – a rare achievement.

We do not have to go far in her novels to find either a rich man or a castle. *Summer Half*, with its school and manor house, is set in Barsetshire, a county which we shall meet again, and which the novelist has provided with pleasingly improbable villages – Winter Overcotes, Little Misfit, Stopingum. The local castle is Pomfret Towers, lovingly described in the 1938 novel of the same name. Huge and cold, the Towers began life as a Norman fortress, got knocked about in the Wars of the Roses and, later, by Cromwell, until an early Earl found rich seams of coal nearby and the building was handsomely restored. The rich, present occupant is the seventh Earl of Pomfret, an enemy of progress and famous for his rudeness (most fictional nobility is eccentric in one way or another). Though there must have been in the 1930s plenty of poor men at the Earl's gate and obsequious women to pop out and bob as the nobs drove in, it is with the gentry that we are mainly concerned. A social weekend of young and old, for example, is arranged to take place 'before the hunting is over'. Why? One's own inadequacies find an echo: 'You've no idea how awful it is, knowing nothing about country life,' moans one of the guests, and Mrs Thirkell assumes, rashly perhaps, that her readers are fully conversant with such matters. Never mind. In her books nothing jars, her humour is irresistible, the jokes are plentiful and hilarious and the reading is easy. I mean no discredit to the authoress when I say that hers were the type of book which, in the days when Boots and other lending libraries flourished, librarians would hand out when requested 'something light'. After all, Wodehouse is the lightest of the light.

There is virtually no servant problem in the novels. On the contrary, maids, both the parlour and the house kind, pullulate. They are addressed by their surnames and appear to have little life of their own. In the larger houses, footmen are fairly thick on the ground, marshalled by a haughty butler who, though not noticeably well educated, can throw off a sentence such as: 'I mentioned to Mr Julian that luncheon was a desiderata, madam,' though Wodehouse's Keggs would have said, more accurately, 'desideratum'. In every room there is a bell, either an oldfangled one (if 'newfangled' why not the opposite?) which possesses wires and requires to be pulled, or an electric one that just needs to be pushed. Both are in constant use to summon domestic help. If they are not immediately answered the delay has to be queried and explained, possible staff adjustments being subsequently arranged by the housekeeper.

The young people, mostly in their early twenties or younger, are a whole world away from their grandchildren of today. They say 'top hole' and 'by Jove' and 'gad!' and 'topping'. They chide a girl friend with 'You great silly!' They are content with small pleasures – a stroll to the stables, a picnic, an impromptu dance with the Axminster rolled back and an HMV portable, and one of those party games where somebody goes out of the room and returns after twenty minutes pretending to be some historical character. Although, like most children of any age, they consider their parents to be effete and half mad, they respect them. Whatever sexual feelings they may have for each other are neither discussed nor revealed to us by the writer. There is plenty of romantic love and moonstruck yearning for the often unattainable, but stronger passions are treated with the delicate touch and sympathetic understanding that one happily finds in other writers of the time such as Ian Hay, E.M. Delafield, Stella Gibbons.

It is unusual, for obvious reasons, for an authoress to write a story set in a boys' public school, and in a brief disclaimer Mrs Thirkell was quick to cover herself against charges of inaccuracy in *Summer Half*:

> It seems to me extremely improbable
> that any such school, masters, or boys
> could ever have existed.

She is much too clever and careful a writer to make many mistakes, and those that exist are fairly trivial – in public schools the keeping of 'pets' is very doubtful, no headmaster would wait until a week before term to engage a classics master, the concept of Matron kissing leavers goodbye is ludicrous, and a Sports Day at the end of June with a sack race and the Dean dishing out prizes is preparatory school stuff, not public.

The school in question is Southbridge, where 400 boys aged 14 to 18 are being educated, and the word 'Half' in the title requires some explanation. It is the word used at Eton and a few other distinguished schools for the more ordinary 'term'. Presumably the school year was originally, for whatever reason (possibly the appalling travel difficulties centuries ago), arranged in two halves, but when it was divided into three, some schools retained the original 'half'. It is not uncharacteristic of Angela Thirkell to side in the matter with Eton.

She gets resoundingly right the full horror of the average school song. It has been the fate of most public schools to find themselves saddled for years, centuries even, with a loyal and exaggeratedly eulogistic song, often in indifferent Latin, and composed by old boys of the school and so traditional that nobody dares to change it for something more acceptable. Of the ones in English, Clifton Collegers sang: 'The men who tanned the hide of us/They shall not lose their pride of us,' while girls from a rather less renowned establishment let fly with:

> Of Bedford High School's fame we hear,
> Of Cheltenham School, a big 'un,
> But what of them? Today we cheer
> The Girls' High School of Wigan

And who can forget the opening line of the Sherborne Girls' School song, 'When Mrs Digby first conceived'? The second line sets worried minds at rest: 'The idea to found a school.'

In the case of Southbridge, Mrs Thirkell refers to 'the revolting *Carmen Southbridgiense*, written in 1854 by the headmaster the Rev. J.J. Damper (better known by his little volume of *Perambulations in Palestine*, now deservedly out of print), and set to music by the school organist, who also taught piano, violin, composition, singing and anything parents asked for. The final lines,

> Alma Mater, Alma Mater
> None than thou wilt e'er be greater,

were justly condemned by the modern school for Latin pronunciation.'

Those readers with hideous memories of daily Latin lessons and of the charmless works of Messrs Hillard and Botting (Mr Hillard also disloyally teamed up with a Mr North), will find, rather surprisingly, a sympathetic voice in the person of the senior classics master, Mr Lorimer:

All classical masters write grammars and exercise a sort of moral blackmail till the school makes it a standard book. Twelve first-class schools use my grammar and unseens. It means there are between five and seven thousand boys per annum who loathe me, who wish I had never been born and who draw insulting pictures of me in the fly leaves of my books.

And how typical of schools is 'the Eleanor Cobbley Special Prize for Latin Verse', and a studious boy who 'disgraced his house by getting a Reading Prize given by the Chaplain.'

Splendid jokes and characters abound. There is a local headmistress, the impressive Miss Pettinger, 'with a voice that could reduce girls to tears when they had stained the honour of the school by not hanging their coats on the right pegs in the cloakroom. She also refuses to give swimming colours to Amber Dandridge (she had cheeked Miss Moore in the bookroom). There is a rather bolshie young master (and remember that in the 1930s it was quite acceptable among intellectuals to be a Communist), who 'takes in a nasty little weekly, all very well informed about What is being Kept From the Public.' There is a delightfully bouncy tomboy, Lydia, who 'had gathered from Shakespeare and other authorities that love was very peculiar and often made people quite potty.' There is the headmaster's beautiful but inane daughter, Rose, with whom many fall in love and for whom everything is either 'marvellous' or 'sickening'. And there is yet another majestic butler who gives weight to his Utterances by embellishing them with capital letters ('Shall I use My Own Discretion?')

Summer Half reminds one of happy and pleasurable pre- and post-war reading – *Before Lunch*, *The Brandons*, *High Rising* and many more. If I were asked to provide just one word with which to describe the novels of Angela Thirkell, I would supply the adjective 'wholesome'. In the field of fiction it is a word that is long since out of fashion, but none the worse for that.

Now read confidently on . . .

Arthur Marshall, Christow 1988

'Thanks awfully,' said Colin. 'Did he – I mean, did you – ?'

'He turned me down. I might have turned him down, but he got in first,' said the applicant, who appeared to be taking his failure in a pleasant spirit. 'I daresay I'll go on the films.'

Colin, watching him from the window as he got into a small car and drove away, suddenly envied people who had been turned down. At least they were not netted and put into a cage with hundreds of boys. It had been madness to think he could be a schoolmaster. Loathsome visions of novels on school life flitted before his eyes. He saw himself falling in love with the headmaster's wife, nourishing unwholesome passions for fair-haired youths, carrying on feuds, intrigues, vendettas with other masters, being despised because he hated cricket, being equally despised because he didn't know the names of birds, possibly being involved in a murder which he could never prove he hadn't committed, certainly marrying the matron. Just as he had made up his mind to escape, leaving word that he was suddenly taken ill, the headmaster's rather terrifying butler opened the door and said, 'Mr Birkett will be glad to see you in his study, sir.'

Of what followed Colin never had any very clear impression. He had a vague recollection of having talked for hours in a voice sometimes shrill with nerves, sometimes unaccountably so husky that Mr Birkett had to ask him to say whatever it was again. He felt that he had said far more about himself and his family than any decent fellow would ever wish to say. He had boasted of his dislike for cricket in a way that would justify his immediate rejection, and told his possible employer that he wouldn't care if he never saw a bird again. When asked, very courteously, if he was engaged to be married, or likely to be so, he had expressed a few ill-chosen views on women, suddenly seen three large photographs of what must obviously be Mr Birkett's wife and daughters, and wished he were dead. As through a veil he had heard Mr Birkett's voice say that the interview had been quite satisfactory, and that he would write to him within the next few days. He had then somehow shaken hands and got away.

The journey between the school and Colin's home was only twenty miles by road, but as Colin had no car of his own, he had to catch a train at Southbridge for Barchester, where he changed into the local line for Northbridge Halt. His father was a solicitor who managed a good deal of the cathedral business in Barchester. When Colin and his elder brother and sister, Robert and Kate, were little their parents had lived near the Close, in the upper storeys of the red brick house where the family business had been carried on for three generations. The firm of Keith and Keith throve, then another girl, Lydia, was born, and Mr Keith decided to move out of Barchester. A small property called Northbridge Manor, belonging to the cathedral, happened to come into the market and Mr Keith, who had early knowledge of this, was able to buy it at a reasonable figure. The house was a square red brick building, about a hundred and fifty years old, with well-proportioned rooms. The rambling servants' quarters had been improved and modernized by Mr Keith, and the garden, which was only separated by a water-meadow from the river, was his particular pride. Here he settled very comfortably, partly as a business man, going in daily to his office, partly as a mild form of country squire. His eldest son, Robert, was a junior partner in the family firm of solicitors, and his younger son Colin, had only left Oxford the previous summer. As Colin had no particular wish for any one profession, beyond a very ignorant desire to be a publisher, his father had suggested that he should read law, with a view to having a barrister in the family. He had been sent abroad

9

for a few months to improve his French and German, and had come home in the early spring and begun reading at home, till such time as his father told him what to do next.

Colin found the law a fascinating form of literature, and rather enjoyed the drudgery till his conscience very unnecessarily rose and pricked him, telling him that young men ought to be up and doing, and not live on their parents. If Colin had been reasonable, he would have mentioned this matter to his father, with whom he was on perfectly good and easy terms; his father would have pointed out that one must live on something while reading law, and why not on one's natural helpers and supporters, and he might have settled down again. But Colin, having as was suitable to his age and education a belief in ideals and unconsidered action which it would take him several years to bring into any kind of relation with life, concealed his trouble from his parents and wrote to friends and ex-tutors at Oxford. Through one of these he heard of a position to be had at Southbridge School under an excellent new headmaster, Mr Birkett. He sent in his application, was weeded out from the rest, interviewed, and as we have seen selected, though his choice had not as yet been confirmed in writing.

Colin was the only passenger to get out at Northbridge Halt. As he walked along the lane that led from the station to the Manor, noting with pleasure some early primroses, he rehearsed to himself the interview he would have with his father. In well-chosen words he would explain that he felt his position as a parasite acutely, that a young man should be ashamed to take a small allowance from his parents as well as partaking of their excellent bed and board for long periods, that his father was ageing, that there were his sisters to consider, that having carefully weighed all these considerations he had decided to give up the law, take a position as a schoolmaster, renounce his allowance, and be on the whole the support of his parents' declining years. His father would then be deeply moved, though in a self-controlled way, the allowance would be withdrawn, Colin would take up his job as Junior Classical Master at Southbridge, and Mr Keith would be able to afford an occasional shrimp with his tea.

When Colin reached home, bursting with self-sacrifice, he found to his annoyance that his father was attending a dinner in Barchester, and would not be back till late, and that everyone else was out. Deprived of an immediate outlet for his noble scheme he had a rather sulky tea by himself, with leisure to continue his imaginary dialogue. But as the exhilaration produced by his interview with Mr Birkett and his walk through the spring lanes subsided, the common sense, of which he possessed a considerable though undeveloped quantity, began to perk up its head.

If he looked dispassionately at his excellent and altruistic plan, he had to admit two facts. The first was that his father, though ready to discuss other possibilities, would like him to be a barrister very much indeed. The family firm had done very well since Colin's great-grandfather founded it, but Mr Keith had a deep wish that one of his sons should go into what is still socially regarded as the higher branch of the law. Robert would make an excellent solicitor and liked the business, so Colin, who had plenty of brains, should be a barrister. It was improbable that he would oppose Colin's change of plan, for he was a reasonable and indulgent father, but he would be disappointed, and that he wouldn't show it would make Colin even more uncomfortable.

The other indisputable fact was that Colin knew his father to be almost a rich man. The business was doing so well that even if Mr Keith suddenly died, Robert could perfectly well carry on. His father would treat his suggestion of giving up his allowance as a piece of silliness, and even if Colin refused to take it his father would probably put it into a bank for him, or leave him something more in his will, or in some way thwart his aspirations. In fact, the more he thought of it the more he realized that the world wasn't properly arranged, and the more doubtful he felt whether anyone would sympathize with him. He went into the darkening garden to commune with nature and in the drive was nearly knocked down by his younger sister, Lydia, returning on her bicycle from the station. Lydia went to the Barchester High School by train every day. As she had to leave the house too early for her father to take her with him in the car, she usually bicycled to the station, left her bicycle with the station-master and picked it up on her way back. Being a Saturday there had been no school, but Lydia had been taking part in the last hockey match of the season. She was wearing the school uniform, supplied by the school without any particular reference to anyone's age or shape, namely a grey silk blouse, a blue gym tunic, and a blue blazer with brass buttons. Her hat was of blue felt with a grey hatband bearing the school symbol, a tree with three leaves and two pieces of fruit, though no one knew why. Everyone hoped that she had stopped growing.

'Hullo,' said Lydia, dismounting, 'any tea left?'

Colin said there was, in the library, though a bit cold by now, and was going to pursue solitude once more when the thought struck him that Lydia, regarded as an audience, was better than nothing, so he turned with her and went back into the house. Lydia threw her hat onto one chair, her satchel of books onto another, banged against the chair so that the satchel fell off, hit the library door with her body, and dropped herself heavily into a chair. While she drank tepid tea and ate a great deal of bread and butter and cake, Colin was able to consider the best approach to the momentous news he had to impart.

'I went over to Southbridge to-day,' said Colin.

'Miss Pettinger is an absolute beast,' said Lydia. 'She gave us a talk about what do you think to-day? Honour! Made us ten minutes late for the match.'

'I went to see the headmaster at the school,' said Colin.

'I should have thought you'd never want to see a headmaster again,' said Lydia. 'I'll never want to see a headmistress, but men aren't quite so foul as women in those sort of ways.'

'Mr Birkett wasn't foul at all,' said Colin indignantly. 'In fact he was particularly decent to me. He –'

'Oh, Geraldine Birkett's father. She's in my form. She says apart from being a headmaster he isn't bad at all. She has special Latin with the Pettinger twice a week, poor mutt, but she says she can always make the Pettinger switch off onto Honour, or Nurse Cavell, or something. Her elder sister is engaged to a master in the school. She seemed to think it rather noble, but I said "Farewell, Romance", and so she had a feud with me for two days. Fancy getting engaged to an assistant master!'

This was getting less and less promising.

'I'm sorry you think assistant masters such a poor affair,' said Colin stiffly, 'as I'll probably be one myself this summer.'

If Colin wanted to astonish his young sister, he had succeeded. Lydia sat, obviously disbelieving but temporarily silenced, while Colin continued, 'I'm tired of being an expense to father, and I think it's high time I did something for myself. So I applied for a job at South-bridge, and I had an interview with the headmaster to-day, and I think it's all right. If it is, I'll start next term, next week that is.'

'I do think it's rotten of Pettinger to make our term

13

begin ten days before lots of the other schools,' said Lydia. 'I don't see why all schools shouldn't have the same Easter holidays. Pettinger and Mr Birkett ought to get together and do something about it. What are you going to teach?'

'Latin and Greek, and some English and history, and I expect a few other things.'

'Anyone can teach English,' said Lydia, 'even the Pettinger. I say, you couldn't help me with my Horace, could you? It was all right for Horace, he could put the words in any order he liked, but we have to get them sorted out, and even then they don't make sense. It's that one about the man who is just and tenacious of his proposition, you know the one I mean, but "man" is in the accusative in the very first line, and that isn't English.'

'Horace was not attempting to write English,' said Colin, even more stiffly.

'Oh, all right, if you can't, you can't,' said Lydia, 'but you'll have to polish up a bit if you are going to teach Mr Birkett's boys.'

So saying she rose, swept a teaspoon onto the floor, and left the room as majestically as a gym tunic will permit. Colin felt seriously snubbed and annoyed. An Ode of Horace, even if it started with an accusative, presented no insuperable difficulty to him, but it would now be impossible to make Lydia believe this. Lydia's views were simple, but unassailable. Being apparently incapable of connected thought, she saved herself a great deal of trouble by a kind of mental toss-up on any question that came under her notice. Black was then black, and she thought no more about it. To distract his thoughts from his disheartening sister Colin decided to have another shot at going for a walk alone, but the noise of the motor outside and his mother's voice in the hall told him that escape was, for the moment, impossible. His mother came in followed by the parlourmaid, who began to remove the used tea-things.

'I have just been to the office,' she said, handing a parcel to Colin, 'and your father asked me to bring you this. Just some tea, please, Palmer, nothing to eat. He said it would tell you exactly what you wanted about something. He has to dine in Barchester at the County Club, but he won't be late. Robert and Edith are dining here. Have you had a nice day, darling?'

Colin recognized the book as one which his father had mentioned to him as giving some very valuable information on Railway Law, but now out of print. Mr Keith must have gone to some pains to get it for him, and this was an uncomfortable feeling, just as he was proposing to desert the law.

'Quite nice,' he said. 'I went to Southbridge.'

'Did you, darling? How nice. Yes, Palmer, just put my tea here, by me, on the little table. What did you do there?'

'I rather want to talk to you about that, mother, I went –'

'Excuse me, madam,' said Palmer, 'but Mrs Crawley rang up to say would you and Mr Keith and Miss Kate dine at the Deanery on Tuesday next at eight.'

'Thanks, Palmer. Please write it down and put it on my writing-table so that I'll remember to speak to Mr Keith about it. Last time we dined at the Deanery was the day the water main burst and the Bishop's cellar was flooded.'

'Yes, madam,' said Palmer, with an intonation implying that though custom compelled her to wait till her employer had finished speaking, she knew perfectly well that Mrs Keith's last sentence was only addressed to Mr Colin, and therefore valueless.

'Well, darling, what did you do at Southbridge?' said Mrs Keith.

'I went to see the headmaster, and –'

'Now, don't tell me his name,' said Mrs Keith, holding the teapot in suspense over her cup. 'I know what it is, because the Dean is one of the Governors, and I remember his mentioning last time we dined there, which must have been more than a year ago, because it was that very night I was telling you about when the main burst, and we haven't dined there since, because once they asked us and once we asked them, and each time we were engaged, that he had just got a very good new man for the school, but what his name was I can't think. I had it just now, but it has gone,' said Mrs Keith reproachfully, as she finished pouring her tea.

'Birkett, mother. He seems a very good sort of fellow. I went to see him because I do really feel I ought to be working, mother.'

'So does your father,' said Mrs Keith. 'In fact he has some plan he wants to tell you about that he has been arranging. But you can read just as well here as you could at Southbridge. No one disturbs you in your own room.'

'I know, mother, but this is different. I shan't earn any money at the law for ages, so I'm going to give it up. I'm going to be a schoolmaster. It's practically settled that Mr Birkett will have me, and then I'll be independent and needn't take an allowance from father. I hope you won't mind.'

'You know I'm not a minder, darling. My Uncle Oswald – you can't remember him, because he died when you were little, he was the eldest son of that immense family my grandfather had, the eldest of the *first* family of course, and my father was the youngest of the third family – was headmaster of a very large mission school in Calcutta and became a bishop. Of course you aren't in orders,' said Mrs Keith, looking affectionately and abstractedly at her younger son, as if she expected to see his collar turning from back to front under her eyes.

'Well, so long as you don't mind, mother,' said Colin, relieved and yet disappointed by his mother's serene want of understanding, 'that's all right. I think I ought to go and do some work before dinner.'

He ran upstairs to his bedroom, tore open the parcel, lit his pipe and settled down to enjoy an enthralling account of two cases connected with the running powers of the now defunct London and Mid-Western Railway, which had been tried before Mr Justice Smith in 1847. He was so truly interested and absorbed that he did not look at his watch till ten minutes to eight, when he had to throw down his book and make a lightning change into his evening clothes. Downstairs he found his mother and his sister Kate.

'Robert and Edith are late,' said his mother. 'Palmer, we will wait for Mr and Mrs Robert. Kate, has Colin told you?'

'Told me what, mother? Did you know that there are only eleven of those wine-glasses with the stars? I can't think what has happened to the other.'

'I knew it was broken,' said Mrs Keith, assuming the air of a prophetess. 'That was the kitchen-maid that had the false teeth. She had no business at all to be washing the wine-glasses. About Southbridge. It seems that the new headmaster is delightful.'

'We might ask him to dinner, mother,' said Kate, whose true self was expressed in boundless hospitality and a care for the well-being of those about her. 'Is he married, Colin? Because it is always awkward if you ask a man and then find he has a wife.'

'I think so. I don't really quite know. I went –'

'I can easily find out at the Deanery,' said Kate, who did odd jobs of secretarial and library work for the Dean when his chaplain was busy or on holiday. 'The Dean is a Governor of the school. Mother, I hope you and father

17

will be able to dine at the Deanery on Tuesday. Mrs Crawley said she had telephoned and she is longing to see you again. Was it nice at Southbridge, Colin?'

'Not exactly nice, but very interesting. You see, I went –'

'Mr and Mrs Robert,' said Palmer.

If it had been a dinner-party, she would have announced Mr and Mrs Robert Keith, but as it was only family, she unbent to their level.

A great deal of family kissing took place. Lydia joined them in an elderly black velvet dress which she had forced her mother to buy against her better judgement, and they went in to dinner. Colin sat between Lydia and his sister-in-law for whom he had a not very interested affection. But this evening he felt sure that he would find in her a sympathetic listener, for would not his renunciation of the allowance put bread, as it were (though he secretly had to admit that it wasn't) into the mouths of her two children? But before he could begin on the subject, Lydia, magnanimously anxious for a reconciliation, had captured him.

'I say,' said she, 'I didn't mean to be a nuisance about that Horace.'

'You weren't. Shall I give you a hand with it after dinner?'

'Thanks awfully, Colin, but I've done it. It wasn't so bad after all. I liked that bit about "impavidum ferient ruinae". It reminded me of the time the plaster all fell off the kitchen ceiling and Palmer screamed so awfully. I do think that's what's so marvellous about Horace and that lot – I mean they really did know what they were talking about. Geraldine Birkett said she thought Horace was a bit over-rated, but you'd think anyone over-rated if you had to do them twice a week with Miss Pettinger. Geraldine gets the wrong angle on things, being with Pettinger as much as she is. It's all because she has to go in for a scholarship, but she has absolutely made up her mind not to get it, and it oughtn't to be difficult, because she never does any prep, only just because of Mr Birkett being a headmaster they expect Geraldine to be brainy, so she gets tortured by the Pettinger. We both think it's rotten, and when we leave school we're going to breed golden cockers together. Her mother has a lovely golden cocker called Sylvia. Did you see her?'

'No. I was really talking to Mr Birkett. He seemed to want me for the job.'

'I must say I'd sooner die than be a schoolmaster,' said Lydia. 'I say, Colin, you won't bring any Young Woodleys and things here in the holidays, will you? Geraldine says the boys are all ghastly, and the masters too.'

With the best will in the world Lydia's conversation was, Colin felt, almost more disheartening than he could bear. Profiting by a moment's pause in his young sister's flow of talk, he turned to Edith and inquired after the health of his nephew and niece. Edith said they were very well. Henry had fallen down and grazed his knee and had very much enjoyed the blood. Catherine, called after her Aunt Kate, had said 'Pussy' to the Dean that morning when out in her perambulator, having taken his Alsatian for a cat.

'But I'm always a bore about the children,' said Edith. 'I want to know about you. Are you getting on with the law? Robert is longing for the day when he can brief you. I suppose you are going up to read in London soon, and eat dinners.'

'Well,' said Colin, 'I went over to Southbridge to-day and saw the headmaster. I think –'

'I don't know him well, but I know his wife,' said Edith. 'She is charming. My brothers were there when Mr Birkett was headmaster of the preparatory school, and they adored him.'

'I liked him very much. We had quite a long talk and he said –'

'Then you can give me really good advice about sending Henry there. We were thinking of putting his name down, but schools do change so and one is never sure. What did you think of it?'

'Well, I didn't see much. I really went to see the head-master about an assistant master's job.'

'I hope he was helpful. Who was it for?'

'Well,' Colin began again, hesitatingly, but his sister-in-law stopped him.

'No, don't tell me,' she said. 'You know I hate prying and I didn't really mean to ask. Let's talk about yourself.'

As Edith's idea of talking about Colin was that she should talk about her husband and children, Colin did not get any further with his explanation. When Edith was not talking about her household, or Lydia giving her views on Latin literature, about which she confessed she was at present awfully keen, both ladies talked across him about hockey and dog-breeding, so he was glad when the meal ended and he was left alone in peace with Robert.

'I haven't seen you for ages,' said Robert, who was very fond of his younger brother and thought a good deal of him. 'You're looking very fit. How are you getting on?'

'Pretty well, thanks. I –'

'I wonder if you've looked at that book father got for you yet? It's a kind of business that isn't much in my line. We haven't had any railway business in the office since the Dean and Chapter opposed the railway coming here in our great-grandfather's time, but it's an interesting subject.'

'Rather!' said Colin. 'There was just one point I couldn't quite follow. I'll run up and get it and see if you could explain.'

He dashed upstairs and was down again in a moment with the book.

'It's here,' he said, pointing to a marked passage.

Robert read it.

'I don't quite get it myself,' he said, 'but I'll tell you who would, the man father is taking as his guest to the County Club to-night, that London barrister, Noel Merton. He has been down here once or twice at the assizes, and father thinks very highly of him. He could settle it in a jiffy. He's going back to town to-night, unfortunately, but I'll ask him next time I run across him. Wait a few years, Colin, and father and I shall be coming to you for Counsel's opinion.'

'That's just what I wanted to talk to you about,' said Colin. 'I do like this law stuff immensely, but I feel so awful living on father and taking an allowance from him and earning nothing. I really ought to be finding a job.'

'Don't be an ass,' said his brother kindly. 'If you've got to be silly about money, don't get it into your head that father is throwing money away. He looks on you as an investment. If you have anything like decent luck and stick to work, you'll be independent by the time you are thirty and doing jolly well by the time you are thirty-five. Then you can be the noble bachelor uncle and put your allowance into what the girls are going to get, or in trust for my kids, or into your wife's settlement, or anything you like. That's all there is to it.'

'I was over at Southbridge to-day,' said Colin, 'talking to Birkett, and he seemed to think –'

'A thoroughly sound man,' said Robert, with a grown-up face. 'I meet him on one or two boards, and Edith's young brothers were under him before they went to Rugby. You couldn't do better than take his advice.'

'I did,' said Colin. 'I had quite a long interview and it seemed pretty satisfactory. He said he would take me on next term. That's only a week from now.'

'Take you on how?' asked Robert. 'If it's coaching you want, you'd better speak to father about going to some good man's chambers. He has something of the sort to discuss with you, but I won't forestall him. Birkett might polish up your Latin a bit, it always comes in useful, but – hullo, Kate.'

'Mother says do come along because she wants to have some bridge,' said Kate. 'Lydia's got to do her history prep and I simply must finish some stuff for the Dean, so it's only Mother and Edith, and they want you.'

'We'll come now,' said Robert, jumping up and putting his arm through his sister's. 'Come on, Colin. We'll have a talk later about this coaching business. It's a good idea of yours, but you must be sure to get the right man.'

Colin followed his brother and sister into the drawing-room, a prey to inward discomfort. While they cut for partners, while they dealt, even, regrettably, while they played, his mind was in a turmoil. It was sadly clear to him that in spite of all his efforts – efforts lasting from about 5 p.m. up to the present moment – not one of his family seemed to have, or want to have, the faintest idea of what he was talking about and what he wanted to do. Even if they had listened, heard, or understood, it was obvious that they didn't care, and that his was one of those miserable personalities which cannot impress itself on the people with whom it comes in contact. How could a man with so little self-confidence ever exert authority over boys? Remembering the ingenious tortures which he had inflicted in his own school-days – not so very far off – on unhappy junior masters, Colin felt sick with apprehension and self-distrust. And it was on account of a foolish scruple about money, a scruple that Robert had set aside as a thing of naught, that he was going to exchange the delights of *Lemon Upon Running Powers* (for such was the name of the delightful work he had been studying with so much enjoyment) for the galling servitude of a school and the brutal tyranny of schoolboys. He still clung desperately to his conviction that young men of twenty-two should not be living on their parents, but if no one else shared his conviction, he was going to be a martyr to himself without any of the fun of martyrdom. There was still his father to consult, and Colin, to his own secret shame, felt rising in him a hope that his father would say 'Don't be a fool, sir' (not that his father had ever said anything the least like that in his life) and write to Mr Birkett by the next post, cancelling his indentures, or whatever the proper phrase was. But even as he hoped, he felt that the hope was dishonourable.

In consequence of this moral strife he played so badly that he and the other players were thankful for an interruption. A car was heard outside and a few minutes later his father came in.

'Well, Edith,' said Mr Keith, kissing his daughter-in-law, 'children well?'

Without waiting for an answer he turned to his wife.

'Helen,' he said, 'can you manage a guest to-night? Young Merton, the barrister I have mentioned to you, who was dining with me, has missed his train. It was really my fault for running things so fine. I ought to have got him away from the Club sooner, but that old windbag the archdeacon talked and talked. You know what the Barchester hotels are like, so I brought him out with me.'

'Quite right, Henry,' said Mrs Keith placidly. 'Kate, dear, tell them to get Robert's room ready as soon as possible. Where is Mr Merton?'

'I left him in the library. I wanted to make quite sure it wouldn't at all upset you.'

'Of course not. Kate, dear, tell Palmer to tell cook that we shall be one extra at breakfast, and then find Mr Merton and bring him up. Sit down, dear, and Edith will tell you about the children, and, Colin, you must tell your father about Southbridge.'

'Southbridge, eh?' said Mr Keith. 'Well, Edith, tell me all about my grandchildren.'

*

Noel Merton was waiting rather uncomfortably in the library. He liked Mr Keith, with whom he had done business more than once, but to like a man in his office is one thing, to spend a night in his house without any luggage another. Luckily the dinner for which he had come down was of an informal nature, so he would be spared the indignity of going up to town on a Sunday in evening clothes, but even so there were delicate questions of toothbrushes and razors that perturbed him. One may be a very rising barrister, a dancer, a diner-out, a man of the world, ambitious, but to appear before a provincial solicitor's family at breakfast unshaven, in yesterday's collar, is a severe trial. As he waited by the fire he began heartily to wish that he had stayed in a Barchester hotel. Mr Keith was delaying unaccountably, and was probably having to placate Mrs Keith, who naturally wouldn't want a complete stranger at half-past ten at night. Kate, having delivered her mother's messages, came into the library and found a tall, elegant young man standing with a melancholy foot on the fender and a melancholy arm draped along the mantelpiece, staring at his own reflection in a mirror. Noel Merton, who was looking not at but through his reflection, became aware of a girl's mirrored eyes meeting his, and turned round in confusion.

'I am so sorry you were left here,' said a very pleasant voice to him. 'Father ought to have brought you straight up. Mother says please will you come up with me, and we are so glad you can stay the night. I am Kate Keith.'

'Thank you so much,' said the melancholy young man, suddenly producing an agreeable smile, undraping himself from the mantelpiece, and taking her offered hand.

24

'My name is Noel Merton, but perhaps your father told you.'

'Yes,' said Kate, leading the way to the drawing-room, 'he said you missed the train. They always alter the trains at Barchester about this time, and no one ever remembers if the 9.35 is the 9.40 or the 9.30.'

'As a matter of fact, it was the 9.30 this time,' said the melancholy young man, 'which is why I am intruding.'

'Helen,' said Mr Keith to his wife, as Kate and the guest came in, 'this is Mr Merton of whom you have heard. My son Robert you know, Merton. This is his wife, that is my other son Colin, and Kate you have already met.'

Everyone said polite things, and a silent struggle took place between Mr and Mrs Keith, she trying to make the conversation general, her husband burning to continue with his guest the technical conversation they had begun at dinner and continued during the drive out. The guest would have preferred, as a third course, to talk with Miss Keith, but she had slipped out of the room, so he exerted himself to be pleasant to his hostess and her daughter-in-law. Suddenly the door was wrenched open, and Lydia's powerful form filled the doorway. On seeing a stranger she began to back.

'Come in, Lydia, and shut the door,' said her mother. 'Mr Merton, this is my younger girl, Lydia.'

'Are you the man Noel Merton that father was talking about?' asked Lydia, crushing the guest's hand in a grip of iron.

He said he was.

'I've awfully wanted to meet you,' said Lydia, 'to ask you if you spell your name with those two little things.'

Noel Merton was instantly equal to the occasion.

'I really ought to,' he said. 'I was christened that way, but as I have to sign my name about twenty thousand times a year, I gave them up and write it plain Noel, without any spots.'

'I thought it might be all covered with bubukles and whelks and knobs,' said Lydia, sitting down ungracefully with her knees apart, and taking possession of the visitor.

'Are you fond of Shakespeare then?' said Noel.

'Rather. I'm frightfully keen on him. Shakespeare and Horace are my favourite poets. Miss Pettinger likes Milton best, but no one takes any notice of her. I say, do you hate Cromwell?'

'Loathe him,' said Noel promptly.

'I say, that's fine,' said Lydia, with a slight American accent. 'I've just been doing an essay about him for the history mistress, and I've made it a stinker.'

Robert, who knew from experience that nothing short of violence would stop his younger sister when she was feeling at her ease, said he and Edith must really go, so they said good night and went, leaving messages for Kate.

'Come along, Lydia,' said her mother, 'it is high time you were in bed, and I'm going too. You'll look after Mr Merton, Henry, won't you?' she added, giving her husband a look which contained so many housewifely reminders about razors, collars, toothbrushes and sundries that he was quite confused.

'I say,' said Lydia, 'you know it's summer time tomorrow. Has anyone put the clocks wrong?'

Mrs Keith looked conscience-stricken.

'I did speak to cook this morning,' she said, 'just after I had read it up in *The Times*, but I don't know if I said to put them backward or forward. I must have known at the time, because I'd just read it, but I can't think now. It's forward, isn't it?'

'Backward, I think,' said Mr Keith.

'I know it breaks my watch to do it one way and not the other way,' said Mr Merton, 'but I can't remember

26

if it breaks it in spring and doesn't break it in autumn, or the other way round.'

'If you go to China you keep on gaining a day,' said Colin. 'Or is it losing it?'

'I know we had to alter the clocks five times an hour going to America,' said Mr Keith.

'Oh, rot, daddy, you couldn't,' said Lydia. 'Not five times an hour.'

'I didn't say five times an hour, my dear,' said Mr Keith mildly. 'Well, yes, you are quite right, I did. But you took me wrongly. What I meant was that I had to alter my watch five times during the voyage, an hour.'

'The captain must have been potty,' said Lydia.

'I think father means an hour five times,' said Colin. 'I mean to alter it an hour five different times. No, I don't. Kate,' he appealed to his sister who came in at the moment, 'is it clocks forward or backward to-night?'

'Forward,' said Kate. 'I know, because there's an hour's less sleep to-night, and the cook is convinced that she will get an hour less in bed every night from now on, till we put the clocks on, I mean back again, in the autumn. I told her she would have an hour more every night through the winter, but she is thinking of giving notice.'

'Gosh! she doesn't understand the thing a bit,' said Lydia. 'Look here, Noel, let's go and explain to her. You'd love the cook. She's a perfect angel, and doesn't mind drowning kittens a bit. Come on.'

'Go to bed now, Lydia,' said her father.

Lydia kissed her father and Colin, wrenched Noel's hand violently from its socket, and accompanied her mother upstairs.

'Going to bed, Kate?' said her father. 'I'm taking Merton and Colin to the library for a drink before we turn in.'

'Mr Merton,' said Kate, with a look of earnest

27

concentration on her pretty face, 'you will find a new toothbrush and toothpaste and safety razor in your room. The pyjamas and hairbrushes are Robert's if you don't mind. We keep them for him, as he is so often here. The only thing I'm not sure about,' she said, wrinkling her forehead, 'is clean collars.'

'Oh, please don't bother,' said the guest, going pink at her cool treatment of his material needs.

'It's no bother,' said Kate simply, 'but I'm afraid father's would be too large and Colin's too small. Colin, when you go up you might see if there are some of Robert's anywhere. And do you mind which train you go by to-morrow, Mr Merton? The Sunday trains are all bad. There's a very slow 11.45 that gets up at four, with no restaurant car, but we'd give you sandwiches, and at 6.37 with a dining-car that gets up at ten. If you'll let me know, I'll order the car.'

Mr Keith pressed his guest to stay till the later train, but Noel said he was dining out and would have to go by the midday train. Kate said good night and the men went to the library.

'Have a drink, Merton,' said Mr Keith. 'Well, Colin, did you get *Lemon*? I gave him to your mother.'

'Thanks awfully, father,' said Colin, 'he's perfectly splendid. But there's one thing I couldn't quite get, and Robert wasn't quite sure either. He said you could help me,' said Colin, turning to Noel and wondering whether he ought to say Sir.

'Let's see,' said Noel, and was able to elucidate the point that had puzzled Colin.

'Well,' said Mr Keith, 'that brings us to the question we were discussing, Merton. This boy of mine has done some solid reading, but he'd be better in London now. Colin, Mr Merton is willing to have you in his chambers and do what he can for you. So unless there is any very grave reason against it, such as your both disliking each other at sight, I think it an excellent plan. And when you have been called, Colin, I hope you will get on as well as Merton has.'

'I shall like my part of it,' said Noel hastily, 'as long as your son does.'

'It's awfully decent of you, sir,' said Colin, hardly knowing what he was saying, so imminent was the deadly moment when he must unmask.

'There's only one drawback,' said Noel. 'For various reasons I can't have you till the autumn. But if your father doesn't mind waiting till then, I expect we shall get on very well.'

'Father,' said Colin in a hoarse voice, 'I meant to tell you I saw the headmaster at Southbridge to-day and I think it's practically certain that I am to have a job as Junior Classical Master. I felt I must do something.'

He then lost all consciousness of time and space. He knew that when he got back to earth he would find Mr Merton scornfully cursing him for his ungrateful flouting of so good an opportunity, and his father either dead of a stroke, or worse, but even more probable, lying senseless on the floor, paralysed all down one side, his face hideously contorted, his mind gone, a hopeless wreck to the end of his days.

'Splendid,' said the voice of Mr Merton coming to him over mountains and down through thundering waters. 'I know Birkett, he's an excellent man. You'll get some experience and be able to do plenty of reading in your spare time. Write to me if you need help on any point.'

Colin began to come to again.

'Well,' said his father, 'you have taken me by surprise, Colin, but it's a very good move. A school is a better atmosphere for work than a home. And with a term's salary you'll be able to go abroad in the summer, or get a little car.'

'But I can't go on taking an allowance, father,' said Colin, becoming articulate.

'That's very nice of you, Colin, but quite unnecessary. No more to drink, Merton? Very well, we'll go to bed. You might take Merton up, Colin. I've got a few letters to write.'

'I think these collars of Robert's might do, sir,' said Colin, after rummaging in a drawer. 'I'm afraid my neck's a bit bony, or I'd have offered you one of mine.'

'Don't let's worry about Sir and Mister,' said Noel, 'unless you'd rather, of course. How old is your sister?'

'Which one?'

'The one in black that wanted to explain summer time to the cook.'

'Oh, Lydia. She's sixteen.'

'Good Lord,' said Noel.

'Well, good night,' said Colin, finding that his guest had nothing else to say.

'Good night, Colin,' said the guest, and retired to Robert's pyjamas, reflecting on the peculiar but not unattractive character of the younger Miss Keith. While brushing his teeth, the feeling of a brand-new toothbrush suddenly reminded him of the elder Miss Keith and her cool, thoughtful care for his needs, and he thought he would like to see both girls again.

Colin went to bed in considerably better spirits. A headmaster of a good school had engaged him on one interview. A successful barrister was taking him into his chambers. What his father might be paying for this privilege, besides the allowance he made him, Colin did not consider. If he had heard the conversation that was going on between Mr and Mrs Birkett, he would have been slightly disillusioned.

'Well,' said that very nice woman, Mrs Birkett, to her husband before they went to bed, 'are you pleased with your Junior Classics?'

'He might be worse. It's a good family. Father's a solicitor in Barchester, well-known old firm. Do you remember the Fairweathers at the Prep School? This man's brother married a sister of theirs.'

'Oh, Edith, I remember her,' said Mrs Birkett, 'a very pretty girl at prize-givings and cricket matches. What is Mr Keith like?'

'Like them all,' said Mr Birkett, refilling his pipe. 'Good University record, no games, likes walking, quite a good mind, I should say. From what he let fall his father wants him to go in for law, and I think he's much more cut out for that than for teaching. He'll do all right for a term though. You can't do boys any harm with Junior Classics. The Latin Grammar is pretty well foolproof. I hope to get Harrison back in the autumn. He mayn't be a brilliant scholar, but he knows boys inside out.'

'Thank you. What I asked was, What is Mr Keith *like*? Presentable? Agreeable? Not likely to fall in love with Rose?'

'I hope not. It's bad enough to have a daughter engaged to one of one's assistant masters without all the rest falling in love. He's a nice-looking young man, nothing against him except his neck.'

'Is it dirty?'

'No, no, he's clean enough. But I do get so tired of those young masters with necks like prep school boys. I never feel a master is up to his work till he takes a fifteen-inch collar. Young Keith will never make a teacher with a neck like that.'

CHAPTER II

Shades of the Prison House

MR MERTON was got to Barchester in time for the slow 11.45, with a packet of sandwiches in his dispatch-case, and family life closed over his head. Rather to Colin's mortification his relations continued to take his new job as a matter of course. No one thought it noble or considerate of him to go and earn some money by teaching, and Kate mistakenly went so far as to say she envied him.

'I do think you are lucky, Colin,' she said, as she sat in her brother's room, sewing his name into the three pairs of new socks he had recently bought. 'It will be frightfully interesting to see what a big school is like from the inside.'

'After all I saw schools from the inside, what with prep school and public school, for about ten years,' said Colin, 'and there's very little to them. Nothing but boys and masters.'

'Still that was when you were young. It ought to be more fun now, because you'll be a master instead of a boy, and there are heaps of very interesting schoolmasters now. I mean some of them are very modern and advanced, Communists and things.'

'I'd rather they were things than Communists,' said Colin morosely. 'We had plenty of Communists at Oxford, all being earnest and writing their novels and wasting time with earnest females.'

'Well, they might be nudists, or believe in self-expression for boys,' said Kate, 'which would be even worse.'

'Judging from my own schooldays,' said Colin, 'there's no need to believe in self-expression for boys. They'd do it anyway, and the less you believe in them the better.

I'm honestly terrified, Kate, when I think I might have some boys in my form that are only half as odious as I used to be. A ghastly, ill-mannered, spotty-faced prig, with an absolutely elementary sense of humour and always growing out of my clothes.'

'You aren't *sorry* you got the job, are you?' asked Kate.

'Oh, Lord, no. I expect it will be quite good fun if it weren't for the boys.'

'Anyway,' said Kate comfortingly, 'you'll have lots of time for reading.'

'I wish I were Mr Merton,' said Colin. 'If I do go to him in the autumn it'll be simply splendid. It must be ripping to have your own chambers and be very busy and go about a lot. Did you like him, Kate?'

'Yes, very much. But he isn't what I'd call very intelligent. He left the toothbrush, which after all no one will want to use, behind, and took Robert's pyjamas. I'll have to write to him.'

'Give him a day or two. I mean if he sees a pair of pyjamas in his dispatch-case that aren't his, he'll see they are someone else's and realize what he's done.'

'Well, I'll wait a day,' said Kate. 'I might hear from him on Tuesday morning. And talking of Tuesday, the parents and I are dining with the Crawleys, and when mother rang up the Deanery to accept, Mrs Crawley said she hoped you'd come too and tell her all about your plans.'

'I suppose mother is broadcasting about my having a job,' said Colin ungratefully. 'I wish to goodness she'd leave me alone. She wasn't a bit interested when I told her, but now she's going to talk about her schoolmaster son till everyone is sick.'

Kate made soothing noises.

'By Jove,' said Colin suddenly, 'I've an idea. Mr Birkett didn't absolutely fix it up. He said he'd write.

And perhaps he will say he has decided I won't do after all.'

'He might. Someone terrifically good might have applied since he saw you. I mean,' said Kate, trying to convey the impression that her brother was the best person in the world for the job, but that there might by a mistake be someone even better, 'someone with just as good qualifications as you and experience of teaching as well. Do you think you can teach, Colin?'

'I don't know. I really never thought about that. How do you learn to teach?'

'I think they go to training colleges,' said Kate, 'or is that to be clergymen? Anyway, they have to begin practising on someone.'

'Gosh,' said Colin, horror-struck, 'I remember now we had a man to teach us for a fortnight when the fifth form master was ill, and he was from somewhere where they teach teaching, and they didn't dare to leave him alone in the room with us, we behaved so badly. Even the drawing master could keep order better than he could.'

Kate sat silent, sharing her brother's presentiments of evil.

'It's such a short time since you were at school yourself,' she said at last, 'that you must be pretty well up to their ways.'

'No,' said her brother. 'The point is that everything changes so quickly. Boys are ghastly polite now, which is much worse than banging their desks or throwing ink. Do you remember that boy of Mrs Morland's, Tony I think his name was, who came to tea last summer with his mother? He had charming manners, but he made me feel about nine years old.'

'There are your socks,' said Kate, kissing the top of his head. 'I must go now. I've got these notes for the Dean to do, and I want to get them finished before to-morrow night, so that I can take them with me. I'm sure school will be all right. After all, heaps of people are school-masters.'

'Look at them,' said Colin, bitterly and unfairly.

*

By Tuesday evening several important letters had been written and received. The breakfast post brought a letter to Kate from Noel Merton.

'Oh dear,' she said when she had read it, 'Mr Merton says it was one of our maids who packed Robert's pyjamas in his dispatch-case, and he is having the pyjamas and the collar washed and sent back. What a mercy I hadn't posted my letter. Palmer, did you pack those pyjamas of Mr Robert's in Mr Merton's suitcase?'

'I packed the pyjamas which was on the gentleman's bed, miss. I am sure I couldn't say whose they were,' said Palmer, clearly showing by a shudder in her voice that she was virginally incapable of telling one gentleman's pyjamas from another's.

'Well, never mind,' said Kate.

As the breakfasters worked through their correspond-ence, it appeared that Mr Merton had written to Mrs Keith, thanking her for her hospitality and apologizing for the trouble he had given. He had also written to Mr Keith, thanking him for the dinner at the County Club, and expressing pleasure at having Colin in his rooms in the autumn.

'Well, I can't see why Noel didn't write to me, too,' said Lydia, who had finished her breakfast and was fidgeting with a knife and a spoon. 'I talked to him as much as any of you did. I'm going to ask him to go to the Old Vic with me some time, because he likes Shake-speare. I could have lent him some of my pyjamas, if it comes to that,' she said, stooping to pick up the knife she had knocked onto the floor; 'that pair I loathe that you got me in Bournemouth, mother, when I'd forgotten mine, and he could have kept them, and there needn't have been any fuss about the washing.'

'You really mustn't call everyone by their Christian names,' said Mrs Keith.

'Well, what am I to call them, mother?' said Lydia indignantly. 'One can't go about calling everyone Mister.'

'You'll be late for your train, Lydia,' said Kate warningly.

Lydia dashed out of the room, shut the door so violently that it sprang open again, and a minute later was seen bicycling at break-neck speed down the drive. Half an hour later the car came to the door to take Mr Keith to his office. Kate went out to see her father off.

'Good morning, Sanders,' she said to the chauffeur. 'Have you taken a letter that was in my writing on the hall table? I don't want it posting after all.'

Sanders said he hadn't taken nothing this morning, but last night when he was going down to the village late, after his supper, Palmer had given him a letter and said he might as well post it. The address was a Mr Merton, he said.

'Oh, thanks, Sanders, never mind,' said Kate.

It was most annoying that this should have happened, and entirely her own fault. No one could blame Palmer or Saunders. Letters were not as a rule posted at night, because they wouldn't get anywhere any sooner if they were, and Sanders always took the family letters to Barchester when he drove Mr Keith to the office. Kate was thoroughly put out. Mr Merton would now think her a fussy young woman, who had suspected him of theft. She worked angrily on her notes for the Dean, with only half her mind on the work before her, till the soothing thought entered her mind that she ought to answer Mr Merton's very polite and considerate note.

Curiously enough the same thought had been in Merton's mind, when with some pains he had composed his letter.

Colin had still had no letter from Mr Birkett and went to the Deanery dinner-party in a subdued frame of mind. It was only a family party, and the conversation ran largely on Colin's affairs, often in a disheartening manner. The Dean spoke of Mr Birkett indeed as an excellent man in every way, and hoped he would get more young masters of Colin's type. There had been a regrettable tendency he said, under the late headmaster, now Master of Lazarus College at Oxford and writing articles of a very foolish kind for newspapers of the left, to appoint men whose degrees were certainly good, but their opinions not what one wanted in those responsible for forming the character of the young. He had reason to know, he stated, that Mr Birkett was not altogether happy about the engagement of his elder daughter to one of his assistant masters, who was encouraging the boys to think rather of politics and the new psychology than of their work.

Mrs Crawley said she was sure boys had by nature such a wholesome contempt for masters as would probably nullify all such teaching. Seeing that Colin looked downcast, she then kindly cheered him up by recounting various anecdotes about nephews of hers who had been at Southbridge, and the trial they were to their unhappy masters.

All this may have been true, and Mrs Crawley certainly made her account of the nephews amusing, but to Colin it was only a nail the more in his coffin. His last hope was removed when, on their return from Barchester, he found a letter from Mr Birkett to say that he would expect him to start work the following week. School began on Tuesday, and he would be glad if Colin would come on the Monday.

'Well, that's all right, father,' said Colin, forcing a smile.

'What's all right?' asked Mr Keith, opening his letters.

'Mr Birkett says he expects me on Monday.'

'Splendid. A very pleasant dinner at the Deanery, Helen. Don't stay up for me, I must write some letters in the library before I go to bed.'

'It is sad that we shan't see you much longer, darling,' said Mrs Keith, 'but you must come home for Whitsun and bring any friends you like. Lydia! Why aren't you in bed?'

'I was, mother,' said Lydia, arriving in a manly dressing-gown, 'but I was reading. I say, Colin, was that Mr Birkett's letter? I saw the Southbridge postmark.'

'Lydia, you oughtn't to look at letters,' said her mother.

'Or at least you oughtn't to mention that you have,' said Colin. 'Yes, it was Mr Birkett's letter, and I am to go there on Monday.'

'I shan't be able to bear it,' said Lydia, beginning to cry.

Her family, concerned, begged her to cheer up, but it appeared that she couldn't, because she had been reading Othello in bed, and was so overcome by the tragedy that the news of Colin's departure was the last straw.

'I'm really enjoying myself,' she protested, amid heart- and ear-rending sobs.

'Well, I'm not,' said Colin, almost sharply. 'Do go to bed, Lydia, and stop being silly. Here's some soda-water.'

Lydia drank the water, blew her nose loudly, wiped her eyes, and went away again. Her mother went up with her to see that her light was turned off, and Colin was left with Kate.

'I have done it now,' he said. 'One thing is it can't last

for ever, but I do wish there weren't any boys at that school.'

By Monday afternoon the school was ready for the boarders, who would be drifting in from tea-time onwards. Mrs Birkett was dispensing tea to any parents who had so little regard for the feelings of their sons as to accompany them to school, while Mr Birkett gave interviews in his study to such parents as absolutely insisted. When Colin arrived in a car from the station, the sinister butler recognized him and took charge.

'Your things will go up to your room, sir, in Mr Carter's house,' he said, 'and Mrs Birkett will be pleased to see you in the drawing-room. She is luckily free from parents at the moment.'

Mrs Birkett, eyeing Colin with the quick appraising glance of a headmaster's wife, agreed with her husband. Mr Keith looked thoroughly nice, but his neck was undoubtedly boyish. With her Colin at once felt completely at home, as generations of boys and masters had done, and was prattling confidently away, when in there came someone so distracting that he stopped in the middle of a sentence.

'My elder daughter, Rose,' said Mrs Birkett, who was used to the impression her daughter made. 'Rose, this is Mr Keith.'

Rose was certainly a ravishing creature, with every attribute of fair wavy hair, dark eyebrows, huge blue eyes, elegant figure, and unexceptionable legs. She shook hands with Colin as if he weren't there and began to eat cake with a hearty appetite.

Rose Birkett was a great trial to her devoted parents, because she simply couldn't help getting engaged. At sixteen she had been engaged to the art master at Miss Pettinger's school. When this was discovered and promptly broken off, to the intense relief of the art master, her parents had sent her to a very good and well-chaperoned school in Munich, where she had been engaged to an officer and a band conductor at the same time. The school had begged her parents to take her back. Before she had been at home six weeks she had become engaged to an assistant master.

Mr and Mrs Birkett did not altogether care for the young man as a prospective son-in-law, but were too exhausted to take steps for the moment, so there the matter rested. The most annoying part of it was that Rose was a very nice, though incredibly foolish girl, and getting engaged was really her only weakness. What significance, if any, she attached to the word 'engaged', no one had yet discovered, unless it meant being taken out in the cars of the successive young men to whom she became attached. Her parents very much hoped she would grow out of the habit in time, but for the present all they could do was to tolerate young Mr Winter and hope for the best.

Colin then remembered what Lydia had told him.

'I think your sister is at Miss Pettinger's with my sister, Lydia Keith,' he said.

'Of course, we know about Lydia,' said Mrs Birkett, as her daughter's mouth was too full to answer. 'She was Ferdinand in *The Tempest* in the school play, wasn't she? We all thought her so good. I do hope you will be comfortable, Mr Keith. You will be in Mr Carter's house. Mr Winter, who is engaged to Rose, is there too, and about forty boys. Matron is very nice, and you get a lovely view from your room over the playing fields and away to the river. We are so glad to have you. I expect you would like to see my husband. He is in his study, just across the passage.'

Colin, intimidated by her efficiency, said good-bye to Rose, who was still eating cake, and went into the fatal room where the interview had taken place. Mr Birkett, protected by his large study table, got up, shook hands across the barrier, and asked Colin to sit down.

'Rather an annoying thing has happened, Keith,' he said. 'Harrison, the man who usually takes the Mixed Fifth, has broken his leg in the Lakes and probably won't be back this term. As you know, I had asked you to take the Junior Classics, but I must keep Winter there, and I'll have to ask you to try the Mixed Fifth for a bit. Do you feel like it?'

'Certainly, sir. But I'd like to know what it is like,' said Colin.

'Well, it's difficult to explain, but it's a bit of everything. All sorts of boys. Some very clever ones that have to mark time a bit till they do their university scholarships; some rather slow ones that have one special subject they are brilliant at. What practically happens is that they all do what they like, so long as they do it intelligently, and you have to help them all, talk to them about anything interesting that comes into your head, try to find out roughly what they are thinking about and tell them not to, or encourage them, as the case may be, and any useful little facts about life – no, I don't mean Facts of Life, all boys seem to be born knowing all about them now – but things you don't know unless you are told, like how to address a Dean, to call a D.B.E. Dame Mary Cook and not Dame Cook, what ordinary trespass is, how income tax is worked, anything that might come in useful. Of course there's a certain amount of routine work as well. Carter will tell you the rest, and if you are in a hole, don't come to me. That's all, I think.'

He picked up his fountain-pen, and, before Colin was out of the room, was immersed in papers.

The sinister butler, who was hovering about, came forward and offered to show Colin the way to Mr Carter's house across the school quad.

'But I know you, don't I?' said Colin, stopping half-way. 'Weren't you a scout at Lazarus? I was there pretty often, and I'm sure I remember you.'

'Yes, sir,' said the butler, 'I was on staircase seven. But when our new master was appointed, the same that was headmaster here, sir, and took to writing for the evening papers, I felt I was demeaning myself by remaining in the College. Our late master used to write for the papers, sir, but toney papers, such as the *Classical Review*. There has been a sad come-down of late, sir, in Oxford. Presidents and Masters of Colleges courting publicity in a way that cheapens Us, sir. So I handed in my resignation to the Bursar, having previously ascertained from Mr Birkett, a very nice gentleman, who also had rooms on number seven in his time, that this situation was vacant. I remember you well, sir, and the High Old Times, if you will excuse the expression, you and the Honourable Mr Norris used to have. Many's the time Mr Norris has done considerable damage to his rooms, but I must say he always made it up handsome. This is Mr Carter's house, sir. He is a very nice gentleman, sir, quiet and learned, and we cannot all have been at Oxford. Mr Winter is, I fear, sowing what one might term his mental wild oats rather late, sir, which makes him trying at times.'

'He is engaged to Miss Birkett, I believe,' said Colin.

'That, sir, I could not presume to say,' said the butler. 'Nor no one else, sir.'

'Well, thanks awfully. Your name is Simnet, isn't it?' said Colin, passing half-a-crown into the butler's hand.

'Thank *you*, sir,' said Simnet. 'The moment I set eyes on you last Saturday week, I said to myself: That is Mr Keith, that used to visit the Honourable Mr Norris on number seven, and he is a gentleman. If you ever need anything, sir, I am to be found in my pantry, when not actively engaged.'

Colin, rather cheered by the prospect of one very useful friend in his new surroundings, rang Mr Carter's bell. As no one appeared and the front door was open, he went in. A long passage paved with hideous tiles ran from front to back of the house, with doors on each side, but they were all shut. In despair Colin opened a door gently and looked in. He saw a large, bare room, with two or three long tables and some lockers, obviously the boys' prep room. It was lighted by two big windows looking onto the playing fields, and inhabited at the moment by four or five senior boys, talking and arranging books. Colin felt like a relapsed heretic before the Inquisition.

'Can I help you, sir?' asked a tall, thin boy in spectacles, with a courteous manner.

'My name is Keith,' said Colin. 'I'm a new master Mr Birkett said I would be in Mr Carter's house. The butler brought me here and I rang the bell, but no one came.'

'They never do on the first day,' said the tall boy. 'My name is Swan, sir, Eric Swan. Tony!' he called to another boy, 'where's Mr Carter?'

The boy raised a serious face from the book he was reading and looked at Colin.

'How do you do, sir,' he said, rising. 'My name is Tony Morland. My mother brought me to tea at your house last summer. I'll find Mr Carter for you.'

He opened one of the large windows and looked out.

'He's going over the cricket pitch with the pro., sir,' he said. 'Eric, take Mr Keith to Mr Carter's study, and I'll let him know he is here. The maids are perfectly hopeless, sir. I'm trying to get things a bit better, but it's an uphill job.'

Swan opened a door at the other side of the passage and stood aside for Colin to go in. A young man in deliberately shabby tweeds, with a white face and flaming red hair, came down the passage.

'What are you doing in Mr Carter's study, Swan?' he said angrily.

'This is Mr Keith, sir,' said Swan, pointedly ignoring the young man's question, and managing to imply that a gentleman always greets a guest before scolding an inferior. 'Morland has just gone to let Mr Carter know he is here.'

The young man walked over to a window and looked out at the school chapel with his back to Colin.

'What are you doing?' he asked, without looking round.

'Waiting to see Mr Carter.'

'Oh, you'll see him when he wants to come. If he's looking at the cricket pitch with Harwood that may be after dark.'

'Don't you like cricket, then?' said Colin, who thought all schoolmasters were athletic, except the old scholarly ones.

'Like it!' shouted the red-haired young man, turning round. 'That's not the question. The money that is spent on that cricket pitch would keep hungry men from starving.'

'I expect it would,' said Colin, 'but probably no one could do it. I think Southbridge is a foundation with its money vested in governors or trustees, and they wouldn't agree.'

'Of course they wouldn't. One is up against that sort of thing all the time. Are you doing Junior Classics?'

'I was to,' said Colin, 'but Mr Birkett says it is to be the Mixed Fifth. I think that was the name.'

'Did he say who was going to take Junior Classics?' said the young man, his green eyes glittering in his pale face.

'Winter was the name I think.'

44

The young man gave an angry laugh.

'Winter,' he said, 'it would be, of course. Oh, there you are, Everard.'

A man of about thirty-five, with fair hair and a thin, amused face, came into the room.

'Sorry not to be here to welcome you,' said the new-comer to Colin. 'Harwood, the cricket pro., wanted me to look at the pitch, and I couldn't get away. I see you two have broken the ice.'

'Look here, Everard,' said the red-haired young man, 'I can't stand it.'

'What?' asked Mr Carter. 'Sit down, won't you?'

Colin sat down, but the red-haired young man remained furiously standing.

'It's Swan,' said he.

'What has he done this time?'

'He looks at me through his spectacles. I can't stand it.'

'But, my dear fellow, if he has spectacles he must look through them.'

'It isn't that. It's the way he looks. I believe he has gone into spectacles on purpose.'

'Now, be reasonable, Philip. You know his mother wrote saying he had been ordered to wear them for close work, and asking me to see that he did.'

'I'm not close work. He needn't wear them to look at me.'

'I can't very well tell him to take his spectacles off every time he speaks to you,' said Mr Carter.

'Then I'll go to the Head,' said the red-haired young man, whose name appeared to be Philip.

'You can't do that,' said Mr Carter seriously.

'Can't I? No, I suppose I can't,' said Philip. 'Things being as they are. But I won't stand it. Keith saw how he looked at me.'

'Did you, Keith?' said Mr Carter.

'No, sir,' said Colin. 'I mean I didn't notice anything.'

45

'You have to notice more than that if you take the Mixed Fifth,' said Philip. 'What do you think I'm to do, Everard? Junior Classics again!'

'You do them very well when you keep your temper,' said the imperturbable Mr Carter. 'I've seen far worse scholars than you.'

'Well, I'll send in my resignation at once,' said Philip. 'To be looked at by boys in spectacles and then have people put over one's head! It's intolerable!'

As he spoke a bell began to ring from the chapel.

'Good God! Orchestra practice and I haven't got my books,' he shouted and rushed out of the room.

'Who was that?' asked Colin.

'Philip Winter. He's an extraordinarily good classic and very keen on music and can't keep his temper. He wanted the Mixed Fifth, but it needs a cooler man. I hope you are cool.'

'I think so,' said Colin cautiously. 'I mean, I don't go off the deep end in a hurry.'

'Good,' said Mr Carter. 'Now we'll have a talk.'

He then plunged into time-tables and technicalities with Colin, who, concentrating on what he was shown, found it all seemed pretty simple.

'You'll do it all right,' said Mr Carter, 'as far as the theory goes. How you will get on with the boys, only time can decide.'

'Are they difficult to get on with?' asked Colin, his original fears reviving.

'I'll have to ask you that question at half term,' said Mr Carter. 'If Eric Swan and Tony Morland approve of you, you'll have no trouble. Don't come to me if you have. And don't go to Birkett, as he'll only send you back to me again. It's a pity you got across Philip so soon, but it can't be helped.'

'I never meant to,' said Colin, surprised.

46

'No, but you've got the Mixed Fifth, and you didn't back him up about Swan's spectacles.'

'I couldn't, sir.'

'I never said you could. And, by the way, it's all Christian names here. I don't like it, but it is the fashion. The housemasters call Mr Birkett Henry, the assistant masters don't, so you may as well get used to it. I'm Everard, and Winter is Philip, as you heard.'

'I'm Colin,' said Colin, 'and if you don't mind my being eccentric I'd much rather say sir than Everard; I suppose Carter isn't done?'

'Hardly,' said Mr Carter. 'You could say Mr Carter whenever you speak of me if you like. That would be considered quite a good eccentricity. Morland and Swan, who of course are Tony and Eric, say Mr to everyone, but if a junior boy did it he would be sat on. Birkett calls all the senior boys by their first names because he knows them. Matron uses surnames. You'll learn it quite soon.'

'Mr Birkett said a few lessons on how to address a Dean or a D.B.E. would be useful for the Mixed Fifth,' said Colin, 'but it looks to me as if lessons on how to address schoolboys and schoolmasters would be more to the point.'

'Like all those moderns who wish to simplify, they have made it much more complicated,' said Mr Carter. 'My father and his oldest friend lived to be over eighty. They were at school and college together and on intimate terms all their lives, but they always called each other Carter and Jones. Come up and see your room.'

He led the way upstairs, stopping to point out objects of interest.

'Lower Dormitory,' he announced, flinging open a door. 'Mark on wall where Harwood once sent a ball from the nets through the dormitory window, crushing an Arundel print of the Martyrdom of St Ursula into a thousand fragments. The mark is officially known as the

Martyr's Memorial. The Upper Dormitory, as its name doubtless suggests to you, is upstairs again. The prefects have cubicles of their own. It is all very civilized. No pillow fights, barring-outs, or if you prefer it barrings-out, stealing of exam. papers, or Damon and Pythias. Not even a passion for the headmaster's wife. I really don't know what boys are coming to. This is where you live. Plenty of shelves for your books. Nice view of English landscape. I won't point out the local landmarks because you'll be sick of them before the half term. By the way, how long are you staying here?'

'I don't quite know, sir. A term anyway, I suppose.'

'Any particular reason for applying for the job?'

'Well, I thought I ought to be earning something. Reading law is no inheritance.'

'No, it isn't,' said Mr Carter thoughtfully, adding, 'So long as it isn't because you like boys,' in what appeared to be a tone of relief.

'Oh, no, sir. As a matter of fact,' said Colin in a burst of confidence, 'I'm terrified of them.'

'You're all right, then,' said Mr Carter. 'Once they've got you where they want you, they treat you very kindly. The wheel has come full circle, Keith. The beggarly usher has his Trade Union now and gets a good salary, holidays half the year round, and quite good social standing. But the boys are our masters. Benevolent tyrants, I admit, but despots. It is far more difficult to expel a troublesome boy than to dispense with the services of an unpopular master. Supper at seven o'clock. A bell will ring.'

Colin found that Simnet had been as good as his word, and his luggage was there, so he unpacked his clothes and lovingly arranged his law books on the shelves. The more he looked at *Lemon on Running Powers*, the more he wondered why he had put his head into a den of lions. If Mr Carter, so wise, so skilled in the great subject of boys, spoke of masters as anachronisms, upholders of lost causes, what chance would he, Colin Keith, have against his pupils? His mind played about the subject, sometimes seeing the masters as the last stand of civilization against a horde of barbarians, mild because of their overwhelming superiority in numbers, but irresistible. And then he wondered if it were not the boys who should be compared with the imperial legions of Rome, steadily marching over all obstacles to surround and capture a handful of terrified tribesmen lurking in their dens, massacre the weakest, and carry off the rest to be palace slaves, treated with the same careless, humane consideration that an expensive, well-educated Greek slave might have received from his Roman master.

The bell rang. Colin went down to supper, which was much less terrifying than he had expected. Mr Carter, Mr Winter, and a couple of other masters whose names he didn't catch were at a sort of high table. The food was unexpectedly good and the boys ate in a very gentlemanly way. After supper the two unknown masters went off, and Mr Carter invited Mr Winter and Colin to come into his study for coffee.

'I'll ask Tony and Eric to come, too,' said Mr Carter, 'they are sensible animals. There is a kind of common room over in the big building for the assistant masters, but no one minds if you don't go. You can always work in your own room if you want to. Tony and Eric, come and make my coffee.'

The two boys stood aside while the inferior fry swirled past them, and followed their housemaster into his study, where they began, apparently in fulfilment of a well-known ritual, to collect from a cupboard cups and saucers, a large glass coffee machine, sugar, spoons, and a jug, which Morland was taking out of the room when Mr Carter stopped him.

'Which jug are you using, Tony?' he said.

'The glass one, sir.'

'All right. The blue one had some dead flies in it.'

'Those must be Hacker's flies, sir. You let him use it last term to keep his flies in for his chameleon. There were a few over at the end of term that he forgot about, and I expect they died. Do you want them, sir?'

'No, no, boy. Don't wilfully play the sham innocent. Get the water for the coffee at once.'

Swan smiled grim approval of his friend's discomfiture, and laid the coffee-things neatly out on a tray, while the masters settled themselves in large creaking chairs. Mr Carter lit his pipe, Philip pulled out a battered packet of cigarettes, lit one, and as an after-thought offered the packet to Colin.

'No thanks,' said Colin. 'To save trouble, I don't smoke cigarettes.'

'Any reason?' asked Mr Carter.

'I don't care for them.'

'So long as it isn't principle,' said Mr Carter.

'Sir,' said Morland, coming back with his jug full of water, 'Hacker says do you think dead flies would be bad for his chameleon, because if you don't he would like to have them, as he has run rather short. He's here, sir.'

A pale boy with untidy hair, a slouching gait, and a slightly vacant look, partly intruded himself into the doorway.

'All right, Hacker, take your flies, and if the chameleon dies don't blame me,' said Mr Carter.

Hacker took the blue jug, muttered some words of thanks, and retired.

'He doesn't look very fit,' said Colin.

'Classical Sixth, sir,' said Swan. 'They all get like that the minute they go into that form. They are awfully brainy, but quite mad, and can't stand up straight. It's the influence of environment on character.'

'What do you mean?'

50

'Keep your mind on the coffee, Eric,' said Mr Carter, 'and don't be clever. When you have seen our Mr Lorimer, Keith, who takes Senior Classics, you will know what Eric means. How did orchestra practice go, Philip?'

'Pretty well. God! I wish I could get those boys to understand three-four rhythm with a dotted crotchet at the beginning. Tᴜᴍ-ti-ty, Tᴜᴍ-ti-ty, with that short second beat. It's the most exhilarating thing in the world, and they go and give the notes equal lengths, young devils.'

'Proputty, proputty, proputty,' said Eric Swan to the coffee machine as he began to pour out the coffee.

'All right, Eric, we all know that you are a specialist on Tennyson,' said Mr Carter.

'Anyway, sir, you couldn't have three notes of equal value in a bar,' said Morland. 'Theoretically, perhaps, practically, no. The first note must have more stress than the others. You can put the stress on the second or third of course, but it comes to the same thing. Any average bar of three comes out as a dactyl.'

'I thought a dactyl was a long and two shorts,' said Philip sarcastically.

'Yes, sir, according to the books: but the long isn't as long as two shorts. I thought of writing a little waltz, sir, called the Virgil Waltz, and the school orchestra could play it on Speech Day.'

'Ingenious idea, Tony,' said Mr Carter, 'but slovenly. How long have you had it?'

'About two minutes, sir.'

'Journalist,' said Mr Carter.

'It all comes of those rotten, up-to-date books on history and economics we have to read in the Mixed Fifth, sir. They ruin a boy's mind and style. I absolutely heard myself telling matron my mind wasn't conditioned to tepid bath water. Conditioned! Is it fair, sir,' he continued to Colin, 'to corrupt youth like that?'

'What happened to the bath water?' Colin asked.

'It improved, sir. I had to draw up a five weeks' scheme for improving the running of the house. First I got matron into my power by letting her rub my ankle which wasn't at all in need of it, and after that it was child's play. Our bath water is now the hottest in any house, sir,' he went on, including Mr Carter in his speech. 'Simnet is green with envy.'

'Good,' said Mr Carter. 'Now it would be a good thing, Tony, if you abstracted your mind from world politics and devoted it to whatever prep you are supposed to be doing. You and Eric can go.'

The boys rose, returned thanks in well-chosen words for their pleasant evening, and departed.

'What do you think of the new arrival?' said Morland to Swan, as they strolled towards the prep room.

'They are all alike,' said Swan wearily. 'This one looks too sensible to stay long. I wonder why all masters go mad sooner or later?'

'It must be mixing with each other,' said Morland, 'We don't go mad, because we keep them at a suitable distance.'

'What about the Classical Sixth?' said Swan. 'They all go mad.'

'Exactly what I was trying to prove, you dull oaf. They live with Lorimer, breathe Lorimer, they even confide in Lorimer, though what they have to confide except false quantities, we shall never know, for they obviously have no human feelings. Therefore they go mad.'

'My attitude to masters,' said Swan sententiously, 'may be summed up in the classic words of a celebrated English general to a small Expeditionary Force some twenty odd years ago: Be courteous to women, but no more. For women, read masters, and there you are.'

'Mr Winter will not love Mr Keith, if Mr Keith is to

have the Mixed Fifth,' said Morland, 'and that will give us something to look at this term.'

'My dear boy,' said Swan in a pained voice, 'don't be childish. To watch assistant masters quarrelling is a sport unbecoming to our age and station. Flies on a window-pane if you like; masters, no.'

*

A short silence followed the boys' departure from Mr Carter's room. Philip, who was nearest the window, said there was still an unknown car with chauffeur outside the Head's house, which meant that the last parent hadn't gone yet.

'What, roughly, is the feeling about parents?' asked Colin.

'What is yours?' asked Philip.

'I hardly know. I happen to like my own, but I was wondering what masters would think of them as a class.'

'There's a lot to be said on that subject,' said Mr Carter. 'I might be a headmaster myself some day, so I have devoted some thought to it. They are, of course, in a sense fellow sufferers with us, because they also are under the monstrous regiment of boys.'

'Their one really impregnable point of vantage,' said Philip, 'is that they provide school-fodder. If they gave up supplying boys, we should have no jobs. Therefore the breed, for good or bad, must be encouraged. We can't do without them. Anyway, thank God, the birth-rate is going down, so perhaps there won't be masters, parents, or boys at all in a few hundred years.'

'Speaking as one who is not a parent, and barely a schoolmaster,' said Colin, 'your side doesn't do badly. I mean the holidays get longer, the fees get larger, you get rid of your boys on odd pretexts like Jubilees and pocket the price of their board. If parents had any solidarity, they'd strike. At least, that's what my father thinks.'

'Yes, but they haven't,' said Mr Carter, 'and for why? One of the strongest primal impulses known to humanity is to get away from, or get rid of, its offspring. Every new child is another shattering blow to its parents' privacy and independence. They will pay pretty well anything to get rid of their children for long periods in every year. The older the child the more the parents will pay. And never will they combine against the benevolent institutions that take their dear children off their hands.'

'If we could afford it,' said Philip morosely, 'we'd pay as much to get rid of their children as they do to foist them upon us. If I had a few hundred a year to play with I'd willingly pay the fathers of one or two of my young charges to take them back again.'

'It's a funny thing,' said Mr Carter reflectively, 'that more schoolmasters are parents than parents are schoolmasters.'

'It sounds awfully true,' said Colin after a moment's reflection, 'but it must be wrong.'

'I can't explain it,' said Mr Carter, 'but it's right. Put it this way. You and I, Keith, are, as far as we know, without wives or children, but at any moment either or both may burst on us. As Philip is engaged, I exclude him from this interesting conversation. Here we are, care-free bachelors in the conventional phrase, but to-morrow either of us may marry the matron or any of the housemaids. Parents, on the other hand, are practically assured that they will not suddenly turn into schoolmasters between Monday and Wednesday. They win!'

'It sounds as if you didn't think too well of schoolmastering,' said Colin.

'I don't,' said Mr Carter. 'It's awful to belong to a profession that marks you. One laughs at clergymen on holiday, trying to be natural. Have you ever seen schoolmasters on holiday? You can't mistake them. Have you ever been on a Hellenic cruise?'

54

'God!' said Philip.

'Or else,' said Colin, warming to the sport, 'they are quite the gentlemanly young Communist and marry the daughters of headmasters and have large families of girls.'

'That's the kind of joke schoolboys might appreciate,' said Philip. 'Try it on the Mixed Fifth.'

He glared at Colin and went out of the room, whistling rudely.

'That's the Red Flag he is trying to whistle,' said Mr Carter. 'It's the kind of tune that hasn't got any tune, but they think it has.'

'I'd absolutely forgotten that he was engaged to Miss Birkett,' said Colin miserably. 'I *have* put my foot in it. I'm most awfully sorry.'

'Yes, it's not bad for your first evening,' said Mr Carter.

CHAPTER III

Supper With the Head

WHY the excellent and intelligent Birketts had produced an elder daughter who was a perfect sparrow-wit was a question freely discussed by the school, but no one had found an answer. Mrs Birkett felt a little rebellious against Fate. She had thought of a pretty and useful daughter who would help her to entertain parents and visitors, perhaps play the cello, or write a book, collect materials for Mr Birkett's projected History of Southbridge School, and marry at about twenty-five a successful professional man in London. Fate had not gone wholeheartedly into the matter. Rose was as pretty as she could be, but there Fate had broken down. Rose was frankly bored by parents and visitors, and always managed to escape when they arrived. She did play an instrument, but far from being a cello it was a piano-accordion, which she handled with a good deal of confidence, but poor technique. As for writing, she was always dashing off letters in a large illegible calligraphy to bosom friends, but her vocabulary was small and her spelling shaky. She was very lazy and was perfectly happy for hours doing her nails, or altering a dress. When she came back from Munich Philip Winter had fallen so suddenly and hopelessly in love that he had to propose to her almost before her trunks were unpacked. Rose had accepted his proposal gracefully, said it would be perfectly marvellous, and wrote to tell her bosom friends about it, spelling her affianced's Christian name with two l's.

Mr Birkett was more concerned for his assistant master than for his daughter, and said as much to the ardent suitor. Philip replied that no one had ever properly understood Rose.

'I daresay not,' said the harassed father. 'I don't understand her myself, and I don't suppose you do. But it is always awkward when a junior master is engaged to the Head's daughter, in fact I'm almost sure it's forbidden in Leviticus. I won't have the school work upset by it, and as Rose is barely eighteen I'm not going to let her marry yet. Forgive my being brutal, Philip, but Rose is a very silly girl, and not good enough for you.'

'I daresay not,' said Philip, 'but she happens to be exactly what I want. I could always resign my post here if it complicates things, but I can promise that I'll keep up to the mark as far as work goes. I don't want to give up the job because I like it on the whole extremely, but I'll have some money when my old aunt dies, and I've been thinking of putting some of my capital into a small prep school.'

'Really,' said Mr Birkett.

'But I haven't decided,' Philip continued, 'whether it would be a crank school or an anti-crank school. I believe anti-crank would pay better now. Parents, even crank ones, are a bit sick of their children not washing behind the ears. I'll have a pure fascist, regimented school. After all, the boys are much more likely to react to the left if they are taught imperialism at school. How soon would you allow Rose to marry me, sir?'

Mr Birkett made the very daring reply that if Rose still wished the marriage to take place he would allow it in the following spring. Philip, while violently deprecating the possibility that Rose's interest in him might wane, agreed to Mr Birkett's conditions.

'You can come to Sunday supper whenever you like,' said the headmaster, 'and take Rose out on Saturday afternoons when you aren't on duty. Otherwise I'll have to treat you just as if you weren't engaged.'

Philip, panting with first love, found these restrictions almost more than he could bear and proposed a romantic elopement to his love. Rose said it would be too marvellous, but on reflexion objected because she wanted a real wedding, with her mother's veil, the school chapel, her six bosom friends for bridesmaids, and the little daughters of the drawing-master to scatter flowers. Also, she said, Philip would look marvellous in a top hat.

After this rebuff Philip told Rose all about his past life, his political views, his hopes, fears and ambitions and especially the prep school. Rose thought a prep school would be marvellous, but wished Philip would get a job. On being pressed as to her idea of a job, she said she didn't know, but perhaps something in the films. Then school had broken up for the Easter holidays and Rose had gone on a cruise to Algiers with her parents. During her absence she sent several picture postcards to her beloved, each bearing the message, 'Marvellous view here love from Rose,' on which meagre fare Philip, working at a little book on Horace, had to content himself. He kept his word to Mr Birkett about sticking to his work, and except for a considerable amount of irritability no one would have known that he was a happy accepted lover.

Towards the end of the Easter holidays Mr Birkett had interviewed Colin Keith and, as we have already heard, inquired anxiously whether he was engaged. In Mr Birkett's view assistant masters ought to reserve their interest in the other sex for the holidays. He himself had wooed his Amy at Easter, won her at Whitsun, and got married at the beginning of the summer holidays, spending part of the honeymoon at Leeds, where there was an Assistant Masters' Conference, after which he was ready to take up the headmastership of the preparatory school to which he had lately been promoted. After suitable intervals Rose had been born at the beginning of the Easter holidays and Geraldine at the beginning of the Christmas holidays, so that the school had been as little inconvenienced as possible. Why all other masters couldn't do the same, Mr Birkett failed to understand, and on hearing that Colin had no commitments he felt a distinct relief, in spite of the thinness of his neck.

Then term began. Rose, finding life a little dull after the close attention of six ship's officers and seven ineligible young men on the Algerian cruise, began to look about her. Mrs Birkett asked Colin to Sunday supper the first week, because he was new, and Rose, in cornflower blue, gave a good piece of exhibitionism for his benefit, refusing food at table and performing on the piano-accordion afterwards. Colin disliked her on the whole and got away as early as possible to his room and the comfortable *Lemon*. Rose, who never noticed anything unless it suited her, informed her parents and her betrothed that Colin was quite marvellous and took to waylaying him in the school quad, to the great interest of some four hundred boys and all the assistant masters except the two chiefly concerned.

Apart from this the first weeks of term slipped away comfortably enough. With a little help from Mr Carter Colin found he could deal quite well with the Mixed Fifth. Swan and Morland set a very gentlemanly tone in the class. Those who felt like working read a surprising number of books and wrote a great many essays. Those who did not feel like working sat in the desks at the back and amused themselves quietly. Colin discovered that he really knew a good deal more about most things than the self-possessed young gentlemen of sixteen and seventeen under his care, and even convicted them on various occasions of crass ignorance. Messrs Swan and Morland, who had made all learning their province, acknowledged a superior, and took credit for the discovery among their

59

contemporaries, especially with Hacker, whose chameleon had thriven on dead flies.

In the summer term the school spent a good deal of its time in or on the river which flowed past the playing fields. The bathing-sheds were on a delightful backwater, and there Swan and Morland, who both hated cricket, would come after school and practise life-saving, or a few fancy strokes, or do a little easy boating.

'Mr Winter and Mr Keith are not fulfilling their early promise,' said Morland to Swan, as they were lazing about in a rickety canoe among the rushes on Saturday afternoon.

'I know, I know. But the Ides of March have not yet gone. Have you noticed our Rose?'

'Not if I could help it,' said Morland.

'She is hounding down Mr Keith,' said Swan. 'Mr Winter hasn't jumped to it yet, nor has Mr Keith. When they do, flies on the window-pane won't be in it.'

'Masters are incredibly dense about life,' said Morland. 'I sometimes think I ought to warn Mr Keith.'

'I always think you oughtn't,' said Swan. 'They've got to learn it for themselves. Let's be an ice-breaker.'

With cries of mutual encouragement they began to push the canoe through the thickest of the rushes, hearing in the noise that their canoe made while forging its way ahead the grinding and cracking of the ice in the St Lawrence, when the first icebreaker comes up the river. Suddenly Morland gave a yell.

'Look out, Eric,' he called from the prow where he was kneeling, 'here's one of your uncles or aunts coming at us.'

A swan's angry face was thrust through the rushes at them followed by a furious hiss.

'He's not my uncle, he's my grandfather,' said Swan indignantly, 'and he says he's cutting me out of his will unless we go at once. Back her, Tony.'

'I'm not frightened of any grandfather of yours,' said Morland, as they quickly backed the canoe into open water again, 'but after all an Englishswan's house is his own castle. I say, Eric, let's take a boat up the river for Whitsun. We can take camping things and sleep in a tent. It'll be very uncomfortable, but my mother is in America, so I might as well do something dashing.'

'We might,' said Swan. 'My people are going to a golfing hotel on the bracing East coast. What curious ideas of pleasure their generation have.'

On that very evening a misfortune took place in Mr Carter's house. Hacker, who was doing extra work for a scholarship exam., sat up late in his cubicle reading Aeschylus, with his chameleon to keep him company. Owing to his position as a house prefect, a position due to his learning and seniority rather than to any gifts of leadership, Mr Carter had allowed him to install a reading-lamp. As his sight was weak he had, without asking permission, changed the electric bulb for an extremely powerful one which almost warmed his small room. About eleven o'clock Hacker, feeling rather jaded, determined to have a surreptitious bath, so he undressed, put on his dressing-gown, and prepared to tiptoe to the bathroom.

'Are you sleepy, old fellow?' he asked the chameleon.

The chameleon looked at him with an abstracted gaze.

'All right,' said Hacker. 'I can't put out the light, or I'll never find my way back in the dark, but I'll cover the light up. Will that do?'

As the chameleon showed no disapproval of this suggestion, Hacker took a large silk handkerchief from a drawer and swathed the bulb of the reading-lamp in it. He then closed his door all but a crack and went softly to the bathroom. If the rushing noise of water from the taps was heard at illegal hours, matron was apt to appear vengefully and send the trespasser back to his room, so

61

the prefects in Mr Carter's house had elaborated a scheme for using the bath late at night without attracting attention. A piece of towelling was fastened onto each tap with an indiarubber band, by which means the water oozed quietly into the bath instead of behaving like Lodore. When the bath had to be emptied, the bather put his sponge over the grating of the waste pipe and let the water percolate gradually, so that matron's ear was not assailed by the roarings and gurglings with which the bath vulgarly emptied itself.

Hacker, having made all these preparations, put the sponge rack across the bath, propped his Aeschylus up on it with his sponge, and sat comfortably in the gently rising tide of hot water. From time to time his spectacles became dim with steam and he had to wipe them on the bath towel. The bath was nearly full, and he had got through six pages of Aeschylus, when an unreasonable doubt assailed him as to whether he had shut the door of the chameleon's cage. He tried to reassure himself, but failed entirely. Visions of the chameleon walking down the passage, climbing out of the window, getting as it had once done into the linen cupboard and there being lost for weeks, flitted through his mind. Suddenly he could bear it no longer. He got quickly out of the bath and as he got out his spectacles fell off. He angrily groped on the floor for them, but his blindness and the steamy atmosphere of the bathroom made it impossible to discover their whereabouts till a sharp crack told him he had trodden on them. He picked them up, but the pieces were useless. The only thing was somehow to get back to his room and find the spare pair which his mother had made him bring, a piece of officiousness that he had deeply resented at the time and even now could barely condone. He managed to find his dressing-gown, huddled it over his wet body, and set off groping down the corridor, leaving the tap still running.

As he neared his cubicle, a horrid smell assailed him. Something was undoubtedly on fire. Inspired by affection for the chameleon he made a lightning decision to risk his own life rather than that of his favourite, blundered into the room, saw with his myopic eyes a smouldering table-cloth with charred fragments of a silk handkerchief burning on it, seized the chameleon's cage and emerged into the corridor and into the arms of Mr Carter, who was just going to bed.

'What's the matter?' said Mr Carter, sniffing the air. 'What the devil are you up to, Hacker?'

'Nothing, sir,' said Hacker.

'Arson, apparently,' said Mr Carter. 'Get the fire extinguisher by the stairs.'

'I've broken my spectacles, sir,' said Hacker.

Mr Carter wasted no time. He strode to the stairs, took down the fire extinguisher and directed it onto Hacker's burning tablecloth. The noise and smell were gradually rousing the rest of the house. The lower dormitory began crowding into the passage. The news rapidly spread that the house was on fire, and Hacker and his chameleon burnt to death, filling the lower dormitory with pleasurable excitement. Swan and Morland suddenly appeared in their O.T.C. tunics, rapidly assumed for an emergency, worn over their pyjamas, and asked what they could do.

'Tell those fools to go back to bed,' said Mr Carter, making a gesture towards the lower dormitory.

As Colin and Philip came out of their rooms at this moment, the lower dormitory chose to understand Mr Carter's words as applying to his junior masters, and fell into paroxysms of giggles. Matron appeared on the landing above, looking so unexpectedly charming in a pink silk dressing-gown that the Captain of Rowing, an unimpressionable boy of twelve stone, suddenly fell in love with her, but as he was a diffident lad and left at the end of the term to join the Nigerian police, he never told his love and the episode went no further.

'What has happened? I can't hear a word you say,' said matron, coming downstairs. 'Don't make all that noise, boys, there's no need to wake the upper dormitory too. What is it, Mr Carter?'

'I can't make out yet,' said **Mr Carter**. 'Hackers seems to have broken his spectacles, but why his room should be on fire I don't know. Anyway, it's out now. You'd better all go back to bed. You too, Hacker. I'll see you to-morrow morning.'

'Please, sir,' said Swan, 'there's a flood coming out of the bathroom.'

'Stop it,' said Mr Carter angrily.

Swan and Morland, encouraging each other with soldierly words of command, made for the bathroom door and flung it open. A delightful scene of horror met their eyes. The bath was overflowing and had evidently been overflowing for some time. Sponges, soap, socks, towels, and a sodden volume of Aeschylus were swept into the passage. The lower dormitory got entirely out of hand and matron had to retreat three steps upstairs.

'It's all right now, sir,' said Swan, emerging wet-legged from the bathroom. 'Someone had left the tap running.'

'Aeschylus!' said Mr Carter, picking up the sodden book. 'And why Aeschylus in the bathroom? Hacker, can you explain this?'

'It was my chameleon, sir,' said Hacker.

'Good God, boy!' cried Mr Carter, 'don't tell me that your wretched animal set fire to your cubicle and flooded the bathroom.'

'No, sir,' said the miserable Hacker.

'If that's all you learn in the Classical Sixth,' said Mr Carter, 'you'd better go over to the modern side. Didn't you all hear me tell you to go to bed,' he said, suddenly turning upon the lower dormitory.

'Some of them have got wet feet, Mr Carter,' said matron.

'They would. Winter, you and Keith send the dry boys straight to bed. Matron, will you deal with the wet ones. And, Winter, stop the dry ones from paddling in the wet. Where's Swan?'

'He went down to see if everything was all right in the kitchen, sir,' said Morland. 'It's just under the bathroom, and we thought some of the wet might have got through.'

Even as he spoke Swan came hotfoot upstairs with the agreeable news that a great patch of the kitchen ceiling had fallen down onto the gas oven and water was still dripping from above. Matron, who had seen the lower dormitory into their beds, now came out again, full of zeal, seeking whom she might devour, and began to harass Swan and Morland till they put on dry pyjamas and got into bed. Hacker, who had rescued his book, found his spare spectacles, put the chameleon back in its place, and got into bed, full of an inarticulate grievance against the fate that wouldn't let one read Aeschylus in peace without bring flood and fire to ruin one's evening, and with but little hope of impressing his doctrine of Predestination upon an unsympathetic housemaster.

'Of course to-morrow would be Sunday,' said Mr Carter to his lieutenants before they separated. 'We'll have to cadge meals for the whole house to-morrow. If Hacker weren't working for a scholarship I'd skin him. I'll have to speak to Lorimer about a suitable punishment that won't upset his work.'

*

Sunday was a little flat after the excitement of the previous night. Matron had been down early and told the cook and the maids the news, adding that the kitchen would have to be cleaned, and there would be no lunch, and only a cold supper. Mr Carter went over to the Head's house directly after breakfast and told him of the damage, which, with a good housemaster's loyalty, he attributed entirely to Hacker's having lost his spectacles. Mr Birkett asked him to come over to supper with one of his junior masters and a couple of senior boys, and arranged for the house to be boarded out for lunch.

'If you don't mind,' said Mr Carter, 'I'll stay in the house and send Winter and Keith over to you with a couple of prefects. I think matron will be glad of my support.'

'I remember much the same thing happening in the junior school when I first went there,' said Mr Birkett, 'only in that case I left the tap on myself.'

Mr Carter then returned to his house and interviewed Hacker, who after lengthy cross-questioning managed to describe the events of the night before.

'Well,' said his housemaster, 'next time you will know that if you tie a powerful electric bulb up in a handkerchief, you will probably be burned to death. I suppose I ought to confiscate your chameleon.'

'Oh, sir!' said Hacker, aghast.

'But I shan't,' said Mr Carter, 'because the wretched thing would die on my hands. But a reading-lamp in your room I now forbid. You can get your reading done at the proper time or not at all.'

'But, sir – Mr Lorimer –'

'If Mr Lorimer can't put sense into your head, it's time someone did,' said Mr Carter. 'You can't even tell a plain narrative of what happened. I'd better ask Mr Lorimer to put you back onto Caesar. He would have given, at once, a clear and concise account of what had occurred, in oratio obliqua. Go and find Mr Lorimer and ask if he can see me.'

The ensuing interview began as a pitched battle between Senior Classics and Housemastering. Mr Lorimer, a middle-aged man with the gait and appearance of a tortoise and an uncanny gift for forcing his pupils into scholarships, criticized with venomous precision the discipline which allowed his favourite for the Montgomery Scholarship to be first burned and then drowned. Mr Carter pointed out that the classics appeared to be no preparation for life, in that they did not, so far as he could see, even train a boy to think. Any child from an elementary school would, he said, have been able to give a clearer account of what had occurred than the head of the Classical Sixth. They then both lost interest in Hacker, and Mr Lorimer gave Mr Carter some of his excellent sherry, while Mr Carter gave some friendly criticism of Mr Lorimer's translation into Greek verse of the new rules about the bathing pool.

'Sorry you can't stay,' said Mr Lorimer. 'I've got to get Hacker through this scholarship. After that you can crucify him if you like.'

'What about this reading he does after lights out?' asked Mr Carter.

'Stop it, Carter, stop it. He'll be stale in another week if he goes on. How I loathe boys and their ways,' said Mr Lorimer, who had been teaching for thirty-five years and took promising boys to his home in Scotland every holidays.

'About mid-term I could kill every boy in my house with joy,' said Mr Carter, who liked being a housemaster more than anything in the world, and usually enlivened the tedium of the holidays by taking boys to Finland, or Mount Athos.

Mr Lorimer then metaphorically tucked up his wristbands, fell upon Hacker, and made him write the history of the fire and flood in Greek and Latin prose and verse, in the manner of the most eminent stylists of both languages, and later in the term Hacker got the Montgomery

Open Scholarship for Lazarus College with no difficulty at all. The incident was soon forgotten, but if it had not been for Hacker's misfortune, Philip Winter and Colin Keith, with Swan and Morland, would not have been invited simultaneously to the headmaster's house for Sunday supper, and the Whitsuntide holidays might have been quite different.

Just as Colin was starting, Mr Carter called him into his study to give him a message for the Head.

'By the way, sir,' said Colin, 'my people asked me to bring anyone I liked home for Whitsun. I don't know if you are fixed up. If not, would you feel like coming? I can offer you two parents, two sisters, a garden with tennis, a river, and church on Sunday entirely optional.'

Mr Carter said he had been leaving the Whitsun holidays to chance, and would be delighted to accept the Keiths' kind invitation.

In the school quad Colin overtook Swan and Morland, clean and serious, on their way to the headmaster's house. As they had been discussing his chances against Rose Birkett, his presence froze their flow of talk, and the courtesy with which they endeavoured to find a subject suitable for a master's intellect was of a paralyzing nature. Luckily for all three Simnet was on the watch, and opened the front door as they came up the steps.

'Good evening, Simnet,' said Colin.

'Good evening to *you*, sir,' said Simnet. 'This is quite like old times, if I may say so, sir. And if I may venture to mention it, sir, the headmaster has a Madeira which he will offer to you during the evening meal, as good as what the Honourable Mr Norris used to have. He got it from the College Cellars, sir, and I have made a Special Study of it. There will be cider for the young gentlemen, sir.'

Swan and Morland looked at each other with real awe. Mr Keith, the tenderfoot of the house, a master whom they were treating with courtesy and no more, was on intimate terms with Simnet, a man compared with whom the Head himself, as was well known, was as naught. In this emotional moment, even the insult about the cider was forgotten, and each boy looked at Colin's back, preceding them into the drawing-room, with something approaching reverence.

Mrs Birkett was alone. Mr Birkett, she explained, had been for a long tramp, and would join them in a moment. Swan and Morland dematerialized, and suddenly reappeared at the far end of the room, absorbed in books. Mrs Birkett gave Colin some sherry and talked very comfortably to him till her husband came in with the School Chaplain, Mr Smith. As Mr Birkett had already met Colin twice that day, once after chapel and once by bumping into him by mistake round the wall of the fives court, he greeted his assistant master with a kind of salute, and said, 'Ha, Keith!'

Colin wanted to reply 'Ha, sir!', but feeling that this would be disrespectful he merely said Good evening.

'Yes, I suppose it is evening,' said Mr Birkett. 'The line of demarcation between afternoon and evening is curiously difficult to define. Smith, you know Keith, who is taking the Mixed Fifth. His father does a lot of the cathedral business in Barchester. And now that summer time is upon us, it is more difficult still.'

'Of course one has to remember that it is really only half-past six,' said Mrs Birkett and Mr Smith together.

'We had frightful difficulty over summer time this year,' said Colin, 'because no one could remember which way the clocks ought to go.'

He had only meant this remark to be a contribution to general conversation, but to his embarrassment, everyone looked expectant.

'So what happened?' asked Mrs Birkett.

'Oh, nothing,' said Colin. 'I mean the kitchen clock

69

had been put on in the right direction, so by breakfast time it was all right.'

'Watch, for ye know not the hour,' said Mr Smith, clapping Colin on the back in a friendly way, and laughing.

'I always wonder what good watching would do,' said Mrs Birkett, 'because if you didn't know the hour, no amount of watching would be any help.'

'It's like looking for the Pole Star if you are lost,' said Colin. 'It's all very well to know where the north is, but if you don't know where you are, you can't tell which way to go, and the north is no more use than the south.'

'Excuse me, madam,' said Simnet, 'I suppose you did not intend to wait for Miss Rose?'

'Certainly not,' said Mr Birkett.

'Pardon me, madam,' said Simnet, whose method of showing his resentment at being interfered with by his master was to ignore him altogether, 'but as Miss Rose has gone out with Mr Winter in his Blue Sports Car, I thought you might wish to be assured of her safe return before commencing dinner.'

'Isn't Rose back then?' asked Mr Birkett.

'No, dear,' said Mrs Birkett, finding herself, rather to her annoyance, reduced to acting as interpreter between her husband and her butler, 'she went out with Philip in his car, but I expect they'll be back any moment now.'

'We'll wait for a few minutes then,' said Mr Birkett.

Simnet remained aloof and impassive.

'Pardon me, madam,' he said, 'but will you wait till Miss Rose and Mr Winter is come back, or shall I use My Own Discretion as to the serving up of Dinner?'

'I'll ring as soon as we are ready, Simnet,' said Mr Birkett, thus winning this particular round. 'But I wish,' he added as Simnet left the room, 'that Rose and Philip would remember to be in time for meals. It has been the same every Sunday. Well, Eric and Tony, what have you found?'

The boys laid down the books they had been looking at and came into the front drawing-room.

'That's a good book you have on Van Gogh, sir,' said Swan, 'but there's a new Viennese one that's even better. You ought to get it.'

'It's from the same publisher that did that lovely book of reproductions of details of pictures of Vittorio da Mantua,' said Morland.

'Too many "of's", Tony,' said Swan.

'Say it yourself then,' said Morland without heat. 'Do you know it, sir?' he continued, kindly bringing Colin into the conversation.

Colin, feeling gross and ignorant, said he didn't, and further admitted that the painter's name was unknown to him. Morland obligingly gave him a list of the few known paintings of that delightful but obscure artist, while the Chaplain conversed with Swan on Van Gogh. Just as Swan was politely explaining to Mr Smith that Van Gogh and Gauguin were separate persons, the Blue Sports Car rushed up to the door, checked and halted. In a moment Rose, untidy and lovely, was in the room, leading Philip by the hand.

'Finished dinner, darlings?' she said, taking a comb from Philip's pocket and passing it through her hair.

'We were waiting for you and Philip, Rose,' said her mother. 'Eric, would you ring the bell.'

'Sorry, darling, but why on earth?' said Rose, flinging her coat and scarf onto a chair. 'Philip and I had a marvellous time.'

'I'm awfully sorry,' said Philip, 'I really am. We went a bit farther than we meant and didn't see what time it was, and anyway I hadn't my watch and Rose's had gone mad.'

'Well, never mind,' said Mr Birkett. 'Dinner ready, Simnet? Come in, everyone, without ceremony.'

Against the deadly ritual of Sunday supper Mrs Birkett had steadfastly set her face for the whole of her married life, and this alone was enough to distinguish her among wives, not to speak of headmasters' wives. In early days she had cooked hot food herself. As her husband rose in his profession and they both inherited legacies from uncles and aunts, she had been able to afford a kitchen maid, so Mr Birkett had not for nearly twenty years known what cold beef, sardines, potato salad, tinned peaches and blancmange (all in themselves, except perhaps the last, excellent and wholesome food) could represent in the way of Sabbath horror. Invitation to Sunday supper was hoped for with frank greed by the school staff and the senior boys, but even Mrs Birkett's hospitality could not seat more than five or six guests at most, and of these some were necessarily apt to be guests from outside the school. It was therefore a piece of luck for Colin that he was taking Mr Carter's place so early in the term.

Philip's position in the matter of Sunday suppers was very uncertain. As the future husband of the Birkett's elder daughter he had an obvious right to sup with them as often as they, or Rose without consulting her parents, chose to invite him, but as an assistant master his rights were doubtful. A careful calculation made in the common room under the supervision of the Senior Mathematics Master showed that Philip's chances were approximately 2·734 per term, and his excess visits to the Head's house already about 500 per cent above the average or mean. Of this situation Philip was uncomfortably aware, and would have been glad to retire from Sunday evenings, but his overpowering love for Rose made it impossible for him to refuse her prayers. On the one occasion when he had made a determined effort to avoid the difficulty, Rose had first begged, then sulked,

72

then burst into tears. Philip, fearing for her reason, nay for her life, had desperately and with loving words tried to explain his position and soothe her wrath, but Rose, who had not troubled to listen to a word he said, cried more loudly than ever, and taking a china pig that she had stopped caring for, threw it right across the room. After this proof of devotion there was no course open to a man of honour but to promise to come to supper as often as her parents invited him. Rose, her lovely blue eyes swimming in tears, said in a choked voice that if Philip liked her parents better than her, he had better marry *them*, and so the episode closed, leaving Philip more madly in love than ever, but none the less sensitive about the Sunday evenings.

Rose Birkett, hanging affectionately on the Chaplain's arm and dragging Philip with her disengaged hand, placed herself between them at table. Mrs Birkett left the rest of her party to sort itself, with the result that Colin found himself between his hostess and Swan, facing Rose.

Mr Smith made the slight preliminary clearance of the throat which is part of a chaplain's duty.

'Mr Keith,' said Rose, turning her large eyes on the new master, 'what sort of a car have you got?'

Mr Smith quickly said grace. Colin wasn't quite sure if a question asked in so irreligious a way had, as it were, any status, and tried to pretend he hadn't heard.

'Because I adore cars – I *am* sorry, Mr Smith, if I interrupted – and I'd adore it if you took me out one day,' said Rose.

'I'm afraid I haven't got one,' said Colin.

'Oh, Mr Keith! But why? Philip has a marvellous sports car, but she's getting a bit old. He has had her seven months. Philip, why don't you sell your sports car to Mr Keith and get a new one? I'll teach you to drive, Mr Keith.'

73

At the thought of Rose teaching Keith to drive, Philip turned quite black inwardly.

'We went over to Barchester last Saturday, sir,' said Swan, addressing himself to the headmaster. 'Mr Carter lent us his car and we had a splendid time. They showed us a lot of old fourteenth-century deeds in the chapter house.'

'We nearly had a crash at the lower bridge,' said Morland, taking up the tale. 'A huge lorry came prancing out of the railway yard at us, but Mr Keith nipped round it like anything.'

'I thought you said it was Mr Carter's car,' said Mr Birkett.

'Yes, sir, but he lent it to us. Mr Keith drove, and he told us an awful lot about the old manuscripts.'

The black wave of jealousy in Philip subsided. If Keith could nip round lorries like that, he would not need instruction from Rose. Swan and Morland hit each other under the table as a sign that they had scored one against Rose, for whom they had the deepest contempt, though outwardly their manners were perfect. That would teach her to try and show Mr Keith how to drive.

'You do drive, Mr Keith? Then why don't you buy Philip's old car?' said Rose, with the pertinacity of the foolish. 'She's got one or two tricks, but I'd come out with you and show you how she works. You can easily get seventy out of her if you know how.'

'What do you say, Winter? Are you thinking of selling?' asked Colin, rather bored, and vaguely hoping to draw his colleague.

'No,' said Philip, rather curtly.

'That's all right,' said Colin cheerfully, 'because I wasn't thinking of buying. A car would be rather an extravagance as far as I am concerned.'

Philip flamed again into inward heat. It would have been intolerable if Keith had wanted to buy his car and

74

take advantage of Rose's offers, and yet somehow it was equally intolerable that he shouldn't want to buy it. As if the Blue Sports Car, though seven months old and perhaps hardly worthy of Rose, were not good enough for an upstart temporary assistant master. The thought of the Mixed Fifth surged up inside him once more. Rose, so sweet, so unsuspecting, must be saved from this interloping scoundrel. He turned to Rose to protect her, but she was deeply engaged with the Chaplain discussing Shakespeare, about whom she said she was potty. Philip, looking round in irritation, caught sight of Swan and glared at him. Swan deliberately took his spectacle case out of his pocket, his spectacles out of their case, polished the lenses and put the spectacles on. He then, for a fleeting moment, looked at Philip. If his housemaster had been there he would at once have recognized what Philip meant when he accused Swan of looking at him through his spectacles, and taken steps to put Swan into a less truculent frame of mind, but Philip was, and knew himself to be, powerless against this monstrous regiment.

'Do you need your glasses at meal-times, Swan?' he asked, in a voice whose brittle calm might deceive masters, but never could deceive a boy.

'Yes, sir,' said Swan mournfully. 'The oculist said to use them for close work, but to put them on if my eyes got tired. I think,' he continued, addressing his headmaster, 'it's the top light, sir.'

He indicated the hanging light above the dining-table, an Edwardian arrangement in art nouveau brasswork with a red silk fringe, which Mrs Birkett had not yet had the courage to petition the Governors about.

'Amy,' shouted Mr Birkett to his wife, 'that light has been put up again. The light gets in everyone's eyes. Tony, pull the thing down a bit.'

'Pardon me, sir,' said Simnet, and with great dignity pulled the light down three-quarters of an inch.

'That's better,' said Mr Birkett. But quite right, Swan, to wear your glasses. Bad light is at the bottom of half the eye strain we hear so much about, and a light hanging from the ceiling is an abomination. I shall mention it to the Governors and ask if we can't have it changed.'

'Do, dear,' said his wife.

'Sir,' said Morland, who knew that Mr Winter was inexplicably irritated by his friend's very modern spectacles, 'don't you think Eric's glasses are a good idea? Show them to Mr Birkett, Eric.'

Swan took off his glasses and handed them to the Head, who examined them with interest. They were indeed a peculiar shape, only lately become fashionable, and Swan had persuaded his mother to order them, although they cost ten shillings extra, on the plea that his sight would be irremediably damaged if she didn't, but really in order to impress his friends, and, if possible, provoke the exacerbated attention of his masters.

'You see, sir,' said Morland, warming to his subject, 'they are made so that you can look up without having to lift your head, or getting the line of the frame across your line of vision. You can get even bigger ones for tennis, when you have to look up a lot.'

Mr Birkett pronounced them ingenious and amusing, and asked permission to try them on. Rose then insisted that Philip should wear them. Sooner than disappoint his Rose he unwillingly put them on, only to be greeted with hysterical giggles from Rose, who said he looked exactly like Harold Lloyd. Philip flushed deeply, took them off, and pushed them across the table to Swan, who remarked innocently that Mr Carter had a pair of the big ones for tennis, and one would hardly notice he had them on. He then picked up his glasses, put them on again, and studied with attention Philip's face from which the red was slowly ebbing.

Mr Birkett, who had not lived with boys for a quarter

of a century for nothing, had rather enjoyed the baiting of his difficult future son-in-law, but the moment had come when, even at Sunday supper, discipline must be maintained.

'You don't need your spectacles now the light is lowered, Swan,' he said.

'Very well, sir,' said Swan. As he put them away he favoured Mr Birkett with a fleeting glance whose extreme candour was almost the equivalent of a wink.

'By the way, Mr Keith,' said Mrs Birkett, after a discouraging look at her daughter which made that lively creature change from the giggles to the sulks, 'do you know anything about Northbridge Rectory? I think it's in your part of the county.'

'It's our church. I mean we go to Northbridge on Sundays. It's an awfully nice sort of rather ugly house with a garden to the river, and an island where people camp a little way up-stream.'

'It is to let for the summer holidays, and we are thinking of taking it,' said Mrs Birkett. 'Do you know if there are drains, or ghosts, or anything?'

'I never heard of any,' said Colin. 'I mean no one goes white in a night, and I know there's an awfully scientific new cesspool, and they've never had typhoid.'

'Oh, Mr Keith, do you live near the Rectory?' said Rose, forgetting the sulks.

Colin said he did.

Rose said that was marvellous, and she adored rectories.

'I had a letter from the Rector yesterday,' continued Mrs Birkett. 'He said he and his wife were going to Matlock for Whitsun, and suggested that we should use the Rectory, with his servants, just for the week-end, and see if we liked it. It is a very kind thought, and quite a good idea, I think.'

No one answered for a moment. Colin, not at all

anxious, though he liked Mr and Mrs Birkett very much, to spend most of the summer near their daughter, was wishing he had given the Rectory drains a bad character, and wondering if he could quickly invent a ghost, when Rose, whose thoughts always came to her as inspirations, suddenly screamed, 'Mummy!' so loudly that everyone jumped except Swan and Morland, who exchanged pitying shrugs.

'Mummy!' said Rose again, 'how marvellous! Oh, do let's go there for Whitsun, and Philip can come too, and we'll go on the river with Mr Keith.'

Mrs Birkett, who had foreseen that they would have to put up with Philip for Whitsun, and thought this would be as good a way as any other, gave a qualified agreement. Philip again hated Colin so much that he nearly stopped loving Rose, till the thought of being in a punt with her made him suddenly feel he couldn't eat any pudding from pure love.

The rule for Sunday evenings was that after lingering a little over the Madeira, the party broke up, because Mr Birkett had Monday before him, so when the men came into the drawing-room, it was only to say good night. Rose was loud in her lamentations that Mr Smith and Mr Keith had to go so soon, and clung to Philip's arm in a heavy and exhausting way.

'Say good night quickly, Rose,' said her father, impatient at the delay.

'Parting is such sweet sorrow,' said the Chaplain, looking benignly at Philip and Rose. 'Good night, good night, everyone.'

Philip tore himself from Rose, and he and Colin left the house together, Swan and Morland walking sedately behind them. Philip, in black anger at the Whitsuntide treat in store for him, kept a sulky silence that Colin, after one or two attempts, stopped trying to break. So the walk back to Mr Carter's house was as uncomfortable as a walk need be. When they got in Philip, muttering good night to Mr Carter and ignoring Colin, banged upstairs. Matron, who had just come in from a day with her married sister, the one whose boy was doing so well in the wireless in the merchant service, was outside the lower dormitory and greeted him with what Swan called her Shushing voice.

'Now, Mr Winter, remember my boys when you come up! Every hour's sleep before twelve is worth two afterwards, you know. But I daresay you are thinking of someone quite different from Our Boys, aren't you, so we must make allowances. Well, good night, Mr Winter, and happy dreams of Someone.'

Philip managed to say good night and shut himself into his bedroom with a bang that resounded through the house. Matron, merely observing aloud to herself that Mr Winter had got it badly, went to see if the lower dormitory had woken up; but how badly Mr Winter had got it she could not guess.

For a long time Philip lay awake, trying, with very little success, to fight the unreasonable jealousy of Colin that was invading his spirit. Reason told him that Colin was guiltless, and every advance had come from Rose, but to admit this was to admit that Rose was not perfect, and this Philip refused to do. He still loved her so frightfully that her image interfered in every moment of his personal life, making him pause while the lather dried on his face, only to wake a few minutes later to the breakfast bell. Into his work he had not allowed Rose to enter, which was perhaps why he was really happier at work than at any other time, though he would have challenged anyone who told him so.

After a few words on house affairs, Mr Carter and Colin went to bed. Swan and Morland had gone quietly upstairs in case matron was lying in wait, but she was not visible, so they could whisper on the landing.

'Rose really is the limit,' said Swan. 'How Mr Winter can stand for it beats me.'

'He's quite a decent chap apart from that,' said Morland, 'but he'll be ruined as a master if this goes on.'

'Take off your shoes and we'll be Bulldog Drummond and Carl Petersen,' said Swan.

This excellent advice was accepted. They put their shoes neatly together against the wall and retired to opposite ends of the dim corridor. With a stifled snarl Petersen rushed forward, only to be met by a smashing counterblow from Hugh Drummond. The two closed, and Petersen's great weight was beginning to tell when the lower dormitory door creaked. Petersen and Drummond hastily picked up their shoes and matron came out.

'We were carrying our shoes up so as not to wake the lower dor.,' said Morland. 'Good night, matron.'

Matron beamed approvingly, and the House was shortly wrapped in a silence which the storm in poor Philip's heart did not audibly break.

CHAPTER IV

Friends on the River

THE correspondence between Kate and Mr Merton, which had begun in so humdrum a manner over pyjamas, had rushed at high pressure into more intellectual spheres. That is to say, Mr Merton wrote to Kate about some of the new plays he had been to, while Kate wrote to Mr Merton about her work at the Deanery and what new books she had been reading. Mr Merton felt that Kate was a distinct acquisition to his large circle of pleasant friends, and Kate felt nothing in particular about Mr Merton except how very nice he was. She had also been to town two or three times to look up things in the British Museum for the Dean, and on each occasion had lunched with Mr Merton at a restaurant where he could point out to her all the theatrical people he knew.

Lydia too had not been idle. A short run of Othello at the Old Vic had caused her to get some of her money out of the Post Office Savings Bank, purchase two dress circle seats for the matinée, and summon Mr Merton to accompany her. As an afterthought she asked her mother whether she might go, choosing the moment when Mrs Keith, already late for an appointment, was getting into the car.

'Why didn't you ask me before, Lydia?' said her mother. 'Saturday? Well, I suppose it's all right. Are you going with the school?'

'Mother! The Pettinger only takes us to Midsummer Night's Dream. I'm going with Noel.'

'Noel who, Lydia? I can't remember all your school friends. Is it Mrs Crawley's girl?'

'Mother! Noel Merton. He's awfully keen on Shake-speare.'

'Do you mean Mr Merton?'

'Well, Mr if you like. Can I go, mother?'

Mrs Keith looked helplessly at her daughter.

'Really, Lydia, I wish you wouldn't be so sudden. You hardly know Mr Merton.'

'Of course I do, mother. And anyway, I'm paying for the seats. And can I have some money for my return ticket?'

'Well, if you are paying for the tickets,' said Mrs Keith, reflecting that White Slavers, whose abundant existence was ever present to her mind, would certainly buy the tickets themselves, and even more certainly not go to the Old Vic, if indeed they had ever heard of it.

'Thanks awfully, mother,' said Lydia, an expert at pinning her mother down at the right moment. 'And can I have the money for the tickets now? It's ten and five the day return.'

'Can't you wait till I come back, Lydia? I'm late as it is.'

'Well, I thought if you gave it me now it would save trouble. If you haven't change a pound will do.'

Mrs Keith scrabbled in her bag and gave her daughter a pound.

'Thanks awfully, mother,' said Lydia. 'Oh, and could Sanders take me to the station to-morrow? If I bicycle in my new suit I'll split the skirt from top to bottom.'

'I can't promise anything,' said Mrs Keith. 'Yes, Sanders, go on.'

'Oh, mother!'

'Well, Lydia, I'll see.'

Satisfied with her work, Lydia waved good-bye to her mother, exchanged a conspiratorial nod with Sanders, and went back to the essay on Cromwell which the history mistress had rightly condemned, ordering Lydia to re-write it in a more historical spirit.

Saturday dawned bright and fair. Lydia had the car and went up to town in very good spirits, lunching in the train on chocolates and sausage rolls, which she had thoughtfully provided for herself out of her mother's pound. In the foyer of the Old Vic she met Mr Merton, who as a student of human nature had put off going away for the week-end till a later train, in order to accept Lydia's invitation. Othello proceeded on its fatal course. As far as Mr Merton could ascertain, Lydia took a deep breath as the curtain rose and held it in a very alarming way till the interval. People poured out to stretch their cramped limbs and get a little fresh air, but Lydia was apparently turned to stone. Mr Merton thought it kinder to let her come out of her trance unassisted, as he had often heard that to rouse the victims of trances too quickly was apt to lead to mental derangement. After two or three minutes she sighed away her long-held breath with a kind of joyful power that made Mr Merton glad that most of the audience had gone out.

'Would you like to walk about a bit?' he said.

'Oh, all right,' said Lydia, getting up with such violence that the whole row of seats shook. 'I say, isn't Othello wonderful?'

Mr Merton said it was.

'I feel as if I'd written it myself,' said Lydia, stumbling into the foyer.

To this Mr Merton found no reply.

'I mean,' said Lydia, in a penetrating voice, 'Shakespeare is so wonderful because he's like Horace. I mean everything he says seems to have something to do with oneself. For instance, when Iago says to Roderigo, "Drown cats and blind puppies", it made me think of our cook and the way she doesn't mind drowning kittens. I couldn't bear to drown them myself, but she says they don't feel it if they are young enough, because she was brought up on a farm. I think Shakespeare must have had an extraordinary mind. I mean he has such a wonderful vocabulary. When you think of all the words you have to look up in the glossary, it just shows. But I don't look up the words as a rule because I think Shakespeare didn't mean you to. I mean he expected you to know them, and if you didn't he didn't mind. I *am* enjoying myself. I expect the second half will be ghastly. I mean it would have been so easy to make everything all right if anyone had had any sense, but Shakespeare's people never seem to have had much sense. I suppose it's partly because of the exits and entrances. I mean they never get their entrance in time to tell anyone what has really happened and then someone kills someone by mistake, and when the person comes to tell them the one they killed was innocent all the time, or someone else in disguise, they only say Othello's occupation's gone, or something of the sort. But somehow when it's Shakespeare it's all right.'

Noel Merton was on the whole relieved to get Lydia back into her place, where she was again stricken to stone. When the lights finally went up she turned a tear-blotched face to Noel and with loud sniffs said it was the loveliest day she had ever had.

'I loved it too,' said Noel, who preferred his Shakespeare in comfortable seats, but would not for the world have told Lydia so. 'Look here, Lydia, I've got to catch a train, so we'll go over to the station together. Would you like some tea?'

He gathered from Lydia that the thought of food revolted her very soul, so he took her across to Waterloo, bought a platform ticket for himself, and put her into her train.

'Thank you so much for giving me such a nice treat,' he said through the carriage window.

'It was all Shakespeare,' said Lydia, in broken accents.

'Shakespeare may have written the play, but he didn't get the tickets or think of asking me,' said Noel. 'That was a very kind thought of yours.'

'I say,' said Lydia, 'you'd better come to us for Whitsun. I'll tell mother to ask you and we'll go on the river if it's fine and talk about Shakespeare.'

'Do be careful, Lydia,' said Noel, a little alarmed. 'Your mother mightn't want me, and anyway I'm not absolutely sure if I'm free.'

'Of course mother will want you,' said Lydia. 'Why not? We've got plenty of room, due reference of place and exhibition, with such accommodation and besort as levels with your breeding.'

'Well, thank you very much,' said Noel, recognizing the language of the Moor of Venice. 'Oh, and would you mind,' he added, as the train began to move, 'giving this book to your sister. I promised to send it to her.'

He pushed a small parcel into Lydia's hand, waved good-bye, and went off to get his luggage from the cloak-room and catch his own train.

Lydia got back in time to make a hasty change of dress and join her family at dinner, during which meal the aftermath of her emotion that afternoon caused her to be extremely uncivil and despise everyone, till her father said she had better go to bed early. Lydia accordingly went into exile as Bolingbroke, undressed as Coriolanus, and got into bed as Richard II. Kate, coming up to kiss her good night, found her in tears again.

'Nothing really awful, is it?' asked Kate.

'Only that I had such a lovely day,' bellowed Lydia. 'Oh, here's a book Noel sent you.'

Kate opened the parcel.

'What is it?' asked Lydia.

'A book he thought I would like,' said Kate, going a little pink under Lydia's bleared but piercing eye.

'Do let me see,' said Lydia. 'Hardy's poems. Gosh! I've read a lot of Hardy. I think he's a bit like Shakespeare, the way no one tells anyone who they really are, or what really happened, till whoever it is is dead, or married someone else. But he doesn't give you that marvellous feeling Shakespeare does. I suppose no one ever was exactly like Shakespeare. I'll never forget Othello.'

'Did he enjoy it?' asked Kate.

'He? Who? Oh, Noel. Of course he did. But I always think no one can understand Shakespeare as well as one does oneself. I'll tell you what I think about Shakespeare, Kate –'

But Kate kissed her sister, turned out the light and went back to the drawing-room. On the stairs she paused, half opened the book, closed it, opened it again at the front page, and when a slight mist before her eyes had obligingly cleared away she read, 'For K. K. from N. M., with his humble duty.'

For the rest of the evening Kate was so stupid that even her mother noticed it.

*

For the next two days Lydia was so disagreeable that her parents began to discuss boarding-school, but by Tuesday morning she had recovered and made a very handsome apology, explaining that the fault was not so much hers as that of the Bard. She added that after all Aristophanes, or whoever it was, had said one ought to be purged by pity and terror if one went to the theatre or whatever it was he said, and would it be all right if Noel Merton came down for Whitsun and would her mother write to him. She then crashed out of the room and went off to school.

Mr and Mrs Keith were so thankful to have Lydia her own exhausting self again that they made little difficulty about asking Noel. Mr Keith did go so far as to say that

Lydia oughtn't to have everything her own way, but when Kate explained very sweetly that it would be nice for Colin to get to know Mr Merton better, he withdrew his objection.

'And Colin is bringing a Mr Carter from Southbridge,' said Mrs Keith. 'I wonder if he is any relation of some Carters we used to know at home.'

No one could tell her.

'There was a Lady Sibyl Carter,' said Mrs Keith, 'that lived not far from us, and my Uncle Oswald had known her people in India. Her father was Governor of a province, I think. I just remember her. She died when I was quite a young girl. I know if she had lived till I came out she would have been a hundred, because it was the year King Edward's Coronation really happened.'

As no one had ever heard of Lady Sibyl Carter before, Mrs Keith was obliged to carry on the conversation by herself. Lady Sibyl turned out to have been the childless widow of an archdeacon, so Mrs Keith's wish to relate Colin's Mr Carter to her deceased acquaintance languished and then died.

'Then will you write to Mr Merton, mother?' said Kate.

'Yes, darling,' said Mrs Keith. 'Why?'

'To ask him here for Whitsun, mother.'

Mrs Keith obediently sat down and wrote to Mr Merton, and Mr Merton, after doing some very untruthful telephoning, wrote that he was free and would be delighted to come.

Southbridge broke up after school on Friday. Mr Carter drove himself and Colin over in his car to Northbridge Manor. After days of cold and rain the weather had pulled itself together. Everything had rushed into leaf and blossom at once. As they drove through the country the green fields were golden with buttercups, the green hedges white with hawthorn, the green banks yellow with cowslips, the green woods full of bluebell lakes and pools. Colin and Everard Carter stopped at Barchester for a late tea and arrived at the Manor about half-past six. The house was empty, and Palmer said she thought Mrs Keith was out playing bridge and wouldn't be back till dinner, and Miss Kate was somewhere about.

Colin said they might as well look for her, and took Mr Carter into the garden, calling as he went. There was no sign of Kate in the rose garden, nor among the vegetables, so Colin said they would look in the water meadows. At the bottom of a sloping lawn, where the daisies had not yet been cut, a little gate opened onto a path which wound among rushes, following the course of a tiny stream, tributary to the river. The flat green water meadows were intersected by channels of varying widths, each with its sluice to flood the fields in season. Beyond the river, whose winding course was marked by a fringe of alders, willows and mountain ashes, rose the line of the downs, crowned by a clump of beeches. As they walked Colin had ceased his call for Kate, and Everard Carter was grateful for the deep silence and stillness of the late afternoon. They came to another little gate and leaned over it, comfortably saying nothing. Everard thinking how delightful it was to get away from his boys and how glad he would be to see them again on Tuesday. Colin feeling unmixed gratitude for a home where no boys existed. Presently Colin cocked his head and listened.

'That sounds like someone in the boat-house,' he said. 'Let's go and look.'

He opened the little gate and they turned to the right along the river bank. Just round a bend was the boat-house, its door open.

'Hullo, Kate,' said Colin, peering into the water-lit gloom, 'I've been looking for you everywhere.'

Kate, who was in the boat, arranging cushions, looked

up, her eyes so dazzled by the shimmer of the water that she could not see Mr Carter.

'Hullo, Colin,' she said. 'I thought you and your friend might want the boat, so I've been doing a spring cleaning. There are still a few more cushions to come down from the house, and we shall need a new oar, I expect. That one that Lydia used as a jumping pole last year doesn't seem to have recovered yet. Are you coming on the river?'

'Rather,' said Colin. 'This is Mr Carter – my sister Kate.'

As their eyes became used to the flickering, green, sun-flecked light, Kate saw a tall man in brown tweeds who didn't look quite as nice as Mr Merton, and Everard Carter thought he saw his journey's end, so he said, How do you do.

Colin said the boat was rather a squash for three on such a warm afternoon. Let Kate steer, he said, and Everard row, and he would take out his dear coracle. The coracle turned out to be a small, almost circular, collapsible canvas boat with no particular bow or stern and one narrow seat across it.

'One's supposed to paddle it,' said Colin, taking off his coat and waistcoat and hanging them on a peg in the boat-house, 'but I find punting more amusing. If you will excuse the apparent vulgarity of my braces, Everard, I will now give you a demonstration.'

Everard took the sculls and pulled out into the river.

'Up or down?' he asked.

'Down,' said Colin. 'There's a nice wide piece at the bend for me to show off on.'

He pushed his canoe out with a punt pole, bending as he came out of the boat-house, and shot off along the river at lightning speed.

'Doesn't he ever fall over?' asked Everard, turning round to look.

'Only if the water is low and there are snags sticking up,' said Kate. 'Lydia, that's my sister, is always upsetting, or else she gets left behind with the punt pole. It's all knack.'

Everard Carter bent to the oars and followed Colin downstream. In a few moments they reached the place where the river broadened, and here Colin was doing a kind of figure-punting by himself, with fantastic bends and swoops of his long body. Everard pulled into the bank and they watched Colin at play. Presently the sound of oars creaking in rowlocks was heard, and a boat with two scullers going at a good pace came up the river. Both ends of the boat were piled high with canvas bags and bundles.

'Campers,' said Kate. 'They often go up to Parsley Island opposite the Rectory. It belongs to Farmer Brown, who lets sites to campers, but we don't often get them as early as this.'

As the boat passed them, one of the oarsmen suddenly said, 'Easy all.' The boat slackened speed, and two hearty voices were raised in the revolting *Carmen Southbridgiense*, written in 1854 by the headmaster, the Rev. J. J. Damper (better known by his little volume of *Perambulations in Palestine*, now deservedly out of print), and set to music by the school organist, who also taught piano, violin, composition, singing, and anything parents asked for. As the final lines

> Alma Mater, Alma Mater,
> None than thou wilt e'er be greater,

(words justly condemned by the modern school of Latin pronunciation who amused themselves vastly by making Alma Mater rhyme with Mr Carter in various libellous ways), came ringing across the water, the singers raised their oars in token of respect.

'Good Lord, it's Swan and Morland,' said Everard. 'What are you doing?'

As he spoke he pulled towards them, and Colin came skimming over the water to their side.

'I say, sir, that's a decent kind of boat,' said Swan, eyeing the coracle with approval.

'Would you like to try her?' said Colin.

'I'd love to, sir, but we've got to get on to camp. Can you tell us how far up Parsley Island is?'

'About a mile. Is that where you are camping? Tell Farmer Brown you are friends of mine. He knows us pretty well. Come down and have tea one day. We live at the Manor, first boathouse on the right as you go up.'

'Thanks awfully, sir,' said Swan. 'Good night.'

'And for God's sake don't sing Alma Mater again,' said Everard, giving it the modern pronunciation, 'or I'll hold it against you both for the rest of the term.'

'O.K. sir,' said Morland. 'Come along, Eric, the stream runs fast, the rapids are near and the daylight past.'

In a few minutes the creaking of the oars had died away, and the water lay untroubled.

'What nice boys,' said Kate to Everard Carter. 'Are they in your house?'

Mr Carter said they were.

'One of them,' said Kate earnestly, 'had a cut on his hand that looked rather horrid. I wonder if they've got any iodine.'

'I expect so,' said Everard. 'Morland has a passion for iodine. Matron complains that it leaks all over his clothes.'

'And the other had a torn shirt with no buttons on it,' said Kate, her soft eyes shining with compassion.

'I expect it was an old one he was using up,' said Everard, uneasily conscious that one of his own waistcoat buttons was hanging by a thread.

'We might go up to the island to-morrow and see,' said Kate.

Everard agreed, indifferent as to the fate of Swan's buttons or Morland's finger, but overcome by admiration for Kate's divine pity.

'Home, James!' shouted Colin, giving his coracle a shove which sent her perilously rocketing up the river. Everard turned and rowed up-stream with the level sun in his eyes, so that he could not see Kate at all except as a dazzling, blinding glory; which was of course what she was. When they reached the house Kate said dinner wouldn't be till half-past eight, as Mr Merton couldn't get down earlier, so the men needn't hurry to dress.

'If you'll give me your waistcoat, Mr Carter,' she said, 'I'll sew that button on for you. It won't last much longer.'

Everard Carter, though fully sharing his junior housemaster's views about the vulgarity of braces, could not refuse. There was in Kate a calm air of competence that he had sometimes admired and even feared in matron, against which there was no appeal.

'It's awfully good of you,' he mumbled, handing the waistcoat to Kate and putting his coat on again as quickly as possible. While wallowing in his bath it occurred to him that never in his bachelor career had any woman succeeded in sewing on buttons for him, except housekeepers or other paid employees. He thought madly of cutting off a button a day for the pleasure of seeing that lovely look of pity in Kate's eyes, of submitting to her authority. He would have reflected on this subject for much longer but that his big toe, becoming entangled in the chain, pulled the plug out of the bath, and the water, with wild shouts of victory, rushed headlong down the waste-pipe. Just as he had finished dressing Colin came in.

'Kate asked me to bring you your waistcoat,' he said, 'and to say the button that was loose was an odd one, so she found one that matched and sewed it on. Come down and have some sherry. It's only the family and Noel Merton, the man I might be going to read with in the autumn.'

Mr and Mrs Keith were in the drawing-room. Mr Keith gave the guest sherry.

'Do come and sit here, Mr Carter,' said Mrs Keith. 'It was so nice of you to come for a dull family party. I have been wondering if you are by any chance a son of an old acquaintance of mine, Lady Sibyl Carter.'

'Not exactly a son,' said Everard, 'because I don't think she had any, and in any case she died before I was born, but I remember my mother talking about her. My great uncle, the archdeacon, who married her, was an Egyptologist and they were both mad.'

'That explains it then,' said Mrs Keith, though what it explained was not clear. 'Lydia, this is Mr Carter. My youngest daughter.'

'How do you do,' said Lydia, who was bursting out of a last year's frock for which she had a great affection. 'I say, mother, the beast Pettinger has given us extra prep for the Whitsun holidays. Geraldine Birkett says she jolly well won't do it. It's a whacking great ode of Horace and an essay about Compare Addison and Pope, with quotations from their works. What good on earth it can do anyone to compare two people who are quite different, and anyway we've only half done Pope this term, so I call the whole thing jolly mean.'

'I quite agree with you,' said Everard.

'But I thought you were a schoolmaster too,' said Lydia.

'But not a headmistress, I am thankful to say.'

'Do you know Miss Pettinger then?' asked Lydia.

'I once had the horror of meeting her,' said Everard gravely.

'You've said it,' remarked Lydia, with her American accent, and was just going to give her amplified views on her headmistress when Kate drew her aside.

'Lydia,' she said, 'have you no stockings on again?'

'Oh, Kate, they all needed darning, and anyway this skirt touches the ground, so it doesn't matter.'

'I mended two pairs and put them on your dressing-table,' said Kate with mild reproach.

'Oh, Kate, what an angel you are. Need I put them on? Don't you hate wearing stockings, Mr Carter?'

'I can't say that I do,' said Everard, 'but then they rarely come my way.'

'Where's Merton?' said Mr Keith, looking at his watch. 'It's five and twenty to nine.'

'He'll be down in a second,' said Lydia. 'I was showing him that ghastly pair of pyjamas mother got me at Bournemouth, and we laughed so much that it made us late, and that was why I had to put on my dress as I came downstairs and never looked on my dressing-table, or I'd have seen the stockings, so that's really why, and anyway one of my suspenders burst.'

Any further domestic details were cut short by the appearance of Noel Merton, looking so elegant, so entirely unconscious of his elegance, that Kate's feelings leapt to her eyes. Everard Carter, seeing her face, felt that his journey must continue, with no visible, no possible ending, and listened with much amusement to his hostess's description of his great-aunt Sibyl. At dinner, seeing that Lydia, who was next to him, was preparing to monopolize not only Noel but the whole table, he devoted himself to her entertainment, and was favoured with many original though not very valuable reflexions on Shakespeare, Latin literature, cocker spaniels, and the incredible horribleness of Miss Pettinger. In this last he was able so heartily to sympathize that he won Lydia's deep respect and even attention. Mr Keith registered mental approval of a man who could get the upper hand of his younger daughter, and when, after the ladies had left them, he found that Everard came of a legal family and had read law himself before becoming a school-master, his approval was complete.

'What made you give up the law, Carter?' he asked.

'I couldn't afford it,' said Everard. 'My people weren't well off and I had a chance in a school, so I took it.'

'Too bad, too bad,' said Mr Keith.

'I don't know,' said Everard. 'We schoolmasters are, I admit, an awful, creeping, degraded race, class-conscious, hardly emerged from the cocoon of the usher, but there is something. I don't yet know what it is. Some of us honestly like boys, some don't. Now, I could bang the heads of any two of the boys in my house or my form together twenty times a day, with the greatest pleasure, and yet I'm wretched without them, I get them at about thirteen, when the shades of the prison house are closing, when they are changing from the frank devils of the prep schools to the more subtle fiends of public school. I see them through mental and moral mumps and measles, I send them on to the Universities, business, the army; spotty, it is true, but improved. Most of them are glad to escape. The few who remember me think of me as an old dodderer, who did his poor best. I have no home but my house, no particular future, for good headmasterships are scarce, and I'm not very ambitious. But I like it better than anything in the world.'

'I wish I did,' said Colin. 'Does one ever stop feeling that boys despise one?'

'Never,' said Everard. 'It is a faint comfort to hug the consciousness that after all we really know a little more than they do. I have got a good many boys out of scrapes, from attacks of religion to calf love, and though they have gone on despising me, they have conceived a faint, a very faint respect for my office. That is perhaps worth while. I don't know.'

'I suppose schoolmastering is a kind of lay priesthood,' said Noel, interested.

'Roughly, very roughly, yes. Just as, roughly, the legal profession is a trade union. That is why you make more mark in the world than we do. You have more solidarity.'

'I thought,' said Mr Keith, 'that schoolmasters were a pretty solid body.'

'I think Mr Carter would say, if he weren't afraid of boasting,' said Noel, 'that in the higher branches of his profession the solidarity becomes mostly a matter of form, a weapon for help in case of real need, but a weapon one would rather not use, partly from a feeling of personal integrity, partly because one doesn't much care to be under the same flag as those who use the weapon politically, without thinking of duty. I imagine that with Mr Carter his sense of his rights would always be outweighed by his sense of duty. I know my old housemaster, whom I confess I regarded in Mr Carter's own words as a well-meaning old dodderer, would have been chucked out of any self-respecting union as a black-leg of the first water. I only realized much later how he had given his time and mind and strength, not to speak of reduced fees in some cases, to boys who needed it.'

'Thank you,' said Everard. 'Do you never work over and above what the letter of your profession demands?'

'Oh, well,' said Noel.

'I must say, speaking as a mere solicitor,' said Mr Keith, 'that in the matter of looks the legal profession scores heavily.'

'That,' said Everard, 'is certainly a point against the ushers. Why most barristers look like very distinguished hawks, or Admirals of the Fleet, while schoolmasters look like anything or nothing on earth, I don't know. It isn't fair.'

'Mr Birkett looks perfectly normal,' said Colin.

'So do I, I flatter myself,' said Everard, 'but that proves nothing. Take any large gathering of us, and you will be horrified by the varieties of ill-made faces and bodies, the booming and squeaking voices.'

'Anyway,' said Colin loyally, 'a lot of parsons look worse. You see them at conferences and things at Barchester.'

'To go back to our talk,' said Noel, 'is it partly being with young people that makes schoolmastering attractive?'

'No,' said Everard. 'It is being perpetually with the young that turns us into boneheads and fossils. Imagine a life in which you rarely talk to people on your own intellectual level. We may sharpen our wits on them, it is one of our few weapons, and an unfair one at that; it is not until they are in their last year that we can sharpen our wits against them. And by that time they are usually so earnest. Age and crabbed youth simply cannot live together for very long, without age either going under or assuming a protective coat of cynicism, and when it comes to cynicism they can beat us at our own game now.'

'Have another glass of port,' said Mr Keith, 'and we'll go to the drawing-room. Well, Colin, what do you think of it all?'

'I think what Everard says is perfectly splendid, but a little frightening. I really like school quite a lot, if only the boys wouldn't look at me.'

'They don't look at you, Colin, they look through you,' said Everard, staring into his port as if it were the sooth-sayer's pool of ink. 'When we are young we all look through our elders, to see what lies beyond. And when we see what is there, we are the elders ourselves. I wish, at the end of this rather boring disquisition, into which Mr Merton has lured me, I could say I have no regrets for my own crabbed youth. There are moments when one misses it quite desperately.'

He spoke with abstracted melancholy, looking not at

Colin, a good dozen years younger than himself, but at Noel Merton, for whom Kate's eyes had shone.

When they reached the drawing-room, Lydia had been dismissed to do her essay on Addison and Pope. Noel didn't play bridge, so he and Kate talked very comfortably while the others played. Everard, conscious of his duty as a guest, played with concentration, his back to the talkers, determined to let no echo of their voices come between him and the cards, and was rewarded by winning seven shillings.

'I never thanked you for sewing on that button, Miss Keith,' said Everard, before they went upstairs. 'You haven't by any chance got the old one, have you?'

'I am so sorry,' said Kate. 'I threw it away. I could look for it if you like. Did you want it?'

'Not particularly. Please don't bother,' said Everard. 'I just thought I might like it.'

He went to bed, humming to himself 'I sent thee late a rosy wreath', and wishing that waistcoat button could be substituted without seriously impairing the poetic and rhythmical value of that well-known lyric.

CHAPTER V

Whitsun Picnic

SELDOM had Lydia passed a more agreeable Whitsun. Her friend Noel, it is true, did not give her quite so much of his company as she had expected, but she did not grudge him to Kate, though what on earth Noel could find to talk to Kate about, she could not guess. On the other hand, Mr Carter, who was almost as nice as Noel, devoted himself to her to a flattering extent, and as Colin seemed to prefer their company, Lydia was certain of an audience. Mr Carter also obliged with some very useful tips about Addison and Pope, and by his and Colin's joint exertions she was dragged through what she had described as that whacking great ode of Horace with the bit about Lacedaemonium Tarentum, a line which at least had the merit of requiring practically no translation. To Colin's great admiration Everard also took a short ode about Lucina in his stride, while Lydia showed in its subject a lack of interest which well became her years.

'Of course I know all about babies,' she said scornfully, 'botany and birth-control and all that. Rot I call it. I say, Colin, let's have a picnic on Sunday up the river. If it goes on being as hot as this it'll be ripping.'

Colin agreed heartily, but suddenly said, 'Oh, Lord!'

'What is it?' asked Everard.

'I didn't tell you,' said Colin, 'that evening I had supper at the Head's house, the day after Hacker left the bath on, the Birketts said they were probably going to the Rectory for Whitsun, with Rose.'

'And therefore Philip,' said Everard.

Lydia asked what they were talking about, and on hearing their difficulties said she didn't see why they were worrying, but if they'd rather go down-stream she didn't mind. This plan was shattered at Sunday breakfast by Mrs Keith, who said she had met Colin's nice headmaster and his wife at dinner at the Deanery the night before, and had arranged with them for a joint picnic to be held on Parsley Island.

'There aren't any campers there yet, so Farmer Brown told your father a week or two ago,' said Mrs Keith, 'and if it keeps as hot as this it will be very nice for you. When my Uncle Oswald was in Calcutta they went up-country every week-end for a kind of picnic, but of course everything went on elephants, because they had a Rajah's son at his school who couldn't go by train because of losing caste or something. There was a very pretty daughter of Mrs Birkett's there, Colin, she said you were a great friend of hers, so I thought that would be nice for you. Your father and I will drive as far as the ferry, and you young people can go up in the boats and take us across. Will you drive with us, Mr Carter?'

Everard, realizing without animus that he was somehow not a young person, though Noel, who was about his own age, was, said he would be delighted, but Lydia protested violently that Everard must come in the boat.

'Really, Lydia,' said her mother. 'Mr Carter, I am so very sorry. Those young people seem to use Christian names almost before they know the surnames.'

'Oh, mother!' said Lydia, 'I couldn't say Mr Carter. Besides Everard doesn't mind, do you, Everard? I mean being a schoolmaster doesn't make you be a mister for the rest of your life, and anyway Everard beat me at tennis, and rode my bicycle backwards all up the grass border without falling off, and I fell off twice.'

'I don't know how often I have told you not to ride on that grass border,' said her father.

'Then,' said Kate quickly, 'I must see about food. Will

you take the drinks in the car, and we can take the food in the boat.'

'What about the thermos that leaks?' said Mrs Keith.

'I got a new one last week, mother, and there's your big one, and that one of Robert's he left here, and that other one in the leather case, so we ought to do. Mr Merton, you like Gentlemen's Relish, don't you? Mr Carter, do you like any special sandwich?'

Everard was torn between wishing she didn't so well remember what Merton liked, and gratitude to her for taking an interest in his own tastes. He also wished that the fact of his having eaten four more sandwiches than Merton yesterday had not so entirely escaped her notice, but to keep himself humble he said he liked Gentlemen's Relish too.

Mrs Keith forced the unwilling Lydia to put on stockings and go to Northbridge church with her and Mr Keith, while the others played some lazy tennis and sat about in the garden, enjoying the blazing heat. By lunchtime it was so hot that everyone was glad of open windows and ice in the drinks. Lydia took off her stockings again and appeared in an exiguous and shapeless garment with holes for her head and arms, considered by her suitable for picnics, and firmly refused to change, on the grounds that she always fell into the river, and the less she had to change the better.

At half-past three, Kate, Lydia, Everard, Noel and Colin staggered sleepily down to the boat-house with baskets of food and a rug. Heavy white clouds were massing over the downs, and Kate said there would be thunder, but she thought not till after tea. She with Everard and Colin packed into the boat, while Lydia annexed Noel for the coracle, and said she would punt him upstream, adding that she had never fallen into the river going up-stream yet. At Parsley Island they tied up the boat and landed. It was a pretty island, with grass and beech trees down to the water's edge and a little thicket on the farther side. On the opposite bank was the ferryman's boat, and a few yards lower down the Rectory exhibited its Gothic revival windows and well laid out garden, embanked with a red brick wall along the river. A punt was moored at the foot of a flight of brick steps. A golden Sunday calm brooded over everything, and when Lydia stopped talking there was no sound but the distant noise of the weir, farther up-stream.

'By Jove,' said Colin, 'those boys are somewhere on the island. Shall we explore?'

'I thought you didn't like boys,' said Everard, lying full length on his back, his voice muffled by the hat he had put over his face.

'No more I do,' said Colin, 'but they might like some tea. I remember what camping was. Bacon and sausages till you burst the first day, and then starvation. Besides, those are rather nice boys.'

'Because they are products of my house,' said Everard.

'I expect you are right,' said Colin seriously.

'I brought some iodine and some buttons and things,' said Kate, 'in case they needed them, so we might go and look.'

'All right,' said Everard, getting up.

The island was not large, and before they had gone far they heard voices. A winding path led them through the thicket to the brink of what looked like a small disused sand or gravel pit. Swan and Morland were sprawling upon the ground, dressed in very dirty shorts. Morland had a disgraceful linen hat tilted over his nose, and Swan wore his spectacles and a green eye-shade. Both were reading. A very small tent with the flaps neatly turned up was near by, and the remains of a fire were smouldering. At the sound of footsteps the readers looked up.

'Hist, brother, Gorgio shunella!' said Swan, recog-. nizing the intruders.

Morland took out of his mouth the piece of grass he had been chewing, marked his page with it, shut the book, and got up.

'Come into the dingle, sir,' he called to Colin. 'Genuine scholar gypsies; baked hedgehogs, drabbed bawlor, poisoned cake from Mrs Hearne's recipe for anyone who likes, and beds for all who come,' he added, pointing proudly to the tent.

The party descended into the dingle. Colin introduced Noel, Kate and Lydia to Swan and Morland, who did the honours of the dingle with true Romany courtesy. Everard and Colin they received as temporary equals, with that fine shade of condescension which only an equal can appreciate. To Noel they were equally polite and agreeable, while managing to convey to him the impression that civility to strangers was the necessary duty of any gentleman. Kate they accepted at once as one of the grown-ups set over them by Providence, and Lydia, after an almost imperceptible exchange of glances, passed as a good fellow, though with not much intellect.

'What are you reading?' asked Noel.

'The score of Stravinsky's *Sacre du Printemps*, sir,' said Swan. 'It's immensely interesting, but I'm not sure if the use of the brass is legitimate. What do you think?'

Noel very bravely said that he didn't know the score, and had only once heard the work, and knew nothing about it.

'Of course, I'm only the dilettante,' said Swan modestly. 'Tony here is the real reader.'

'Gosh!' said Colin, who had looked at Morland's book, 'you're reading *Lemon* too!'

'He's jolly good reading, sir, don't you think?' said Morland, pleased to find another railway enthusiast. 'I've always been very keen on railways, ever since I had a clockwork train, and I like reading everything I can find about them. *Lemon on Running Powers* is awfully interesting. I find it a bit stiff in bits, but of course you wouldn't, sir.'

'Well, I did,' said Colin, 'and I had to get Mr Merton to explain it.'

Colin and Morland would have liked a long talk about *Lemon*, but Kate interrupted to inquire after Morland's hand, which had a very disgusting piece of sticking plaster on it.

'It's splendid, thank you,' said Morland. 'Eric had a little bottle of peroxide with him, so we put it on and watched the rotten part fizzling. It was ripping. Would you like to see the tent?'

Ignoring the fact that she could already see it quite well, Kate allowed the boys to show her everything; their clothes and camp equipment neatly folded, and the trench they had dug in case of rain. When she had admired it all, she inquired if any mending were needed. They thanked her, but said no.

'Your shirt didn't seem to have any buttons the other day,' said Kate to Swan.

'Oh, that shirt doesn't like buttons, thanks awfully. What, Tony?' said Swan, as his friend hit him. 'Oh, yes. It's awfully kind of you, Miss Keith, and if you did happen to have any black wool about you we'd be very grateful if you could mend a sock. You see, we only brought one spare pair, and Tony burnt half of it when he was using it to take the frying pan off the fire, when we were doing sausages.'

Kate said she had her sewing things in her bag, and would love to mend the half sock. The boys were then formally invited to the picnic, an invitation gladly accepted. The picnic-party returned to the boat, leaving Swan and Morland to make themselves a little tidier before entering society.

By the time tea was laid the Keiths had arrived in the car with the thermoses. Colin went over to the bank to fetch them. A few minutes later the ferryboat was seen coming across with Mr and Mrs Birkett, who explained that neither of them punted, so they had left the punt for their daughter and Mr Winter, who had gone out in the blue sports car. Swan and Morland, in blue short-sleeved shirts and flannel trousers, joined them. Mrs Birkett begged that no one would wait for her unpunctual young people. Swan and Morland were very helpful in passing things, and then tacitly withdrew with Lydia and a large plate of mixed food to a slight distance, leaving the grown-ups to themselves.

'Lydia,' Kate called across the grass, 'where did I put the Gentlemen's Relish sandwiches?'

'I don't know,' shouted Lydia through a large mouthful of something. 'Have the last sandwich, Tony.'

'Rather,' said Morland. 'I say these sandwiches are pretty decent. What are they? Anchovy?'

'Dunno,' said Lydia. 'It says on the paper. Kate always writes on sandwiches what's in them, as if one couldn't taste.'

'Patum Peperium,' Morland read on the greaseproof paper. 'It would make a good verse for the *Carmen*, Eric.'

> 'Patum Peperium, Patum Peperium,
> When they stink you'd better bury 'em.'

This brilliant effusion was a great success with both Swan and Lydia, and led to a very intellectual discussion of Horace, in the course of which it was unanimously agreed that if he hadn't written in Latin he would have been a jolly good poet. The noise and laughter made Mrs Keith ask what it was.

'Only Tony making a poem about Patum Peperium,' said Lydia.

Kate jumped up and went over to the classical department. The incriminating paper lay at her feet.

'Oh, Lydia, you've eaten all the Gentlemen's Relish,' she said.

'It said Patum Peperium,' said Lydia.

'My good girl, don't you know that Patum Peperium is the Latin for Gentlemen's Relish,' said Swan. 'These girls' schools! We're awfully sorry, Miss Keith. We didn't know they were special.'

'As long as you enjoyed them, it's all right,' said Kate. 'There's fruit salad when you're ready, but you'll have to come over and get plates and spoons. I've got the mending for your sock, Tony, if you let me have it.'

Morland handed her the sock, which she put in her bag.

'Gosh!' said Swan, pointing to the river. 'There's our Rose in a punt.'

'Is that the one that's engaged to a master?' asked Lydia.

'Yes. And there is the master, our Mr Winter, punting her. Look at him, Tony, the water's running down his sleeves.'

Philip Winter, not an expert punter, was indeed nearly wet through already, with a sluice of water running all over him every time he lifted the punt pole. He tied up the punt and he and Rose came ashore. Rose, in pale pink organdie with a large floppy hat, looked so perfectly the River Girl that an audible gasp went up from her audience.

'Well, I'm glad I don't look like that,' said Lydia, who was sitting on the ground, her feet straight out in front of her, her face, neck, arms and legs bright red, and her hair tied back with an old tie of Swan's that she had borrowed.

'It wouldn't hurt you to tidy up a bit,' said Swan, 'though I admit our Rose is more the pink limit than ever to-day.'

The presence of three young men, one of them a stranger, gave added lustre to Rose's lovely eyes and an added flush to her well made-up cheeks. She at once embarked on an animated conversation with all three, ignoring her damp affianced in a way which, used though he was to her peculiarities, he could hardly bear. Lydia and the boys, attracted like savages to something new, came over and established themselves among the party, gazing with the unmoved and scornful stoicism of Red Indians upon the enchanting Miss Birkett.

Kate, who couldn't bear to see anyone neglected, addressed Philip, asking him if he had seen the Whitsun decorations in Northbridge church.

Philip said it was horrible to see flowers torn from their natural setting and slowly dying of thirst.

Kate, who had a kind heart for everything, said she hated that, of course, but that in Northbridge church all the flowers had their stalks either in jam-jars of water or in damp moss.

Yes, said Philip, while human beings were dying slowly in the depressed areas.

Lydia, resenting Philip's way of taking her sister's kind advances, said loudly that it was awful about the depressed areas, but she didn't see that jam-jars of water or damp moss would be any good to their inhabitants, even if some people did like being wet.

Philip, his damp shirt clinging to his shoulders, sore at his Rose's immediate neglect of him for a gilded stranger (for so he inaptly called Noel in his own mind), made a scornful noise and said, pointedly ignoring Lydia, that the money spent on flowers would have supported several families for a week, but he supposed Miss Keith knew nothing about such uncomfortable subjects.

Kate, having to disappoint him, said that far from money having been spent on flowers, they were all gifts. And what was more, Lydia put in, her sister had done charitable work in Barchester ever since she left school and been into all sorts of perfectly ghastly places that she didn't suppose Mr Winter had ever heard of, and she didn't have to read the newspaper to know about distressed areas.

'Good old Lydia! Muscle in!' said Swan, softly enough for Philip to have to pretend that he hadn't heard.

Philip, looking angrily at Lydia, said it was easy for people with great gardens and acres of hothouses to give from their superfluity, and the poverty in Barchester was (which he seemed to consider discreditable to it) as nothing compared with the poverty of the distressed areas, and that social problems could not be tackled by amateur charitable organizations, and as an after-thought, that fascism got no one anywhere.

Kate was so puzzled by the sudden introduction of fascism, and the way in which Philip was now arguing on three different subjects at once, that she was silent for a moment. But Lydia, looking at Philip as if he were a blackbeetle, said no one with any sense would be a fascist.

'Nor a communist either,' she went on, stunning the rest of her auditors with the power of her voice. 'I'm all for the Empire myself. I mean when people are young I suppose they've got to be something, but the sooner they get over it the better. And as a matter of fact the flowers all come from the cottage gardens, and the best ones came from the allotments down by the railway. And if people aren't as distressed in Barchester as they are in the north of England, that's a jolly good thing for Barchester, and anyway if they wanted they could be just as dis-tressed as anyone. And as for charitable things, they do the best they can, and that's more than can be said of everyone that talks a lot. I say, Eric, let's have races. We'll punt the boat, and Tony can punt the canoe, and whoever falls in first wins.'

As the three younger members withdrew, Mrs Keith, who hadn't heard the beginning of the conversation, but had been agitated by her younger daughter's attack on a guest, turned to Philip, and asked him kindly whether he had seen the Whitsun decorations in Northbridge church, which she thought quite lovely.

'Don't you feel the brutality of tearing flowers from their natural surroundings to perish slowly of thirst,' said Philip, torn by the sight of Rose's triple flirtation, miserably conscious that he could hardly control himself, anxious to wound someone.

Mrs Keith looked at him with interest.

'No,' she said thoughtfully, 'not if they give pleasure. You must excuse my disagreeing with you, but I find that a purely sentimental point of view. If it were human beings I could sympathize, like Negroes being sold down the river, or child marriage that my Uncle Oswald used to think so unfortunate. But, of course, in England child marriages are not allowed.'

'People are suffering and dying day by day in the distressed areas,' said Philip, sticking to one of his points.

'But that is so sentimental again,' said Mrs Keith. 'They are suffering just as much here, only because it's the South no one is interested. Henry,' she called to her husband, who had been talking to the Birketts, 'Henry, what is the number of people out of work at Hogglestock? Mr Winter is interested in unemployment.'

'About three hundred, I'm afraid, since the boiler works closed down,' said Mr Keith.

'There!' said Mrs Keith.

'They are doing all they can for them in Barchester,' said Mr Keith. 'The Dean's grandfather used to be a curate at Hogglestock when it was a very poor agricultural community, and Crawley has always felt a special interest in it. What touched him very much was that some of the Easter flowers in the cathedral were offered by the men there, who had grown them in their enforced leisure. The committee on which the Dean and I serve had provided garden tools and seeds.'

'They asked for bread and you gave them stones,' said Philip sternly.

'Not stones, *seeds*,' said Mrs Keith. 'I wonder, Mr Winter, if you are related to my Uncle Andrew. He was the youngest of my grandfather's second family. My father, who was the youngest of the third family, was very fond of him. His second wife was a Miss Winter whose parents had lived in Bermuda and were supposed to have a trace of black blood.'

'My father is a clergyman,' said Philip, rather sulkily.

'Then he wouldn't have black blood,' said Mrs Keith. 'At least, I'm not sure, for I know I met a black bishop once, at the Palace at Barchester, but then, being a bishop makes a difference. I don't think they'd allow it in the lower branches.'

'My father has no black blood,' said Philip, determinedly.

'Of course not,' said Mrs Keith. 'Kate, I do think it's going to rain.'

'I'm sure it is,' said Kate; for the fat white clouds had turned black while they were talking and were surging up in the sky, while a chill wind began to blow. 'You and father had better go back.'

Mr Keith said he would take the Birketts and his wife over in the Rectory punt, leaving the picnic-party to collect the boats and bring them home. Rose had no objection to being left with so many gentlemen, and no one took any notice of Philip, who began to collect the tea-things in a hopeless way. Kind Kate, who saw what the matter was, and bore him no grudge for his recent attacks on the church decorations and charitable committees, knelt beside him, packing up the remains of the feast in friendly silence.

'I'm sorry,' said Philip presently, in an ungracious voice.

'Lydia can be most trying,' said Kate.

One or two big drops fell. Kate looked anxiously up the river, but the racing craft were not yet in sight.

'Philip,' said Rose, addressing her lover for the first time since the picnic began, 'can't you get a boat? My frock will be spoilt.'

Short of swimming across and getting the punt there was no escape till the boat and canoe came back. Colin said he would shout for the ferry, but it was well known that old Bunce took himself off duty every day from five to seven, these being the hours when the ferry was most in demand, and worked on his allotment a quarter of a mile away, besides being stone deaf. They all shouted, but no one appeared.

'Oh, Philip, you are sickening,' said Rose. 'It's going to pelt, and you know I'm frightened of thunder.'

'I'll go up to the end of the island and yell to Lydia,' said Colin. 'They can't have gone farther than the weir.'

He buttoned up his coat and ran off. The heavy drops were spattering on the tree beneath which Rose and her cavaliers were standing. Rose had taken off her flowered hat and was holding it in her hand.

'You are sickening not to have brought a coat, Philip,' said Rose. 'Isn't he sickening, Mr Merton?'

'Have mine,' said Noel, taking off his grey flannel coat with a good pretence of willingness, and putting it carefully round Rose's exquisite shoulders.

'Thanks most awfully,' said Rose. 'Oh, Mr Carter, could I have your coat to cover my hat? It will be absolutely spoiled if it gets wet.'

Everard saw nothing for it but to take off the coat and give it to Rose, who wrapped her hat carefully in it. Philip, nearly beside himself with mortification and rage, strode off after Colin, leaving Kate to pack the last of the tea-things into the basket.

'Miss Keith,' said Everard, 'you'll get wet. Come under the trees.'

'Where is your coat?' asked Kate severely. 'You'll be drenched.'

'Rose Birkett, confound her, has taken it to cover her hat,' said Everard.

'There's the rug,' said Kate. 'I'd put it under the tea basket to keep it dry. It's rather old and dirty, but if you don't mind —'

Everard seized the rug, rapidly unfolded it and put it round Kate. Kate snatched up her bag from the ground and they ran under the trees, where Kate knew a good log they could sit on. Lightning split the clouds and thunder crackled across the sky. Then the rain came down in a steady drench.

'You'd better have some of the rug,' said Kate, unfolding it to its fullest extent and throwing part of it across Everard's shoulders. 'I don't think much rain will come through the leaves, but it's silly to get wet. These storms never last long. Now I can get that sock of Tony's mended.'

From her bag she took some black wool, a darning needle, and a black sock into which she thrust her hand. A small charred circle in the leg had crumbled away, leaving a hole. Kate looked at the sock more closely.

'Oh, Mr Carter,' she said, 'someone has been mending this sock with navy blue wool!'

Everard was hardly in a state to understand anything. Pure chance had set him there on a log, a very shabby old rug folding him and Kate away from the world. The words 'expiring frog' floated in his mind, which was otherwise a thundering void, flecked with points of light. He pulled himself together enough to say in a weak voice, 'I'm sorry.'

'Oh, it isn't your fault,' said Kate tolerantly. 'I don't suppose you can think about boys' socks as well as everything else. I'll just unpick this and darn it again properly.

Can you imagine anyone using navy blue wool for a black sock!'

Everard was so deeply conscious of Kate by his side that he could only just summon enough strength to say 'No.'

'I suppose you haven't any real control over the matron,' said Kate. 'I don't see how a man could have. But really, navy blue wool –'

'Do you mind if I smoke,' said Everard, hoping to calm himself. He took a cigarette and lit it, but his hands shook so much that Kate looked up from her work.

'You have got a chill,' she said anxiously. 'I do think Miss Birkett is a little unreasonable to want two coats, but she is so very pretty. The rain won't last much longer. Look, it's clearing towards Barchester. I can see the sun on the cathedral. Put the rug more round you.'

'I don't think I could bear to,' said Everard, feeling that to be a fraction of an inch nearer Kate would make him say or do something that would banish him for ever from the society of honourable men.

'If you really aren't cold –' said Kate doubtfully. 'Oh, that button you wanted. I found it in the waste-paper basket.'

She fished in her work-bag and extracted the button.

'They seem rather careless at your school,' she said. 'Fancy sewing a button that doesn't match onto a waist-coat! But this one might come in useful for something, so I kept it for you.'

Everard took the button. The ineffable bliss of touching Kate's fingers, if only for a moment, so wrought upon his senses that he immediately dropped it.

'Oh dear,' said Kate, 'it must have fallen on the ground.'

Everard scrabbled among leaves and moss and twigs in vain.

'Perhaps,' said Kate, 'it has fallen into the turn-ups of

your trousers. Colin lost sixpence like that once, for ages.'

Everard rummaged round his ankles and rescued the button. As he wasn't wearing a waistcoat he tied it up in the corner of his handkerchief.

'They really are dreadful, Mr Carter,' said Kate, her eyes flashing with honest indignation.

'Who?'

'The people who do your mending. Look at that handkerchief. The corner is right off!'

'I think the rain has stopped,' said Everard, getting up so suddenly that Kate was afraid she had hurt him by her criticisms of the school mending.

The rain had cleared as quickly as it came. Brilliant sunshine flooded the landscape, and the shouts of the returning travellers could be heard. The boat, with Swan, Colin and Philip on board, soon appeared, and the coracle, propelled by Morland and Lydia, followed hard upon it.

'Did you get wet?' asked Kate as the boat and the coracle drew up.

'Not a bit,' said Lydia. 'We went into the cottage at the lock and had parsnip wine. And I didn't fall in at all. And we picked Colin and this one up at the end of the island.'

'You jolly nearly did fall in,' said Morland, 'if Eric and I hadn't grabbed you. It all comes of drinking homebrew with the tenantry.'

'Ass!' said Lydia, in high good humour, nearly up-setting the coracle with the violence of the blow she aimed at him.

'Well, we'd better get home,' said Kate. 'Oh, where are Mr Merton and Miss Birkett?'

'I'll find them,' said Philip, springing on shore, damp and angry, and making hotfoot for the tree where he had last seen his beloved; but she was not there. The beloved, had he known it, was now some distance away, comfortably seated on Everard's coat, her hat on her lap, Noel's coat over her head like a shawl. Noel himself was leaning against a tree which protected him from the shower. He had amused himself quite sufficiently with Rose. Never in his life had he met anyone so entirely foolish, and seldom anyone so absurdly pretty. He had, for his own interest, tried at least twenty different conversational openings, to none of which had Rose made any response, till he wondered if she were really half-witted. Her entire vocabulary appeared to consist of the words Marvellous and Sickening, with a smattering of light badinage of the 'You did', 'I didn't' description. In vain had he tried school, weather, the cinema, the Royal Family, boating, cricket, till at last, just as the storm was passing, he hit upon Shakespeare.

'Oh, I do adore him,' said Rose. 'He's marvellous. I saw him fourteen times.'

'Saw whom?'

'Shakespeare. At that theatre in London, you know. John Potter was absolutely marvellous in it.'

'Oh, Hamlet.'

'Yes. Of course, it's sickening the way Hamlet dies at the end, but it's too marvellous the way he does it. I'd love to go again about fourteen times more. Don't you think Shakespeare is absolutely sickeningly marvellous?'

'Absolutely,' said Noel, at which moment Philip surged out from among the bushes, and stood flaming in wrath.

'I've been looking for you everywhere, Rose,' he said, taking no notice of Noel. 'Where have you been?'

'Here, of course,' said Rose, opening her large eyes wide. 'Mr Merton simply adores Shakespeare. Are you wet, darling? I've had a marvellous time with Mr Merton's coat.'

'Well, you'd better come along now,' said Philip, 'before it rains again.'

He held out his hand to Rose, but she got up lightly,

without assistance, and taking the coat off her head handed it to Noel.

'Thanks most awfully,' she said. 'Philip, you were sickeningly silly not to bring a coat.'

Philip, who would willingly have flayed himself alive to provide a shelter for Rose, had to bear the sight of the gilded stranger callously putting on the coat that was hallowed for ever by the warmth and fragrance of his lovely idol.

'Come on,' said the idol, 'it'll be dinner-time soon, and I must get the bath before mummy has it. There are only two baths at the Rectory, Mr Merton. Isn't it sickening?'

'You didn't bring my coat, did you?' asked Everard, as Rose and her admirers came down to the water.

'No. Where is it?' said Rose. 'Oh, I was sitting on it. Philip, be an angel and fetch it.'

But Noel, with a fellow feeling for that nice chap Carter, who had also had to do without his coat to please a silly little sparrow-wit, had already run back and fetched Everard's coat. When the owner put it on, everyone could see a large, damp, greenish stain on the back.

'Oh, Mr Carter's coat must have got wet,' said Rose.

'Yes, isn't it sickening?' said Noel politely.

Everard said nothing, but his dislike for his headmaster's daughter became perceptibly stronger.

Rose and Philip were landed at the Rectory steps, and the rest went back to the Manor, only to discover that Mrs Keith had asked the whole Rectory party to come in after dinner.

'Now I know why people leave home,' said Colin to Noel and Everard, as they were having a drink before going up to dress for dinner. 'As if it weren't bad enough to have Rose for tea. Now we'll all have to dance with her. If I weren't a so-called gentleman I could say a great deal.'

'Anything you could say is simply nothing compared

with what I've got to say,' said Noel. 'I had to stand bare to the blast under a tree in a thunderstorm while that Beautiful Pink Devil sat on all the coats and drivelled about Hamlet being marvellous till I could have thumped her on the head.'

'Anyway, she was only wearing your coat,' said Everard, 'not sitting on it. I always wondered what Sir Walter Raleigh really felt like, and now I know. How Philip can stand it I can't think.'

'He's smashingly in love just now,' said Noel. 'I hope he won't marry her, because if he does he will very rightly murder her, and though his manners are not very good I wouldn't wish a dog to swing for the pink fondant. Let's have a sweepstake. Half a crown each, and whichever has to dance with her most gets it.'

The three half-crowns were handed over by the conspirators, who bound themselves by an oath to use no unfair methods of avoiding Rose.

'Although,' said Everard, 'I've never seen a seven and six I would more willingly forgo.'

While Everard was dressing for dinner there was a knock at the door and Palmer came in.

'I beg your pardon, sir,' she said, not looking at Everard, who was all dressed but his dinner jacket, in a way that made him feel like a professional seducer, 'but Miss Kate asked me to ask you for your coat. She says there's something nasty on it.'

Everard gave her the stained coat, and was so moved that he parted his hair on the wrong side and had to do it all over again. From his other trousers pocket he took his handkerchief, unknotted it, took out the button, looked lovingly at it, and put it away in the box where his pearl studs lived.

Dinner was languid. Mr Keith was sleepy after the picnic, and the three younger men annoyed at the prospect of Rose and her difficult admirer being thrust on

them. Kate was thinking how very sorry she was for poor
Mr Winter, and how best she could get the stains out of
Mr Carter's coat, and whether there would be enough
drinks for the evening if everyone came. Lydia, a healthy
but hideous sight, red with sunburn on every visible inch
of skin, was thinking of further arguments of a knock-
down nature to use against that horrid Mr Winter. Mrs
Keith, hospitably pleased at having invited the Birketts
and their pretty daughter and her fiancé, noticed nothing, and gave Everard a very interesting account of her
grandfather's family by his second wife.

Dinner at the Rectory was not much better. Philip had
quite lost his temper and made a scene in the garden
after he and Rose had landed. It could not be called a
quarrel, because Rose never listened to anything he said,
and therefore was a merely passive, though highly exas-
perating, party to the affray. It began by Philip sneezing
twice, which caused Rose to say for perhaps the tenth
time that he was sickening not to have brought a coat.
At this Philip had gone even whiter than usual and
accused her of being heartless. Rose said, well, now he
was sneezing, which showed, and it would be absolutely
sickening if he got a cold, and not to come too near her
as she didn't want to catch it. Philip said if everyone
caught cold and died it would be her fault, as she hadn't
the sense to bring a coat herself and took other people's.
He hoped Mr Carter and Mr Merton would both die,
and serve her right, and serve them right, too. He added
as an afterthought that he hoped young Keith would die
too. Rose said she would never be ready for dinner in
time and must have her bath, and blowing Philip a kiss
went indoors. Philip's gloom at dinner was so marked that
the schoolgirl prattle of Geraldine Birkett, who had been
let loose for the Whitsun holiday from Miss Pettinger's
school where she boarded, was for once gratefully
encouraged by her parents.

When they arrived at Northbridge Manor Colin and Noel had cleared one end of the drawing-room for dancing. Lydia, who despised dancing, had retired to her room. For Philip the evening was an unmixed failure. His cold was getting worse every minute and he was turned down as partner on the ground of infection by Rose, who annexed Colin as a suitable victim. Colin could not very well refuse a guest who was his headmaster's daughter, but he wished Rose were a better dancer. Everard had the displeasure of seeing Noel and Kate dance very exquisitely together for a long time. Colin, to his great relief, was presently cut out by his father who, a dancer of the old-fashioned bumpy style himself, did not mind Rose's rather clumsy movements, and enjoyed the company of so pretty a child. Philip's miserable appearance became so obvious that Mrs Birkett said she must take him away, and by eleven o'clock the party was over.

'Your sister dances unusually well,' said Noel to Colin over a drink, after Mr and Mrs Keith had gone to bed.

'She's pretty good,' said Colin. 'We practise a lot together. As for our Rose –'

'Your father cut us all out,' said Noel. 'I think that bet is off.'

'Fair play!' said Colin indignantly. 'I danced, if you can call it dancing, with that waxwork for a quarter of an hour at least.'

'I think Mr Keith ought to have it,' said Everard.

'No, no,' said Noel, 'money will be returned at the doors. Half a crown each is not to be sneezed at. And talking of sneezing, Winter looks as if he would have your blood for dancing with Rose, Colin.'

'I'd rather he had father's,' said Colin, with great want of filial feeling. 'I've got to live with Winter for the rest of the term. Father hasn't.'

They all went to bed, Noel to reflect quite unemotionally upon Kate's perfect footwork, Everard to try to

CHAPTER VI

Tea at the Sports

PHILIP's cold yielded to hot whisky and aspirin, and he was well enough to go back with the Birketts on Monday evening. Mr and Mrs Birkett were delighted with the Rectory, and decided at once to take it for August. Their kind hearts made them invite Philip for the first fortnight of the holidays, after which he had luckily arranged to visit Russia to see what it was really like; or rather, to confirm his impression that it was exactly like what he thought it was like. Their feelings towards their future son-in-law were a mixture of increasing sympathy and exacerbation which would make his stay with them extremely difficult and uncomfortable as far as they were concerned. Philip himself appeared for the present to be so eaten up with self-pity that he would be unhappy wherever he was. Little as Mr Birkett liked discussing his private affairs with an outsider, he found himself obliged to ask Everard if he couldn't do something about his difficult assistant.

'I am really at my wits' end,' said Mr Birkett, having taken Everard off for a Sunday afternoon tramp over the downs where no one could hear them, 'and I shall shortly be at the end of my patience. I would like to thrash Rose.'

'And I would like to thrash Winter,' said Everard, 'but I must say that he isn't letting it interfere with his work. The Thirds and Fourths did extremely well in their test papers last week. But he makes up for it by being more than usually trying out of class. The boys are taking a broad view of it all, and I understand unofficially that Swan and Morland have said that Mr Winter is not to be baited because he is off his nut.'

'Has Swan been looking at him through his spectacles lately?'

Everard laughed.

'No. But if Winter can't stop nagging at Keith, Swan probably will. Keith has somehow acquired the respect of Swan and Morland.'

Mr Birkett, who noticed a good deal, remembered the evening when Colin Keith had defeated Rose at supper, but did not give his daughter away.

'Well, it's only for a few weeks more now,' he said with a sigh. 'And next term I hope we'll have Harrison back. I'm sorry it means more changes in your house, but it can't be helped.'

'Is Keith definitely not staying with us?' asked Everard.

'I had a talk to his father at the week-end. He is really anxious for Keith to stick to law, and I don't think this is his right place. He does his work well and apparently from what you say the boys approve of him, but he'll never make a real schoolmaster. If he didn't give it up now, he'd give it up later, and that would be a waste of time.'

'I'll be sorry to lose him, but I daresay you are right,' said Everard. 'He's a nice type of young man.'

'They are a very nice family,' said Mr Birkett. 'By the way, Hacker has got the Montgomery scholarship.'

'That's good news,' said Everard. 'I can do without him nicely. His chameleon was lost again last week, and someone found it and tied it up in red paper with its head sticking out, and put it in Winter's desk with a note to say that it had gone Red in sympathy with his political views.'

'Devils,' said Mr Birkett, in a loving voice.

*

As Everard strolled by the river after tea he came upon Philip, sitting on the edge of the swimming pool, moodily watching Morland and Swan saving each other's lives. Philip looked at him with such a drawn, harassed expression that Everard stopped.

'Mind if I sit here a bit?' he said.

Philip said nothing, though it was obvious that he would shortly burst unless he said something.

'Hacker's got his scholarship,' said Everard. 'Lorimer will be unbearable. I shall tell him that it is all due to your grounding of Hacker when he was a junior.'

'To hell with juniors,' said Philip.

'I've often thought so myself.'

'I'm sorry,' said Philip, plaiting some pieces of grass industriously as he spoke. 'Look here, Everard, I'm going mad.'

'No, you're not,' said Everard.

'You don't know how ghastly being engaged is,' said Philip.

'Odi et amo,' said Everard.

'More than you'd think,' said Philip. 'Everard, I can't go on like this; I can't, I can't!'

'Don't then,' said Everard. 'It isn't worth it.'

'I know,' said Philip. 'But there one is. Also one cares; very, very much. Thanks, though.'

Everard strolled on, intensely annoyed with love and lovers. If he had the felicity to be engaged to Kate – but he shook the thought off and went to congratulate Mr Lorimer on his pupil's success.

'Well, Lorimer,' he said, 'this is very good news about Hacker. I suppose he will now go like a meteor through the university, get a fellowship, and never be heard of again. Have you anything on hand at present?'

It was Mr Lorimer's weakness to desert from time to time the Latin for the English Muse, and drop into poetry of an occasional and weak-kneed nature. For these unworthy productions he had all an anxious father's feelings, and got nearly as much pleasure out of seeing his verses in the School Magazine as he did when his pupils swept the scholarship board. Everard, well aware of this amiable failing, sometimes liked to pull Mr Lorimer's leg.

Mr Lorimer guiltily shuffled some papers on his desk.

'Nothing, nothing,' he said.

'Rubbish,' said Everard. 'I can see poetry sticking out under the blotting paper. What is it? A new version of the *Carmen*?'

'No, no, a mere trifle, a little occasional piece written after supping with the Head last Sunday.'

'Well, I shan't ask you again,' said Everard, 'so this is your last chance. Out with it.'

Mr Lorimer put on his pince-nez and began sorting the papers.

'Parody,' he began, in his high drawling voice, 'is perhaps an unworthy garment for the Muse to wear, but even the Muse may disport herself in seasonable time and place. The English language has not the mordant and terse qualities required for the epigram, but for parody our language is perhaps peculiarly fitted. I have, not altogether uninspired by current events, been indulging in an attempt at parody, choosing as my model, or perhaps more correctly my victim, the one English poet in whom, to my thinking, the epigram approached the feeling of the Greek, whose choice of Ianthe as a name to personify an abstraction of female charm shows the trend of his thought; a man of wide reading and powerful mind, if not a scholar in the profoundest sense of the word, and estimated to-day, except by the few that really value him, at considerably less than his proper worth.'

'Eighteen letters. Walter Savage Landor,' said Everard. 'I daresay there's an anagram of it, but I can't be bothered. Let's hear the parody, Lorimer.'

Mr Lorimer, a little self-conscious, picked up a paper.

'I must explain,' he said, 'the circumstances to which

this opusculum owes its origin. I was supping, as I mentioned, with the Head. Winter was there, and Birkett's daughter, to whom he is so regrettably engaged. After observing Miss Birkett's personal appearance, her very limited vocabulary, and her total want of consideration for the gentleman to whom she has plighted her troth, I came home, and in the heat of the moment wrote down the following lines. They need polish, they need polish, but they are not without their point.'

He gazed happily out of the window at the invisible peaks of Parnassus, and then composed himself to study his little work, pencil poised over the paper, which already bore the marks of many corrections and emendations.

'I haven't heard your poem yet, you know,' said Everard, after the lapse of three or four minutes.

'My dear fellow, my dear fellow,' said Mr Lorimer, confused, 'forgive me. The lines, not of the first water you will say, but such as they are a poor attempt to reproduce, by the medium of parody, the feelings aroused in me on Sunday night, are as follows:

> 'Ah, what avails the painted face,
>   Ah, what the curving spine –

she slouches terribly, you know,

> 'What every want of every grace,
>   Rose Birkett, all are thine.

I think they are good,' said Mr Lorimer, in a broad-minded way.

'Excellent,' said Everard. 'Have you any more?'

'I was thinking,' said Mr Lorimer, a little shyly, 'of going on to the second stanza, but inspiration is lacking. I have got as far as

> 'Rose Birkett, whom our hating eyes
>   Unluckily must see . . .

but the Muse has fled.'

'She will come back,' said Everard. 'I gather that your feelings about the lady are much the same as mine.'

'That Lesbia; neither more nor less,' said Mr Lorimer angrily.

'I saw Catullus by the boat-shed just now,' said Everard. 'My impression is that he would be thankful to be out of the whole affair, but feels in honour bound, and still loves where he can't like.'

'The best Junior Classical Master I've had since Turnbull was killed,' said Mr Lorimer, thinking of the dark days of the war. 'He was disappointed at not getting the Mixed Fifth, but his work is excellent, first-rate. No one else could have got into Swan and Morland's heads last year even the miserable modicum of Latin that the School Certificate, that filthy spawn of the devil, demands. And he sent Hacker to me ripe for development. Hacker owes the Montgomery as much to him as to me.'

'He'll be glad to hear you say that,' said Everard.

'No, he won't. He would rather hear that painted Jezebel,' said Mr Lorimer, now thoroughly roused, 'saying that everything is marvellous or sickening. If I had my way – '

Here Mr Lorimer paused, unequal to finding words for his feelings.

'Well, I must be getting along,' said Everard. 'We can only hope for Fate to do something.'

'I'll make a waxen image and stick nibs into it,' said Mr Lorimer vengefully. 'And I'll just run my eye over the Eighth Eclogue again. One might get some hints there.'

*

Towards the end of June the annual school sports took place, to the intense annoyance of the masters who were working their forms up for the summer examinations.

Boys began to come in late for lessons on the plea that they had been competing in the heats. Mr Lorimer said that anyone who didn't want to take part in the preliminaries could say he had been kept in, and defied the sports committee. Swan deliberately came last in his trials, and so to his fury found himself put down with Hacker for a consolation race. Morland, by well-timed references to a poisoned insect bite, got matron to put a large bandage on his leg and so scratched from all events.

It was Everard's habit to keep open house for parents and old boys on sports day, and any master or prefect could have tea in his own room. Colin invited Lydia and Kate, who had not yet seen the school, to be his guests. They accepted with enthusiasm, and Lydia asked if she might bring Geraldine Birkett, who was getting the afternoon off from school, with her.

'You wouldn't care to have tea with me and my sisters, sir, I suppose,' he said to Everard, 'or a drink afterwards?'

'Nothing I'd like better,' said Everard, 'but I have to be more or less on duty as housemaster. Let me come in later if I can.'

Swan and Morland were invited, and greeted with pleasure the idea of seeing Lydia again, and Colin had the kind thought of asking Hacker to come with his chameleon. He wanted to ask Philip, but did not know how his thorny colleague would take it. At last, the night before the sports, having finished his school work, he knocked at Philip's door.

'Come in,' said Philip, not looking up from his work.

'I'm having my sisters to tea to-morrow and one or two senior boys,' said Colin. 'If you'd care to look in it would be very nice. Or for a drink after sports.'

'Oh, you don't want me,' said Philip ungraciously.

'Is that yes or no?' said Colin, trying to make his voice sound ordinary, but as Philip only muttered something about wishing one could get a moment's peace, he withdrew, feeling uncomfortably that he had intruded and wishing he had left things alone. It was impossible to say to Philip that Rose was an infernal nuisance, and that if he thought one cared about her he was wrong, and one was very sorry for him being in love with such a selfish girl. That was a thing one simply couldn't say, and Philip, who was rather good at boxing, would probably fly at one and punch one's nose. So he returned to his law books and was soon immersed in a chapter that needed all his concentration. Presently he became aware that someone had knocked more than once on his door and he in his turn called out, 'Come in.' Philip, looking half defiant, half apologetic, stood in the doorway.

'Do you mind if I come in?' he asked.

'Not a bit,' said Colin. 'What will you have? I've sherry and I've whisky, but no soda water.'

'No thanks,' said Philip. 'Look here, Colin, I didn't mean to be gruff just now. I was thinking about some work I'm trying to do, and it made me a bit stupid. May I come to your party to-morrow? I'd like to see your elder sister again. She seems awfully kind.'

'Splendid,' said Colin. 'Lydia's a good chap, too, but a bit overflowing.'

'Are you working?' asked Philip, always ill at ease.

Colin said he had finished his school work and showed Philip what he was reading. Philip began to thaw and spoke with enthusiasm of the work on Horace that he always had in his mind. Colin said Lydia would be interested in that, and they were beginning to talk quite pleasantly, and Philip had accepted some whisky and tepid water, when another knock came at the door. One of the maids came in with a note.

'Please, sir,' she said to Colin, 'this note came for you from the headmaster's house, and please is there an answer.'

Colin opened the letter, read it, and looked annoyed.

'No answer,' he said. 'Or I'll answer it later.'

'Yes, sir,' said the maid. 'Oh, and matron said would you come and speak to her for a moment. She says she won't keep you.'

'All right,' said Colin. 'Excuse me, Philip, I won't be a moment.'

Philip wandered about the room looking at Colin's books. Then he sat down again near the table and saw the letter his host had just received. He knew only too well the flowing ill-formed writing. On a sudden impulse he looked at it, knowing he was behaving quite disgracefully.

DEAR COLIN [it ran]. Do ask me to your party to-morrow because Geraldine says she is coming to tea with you with Liddia with heaps of love from Rose.

When Philip had read it he drank the rest of his luke-warm whisky. He would have had some more, but his host had hospitably given him the last drop in the bottle.

'She only wanted me to get the broken cork out of a bottle of syrup of figs,' said Colin, coming back. 'No one had the gumption to push it right in and find another one. Anything wrong?'

'I have read your letter,' said Philip, pointing an avenging finger at the document.

'Well, you shouldn't,' said Colin. 'You're as bad as Lydia. It's bad enough having that girl sending round letters by hand, making me a laughing-stock without having you reading them.'

'She has never written me more than a postcard,' said Philip.

'Well, I can't help that. God help anyone she writes to in that awful writing. Don't do it again, Philip, that's all.'

'How dare you speak about her like that?' said Philip.

Colin, after more than half a term of pinpricks from Philip, was near the end of his temper.

'Look here,' he said, 'you are a boxer and I'm not, but I'm heavier than you and a good deal fitter just now, and if you go on like this I shall have a fight with you, and I don't know the rules, so I'll probably roll on you and bite your ear.'

'It's like hell,' said Philip.

'All right, it *is* like hell. But if you think I ever want to see the writer of that note again, I don't. I wish you and she were on a desert island and couldn't get back. I'll have to say yes, because she's the Head's daughter and one must be civil, but my party will be entirely spoilt. You may well say hell.'

'Is it any good apologizing?' said Philip.

'Oh, rot,' said Colin. 'Have another drink. Bother, there's no more whisky. Have some sherry.'

'No thanks,' said Philip. 'I'll come to your party if you'll let me. I swear I don't mean to be a fool, but you don't know how appalling it is to be engaged.'

'Well, don't be engaged,' said Colin, 'and do go to bed.'

'Would you like to hit me?' said Philip hopefully, with the gesture of one who bares his breast to the sword.

'Of course not, you fool,' said Colin, 'and for God's sake do go away. I've got to answer that blasted letter. Would you like to see me do it? No, blast it, she can wait till to-morrow.'

He tore the letter into a great many little bits and threw them into the waste-paper basket. Philip went back to his room, and to bed, where he lay staring into the darkness. Half of him would have given anything in the world to be free from his Rose. The other half was still instinctively jealous of anyone she looked at, but he believed Colin now and felt safe with him, and this was the first sign of sanity he had shown since the beginning of the winter term when his engagement took place.

Colin felt extremely annoyed with Philip, and also

extremely sorry for him. Once or twice before going to
sleep he got out of bed, went gently to Philip's room, and
listened at the door in case he had committed suicide.
Complete silence gave him no clue as to what was going
on, but he found it reassuring.

*

The day of the sports was fine and warm, and matron
said she knew someone would faint before the day was
over. After a very sketchy morning school and a hasty
lunch, the whole school prepared for the event. The com-
petitors gathered on the grass under the elms and brought
out bottles of fearful oil or embrocation, with which they
pinched, rubbed, and massaged their own legs and those
of their friends. The spectators borrowed each other's
hair fixative, and made such a noise that matron turned
them all out of both dormitories. Mr Birkett had a large
lunch party, including the Dean and other Governors.
Everard entertained a number of old boys in his study.
Philip was out on the ground helping at the sports
secretary's table. Colin felt rather lonely, and thought
wistfully of Noel Merton's chambers, untroubled by boys.

While the first events were being run or jumped, there
were not many visitors, but by three o'clock the fringe of
spectators round the field was several deep. The sun
shone, a light breeze blew, the Barchester Police Band
played the same selections from Gilbert and Sullivan that
it played every year. Colin, looking in the wrong direction, was pounced upon by Lydia and was no longer
alone. Lydia had been for once forced into the right
clothes by her mother and Kate, and was looking
extremely handsome in a gay flowered dress. With her
were Kate and a speechless girl, whom Colin rightly
guessed to be Geraldine Birkett. Colin managed to find
places for them, and they sat talking while the sports
went on. In the distance they saw Rose enjoying herself.

As they walked towards Mr Carter's house for the tea interval, Kate explained that Geraldine Birkett was very devoted to Lydia.

'I think Lydia finds it a bit trying,' she said, 'because Geraldine follows her about at school all the time and never says anything, but Lydia is really very kind-hearted and puts up with it, and Geraldine does her maths which she can't do. Mother let us have the car to-day and we offered to bring Geraldine, but I didn't know she was going to stick so tight. I thought she would be joining her own people.'

'It's better than Rose, anyway,' said Colin. 'She has invited herself to tea.'

Kate looked anxious, but said nothing.

The tea in Colin's room looked perfectly delightful. There were mustard and cress sandwiches, cucumber sandwiches, jam sandwiches, bloater paste sandwiches, cakes with pink icing, a chocolate cake, a coffee cake, and two plates of biscuits. Colin, poking about in the village, had found a grocer who kept those joys of his early childhood, animal biscuits and alphabet biscuits, and had bought a pound of each. There was also a huge bowl of strawberries, a large jug of cream, and on the dressing-table beer and sherry for the later comers.

Swan and Morland, who were already in the room, made Kate and Lydia welcome. Geraldine they greeted with a nicely mingled shade of conventional respect for the headmaster's daughter and suspicion of any sister of Rose's. Geraldine moved closer to Lydia, twisted her own legs round the legs of her chair, and prepared to enjoy the party. The next arrival was Hacker with the chameleon. Colin, who had previously primed his guests about Hacker's attainments, formally introduced him. Kate very sweetly congratulated him on his scholarship, calling him Mr Hacker. Hacker, after silently and despairingly twisting himself about, suddenly found his voice, an octave lower than where he expected it, and said something about Mr Lorimer.

'I am so sorry,' said Kate. 'I thought Colin said Mr Hacker.'

'Mr Lorimer is the Senior Classical Master,' said Colin hastily. 'Hacker is working under him. He coached Hacker for the scholarship exam.'

'Hullo,' said Lydia, 'what's that you've got?'

'It's his chameleon,' said Swan, seeing that Hacker was in a state of palsied imbecility owing to shyness. 'It's a good sort of fellow and eats flies. Got any flies, Hack?'

Hacker pulled from his pocket a small glass jar with a screw top and held it up. In it four or five flies were walking about upside down.

'How loathsome!' said Lydia, her eyes shining with interest. 'Make it eat.'

Hacker took the chameleon out of its cage and put it on the table. He then partly unscrewed the jar and let a fly come out. The chameleon licked it off as it emerged and looked as if nothing had happened.

'What's its name?' asked Lydia, as the chameleon finished the flies.

Hacker went scarlet.

'Gibbon,' said Morland, adding, 'Can't you talk, you ass?' in a loud aside to Hacker.

'Did you call him after Gibbon?' said Lydia.

Hacker looked piteously at his friends.

'You must excuse him,' said Swan kindly. 'The Classical Sixth are all like that. He had to read Gibbon for his scholarship, and got quite romantic about him, so he called the chameleon Gibbon. It used to be Greta Garbo, but he took that one off.'

'That beast Pettinger said Gibbon was beyond me,' said Lydia, 'but he wasn't. In fact I think he's jolly good. He seems to have a very comprehensive grasp of things, if you know what I mean. I say, Colin, can we begin?'

Colin said they ought to wait a little for Rose, and just then Philip came in, asking if anyone had seen Rose. He had been at the table with the sports secretary all afternoon and unable to look for her.

Kate, who had seen Rose surrounded by admiring old boys and gallant fathers, felt sorry for Philip and said nothing, but Lydia, in whom the memory of her encounter with Philip was still rankling, had no such inhibitions.

'I shouldn't think she'd be here for ages,' she said. 'There are about twenty people asking her to have tea with them in the tent. Look.'

She haled the unwilling Philip to the window and pointed out a large, noisy group. Among the white flannels, grey flannels, and even a few frock coats and top hats, he could see the billowing cloud of yellow organdie that enveloped his love.

'Yes, I see her,' he said. 'Well, Colin, sorry I'm late. I hope you haven't been waiting tea for me.'

Swan came up to Lydia.

'Look at the Dean of Barchester down there,' he said, pointing to a group on the grass. 'He's telling everyone what a good school it is, because he's a Governor. Gas and gaiters we call him on Speech Day. I say, Lydia, be decent. It isn't fair to rag Mr Winter about Rose. He may be a bit short in the temper, but he's a *decent* master, and Rose is just one large yellow mistake. Tony and I are thinking of taking serious steps about it. We can't have the house upset by a brainless vanilla ice,' he said, looking vengefully at Rose's yellow dress, which was floating in their direction.

'You mean she isn't playing fair?' said Lydia.

'Fair, my good girl! Blonde is what she is playing. You'll be decent to Mr Winter, won't you? Come on, tea's ready.'

Lydia nodded gravely and took her place at the tea

table. A violent revulsion was taking place in her down-right mind. When she had first seen Philip at the picnic she had taken a strong dislike to him on what she considered extremely adequate grounds. He had dared to speak in an uppish way to Kate, for whom Lydia, in her young arrogance, had a very protective, if slightly condescending, affection. Lydia had flown to Kate's rescue and administered to Philip what she considered an awfully good snub, or, as it was called in school circles, a blip. After this, everything he did was wrong. A man who got water down his sleeves when he punted she could not endure. If he had fallen in like a man, as she so often did herself, she could have forgiven and sympathized, but for so mean an action as not handling a punt pole correctly, she had nothing but scorn. The fact of his being engaged to Rose Birkett further lowered him in her estimation. With no envy of Rose's looks and power of attraction, she felt that a man who could fall in love with someone who was so obviously not a good fellow, was below the normal standard of intellect. And worst of all, she had gathered that Rose was persecuting Colin. If Rose tried that on, Lydia would defend him tooth and nail. If you were engaged, even to so low a worm as Philip, you were engaged, in Lydia's simple code, and you jolly well stuck to him and didn't go about making eyes at people's brothers. Therefore her feelings towards Philip underwent her usual rapid revision, and she decided to treat him kindly and reserve her heavy artillery for Rose, regardless of the fact that Philip cared for her. That he could for a moment care for such a washout as Rose went against him, but Lydia had gathered from Shakespeare and other authorities that love was very peculiar and often made people quite potty. If Desdemona could fall in love with Othello, Philip might be excused for falling in love with Rose, whose worst enemy could not call her black. Having thus arranged her so-called thoughts, in much less time than it takes to write about them, she dismissed them to the back of her mind and settled down to enjoy Colin's very good tea.

Kate was pouring out, and with her usual instinct for the defenceless had got Philip and Hacker one on each side of her. Hacker's chameleon, who had previously been put on the iced cakes, obstinately refused to turn pink, and was put back in his cage, and the serious business of eating was just getting under way, when Rose came in, leading by the hand, for such was her usual engaging and artless way, no less a person than Noel Merton.

'Oh, Colin,' she said, ignoring everyone else. 'I've brought Noel. He is staying with the Dean, and tea in the tent looked so sickening that I knew you'd be an angel and not mind.'

Noel, feeling that his fair guide's explanation, though obscurely phrased, would probably be understood by the party, merely apologized for gate-crashing.

'When Mrs Crawley asked me for the week-end,' he said, 'I didn't know I was to have the treat of coming to the sports. May I come to tea?'

Colin, as host, welcomed him, and there was a little clamour of greeting. Noel looked towards Kate, but the places by her were occupied and Rose, who had already put herself next to Colin, pulled Noel into the chair on her other side with a firm hand, and cast her lovely eyes round the table.

'How do you do, everyone,' she said vaguely. Her eyes then fell upon the face of her affianced, to whom she remarked, 'Oh, Philip, darling, are you there, I thought you were doing the sports,' and took no further notice of him. Lydia, bristling with her new opinions, looked at Philip, saw him wince, and prepared for his defence. For a time no chance offered itself. Rose was using her charms to her right and left, while Philip sat and wondered why he cared for her so much.

Swan and Morland were engaged in sorting out the alphabet letters and talking in low voices. Kate, having done her unsuccessful best by Hacker, turned to Philip and made soothing conversation to which no reply was needed. Geraldine, who had hitherto remained perfectly silent, pointed to the chameleon, sitting in his cage with his eyes shut, and said confidentially to his master, who was next to her, 'I like him.'

Hacker looked at her with the first dawnings of humanity in his expression, but could not articulate. Geraldine, enchanted to find a companion even more tongue-tied than herself, said again, 'I like him. What's his name?'

'Greta Garbo,' said Hacker in a hoarse voice, and then remembering the change of name said hastily, 'Gibbon, I mean.'

Geraldine looked gratified, and was about to make another remark, when Swan said:

'O.K., Tony. I'll explain and then we'll start.'

'What is it?' asked Kate, who had been looking at the letters that lay before them.

'It's called Alphabet Race, Miss Keith,' said Morland. 'You get all the letters of the alphabet, or if you can't get the exact letters you get twenty-six, we had to have three M's, because there wasn't a J or an L, and then you see how many you can get into your mouth. My record is twenty-three, and we're out to break it. Only one at a time are the rules. Will you start us, sir?' he said to Philip.

Philip jumped nervously. Morland repeated the request, and Philip gave the word, upon which both boys began to cram their alphabets, a letter at a time, into their mouths. Everyone watched, fascinated, while the letters disappeared, and Rose found herself for once without an audience. At twenty-four Swan gave up, while Morland managed to cram a twenty-fifth into his mouth.

They then sat, proud but disgusting sights, for a triumphant moment.

'That's very good,' said Colin. 'And now you had better both go and do your chewing in the passage before you burst and choke, and then come back for strawberries.'

Swan and Morland, obviously on the verge of apoplexy with suppressed giggles, made a plunge for the door and banged it behind them. Matron, who was passing, thought they had whooping cough, and what with crumbs in the windpipe and tears in the eyes, they had great difficulty in explaining what had happened. There was such a noise in the passage that Colin came out to see, and invited matron to come and have tea. Matron said, a little boastfully, that she had a senior boy with a sprained ankle, and a junior boy who was bilious with excitement, and a visiting father in holy orders who had fainted from the heat, but she would love to have a tiny peep at Mr Keith's party.

'Do you mean a monk?' said Swan hopefully.

'Not that kind of father. Matron means a parent, you ass,' said Morland. 'It's young Holinshed's father. He went all religious and turned into a clergyman. It was all right, because he is rather well off, but Holly says they have family prayers and grace, and it's ghastly.'

Matron was introduced. Hacker rose and offered her a chair, which she accepted gracefully, saying you always knew the boys in Mr Carter's house because they were such gentlemen, so that Hacker, knowing what his friends would say to him later, wished he hadn't been polite. Kate gave matron some tea and asked her if she had much trouble with the laundry. This was an inspiration on Kate's part, for matron waged a ceaseless warfare against the school laundry, who, in her opinion, had installed special machinery, with spikes and scythe blades to destroy the sheets, towels, table napkins and personal wear of the house. Kate sympathized so heartily that matron told her the number of pillow-cases that had to be renewed every year because the boys would put stuff on their hair whatever she did, and how difficult it was to make the upper dormitory boys wear their pyjamas in bed in the summer term. Emboldened by this confidence Kate mentioned that she had darned a black sock for one of the boys in the Whitsun holidays and found that it had been mended with blue wool.

'I'm not surprised,' said matron, 'and I'm very glad you mentioned it, Miss Keith. That will be Jessie. She's a good girl, but she's vain, and she won't wear her spectacles. I've told her again and again you can't tell navy blue from black without your glasses, Jessie, especially I said by artificial light, but it's no good speaking. I can't keep an eye on everything, and I shall tell Jessie it has been noticed by outsiders. There was a really dreadful affair, Miss Keith, last term, when Mr Carter's black silk socks had a little place in them, and she simply pulled the edges together, and never tried to darn it properly. Mr Carter never complains as a rule, but this time he did, and I was really ashamed. It is nice to have a talk with someone who takes an interest.'

So absorbing was this delightful technical talk that Kate's sisterly ear did not at first hear the noise her sister Lydia was making. Rose was a little put out at the transference of interest from herself to the biscuit eaters. For her father's pupils she had little use. None of them had cars, and most of them were too young to be interesting. Of the senior boys, the athletic ones were working far too hard to have any time to look at Rose, while most of the studious ones were such as she was not going to waste her time on. There were a few older boys, Swan and Morland being of the number, who seemed to Rose worthy of a little attention, but perversely they considered her worth none at all. As Swan truly remarked to Morland, the peak period for headmaster's daughters was over. 'And, mind you,' he added, 'the same applies to wives. No one but a born poop would cast an eye on anything that came out of a headmaster's or a housemaster's house.'

'What about Mr Winter?' Morland had asked.

'Oh, he's simply a throw-back. Most of those young Communists are. They are so jolly earnest that they don't know where they are. I mean, it simply isn't done now to fall in love with anything inside the school. Mr Winter thinks he is all up to date because he takes in a nasty little weekly all very well informed and printed in typewriting so that you can't read it, all about What is being Kept From the Public, but as for knowing anything about life –'

'I say,' said Morland, losing interest in the puerilities of his superiors, 'your young cousins down by the bathing pool are coming on nicely. Let's go and take them some biscuits.'

'My half uncles and aunts, you mean,' said Swan. 'Do get the relationship right.'

*

So Rose, fortifying herself with some more powder and lip-stick, turned to Noel and asked if he had seen any shows lately. Noel replied that he had seen John Potter's new Shakespeare production.

'Oh, I love Potter, he's too marvellous,' said Rose. 'I saw him fourteen times in Shakespeare.'

'So you told me when we were under the tree, the day of the thunder-storm,' said Noel.

'You were marvellous, giving me your coat like that,' said Rose, casting a sheep's eye at her preserver.

'I could do no less,' said Noel, half amused, half remorseful, as he saw Philip looking in his direction, but quite unable to resist the pleasure of drawing Rose.

'Isn't it a marvellous bit where he sees the Ghost?' said Rose.

'Who? Oh, yes, Potter.'

'He looks so divine in black,' said Rose.

'Black? But he is in armour in that scene.'

'Oh, no, Noel. He is all in black, with battlements.'

'Well, all I can say is that last night he was in armour in his tent, quarrelling with Cassius,' said Noel.

Lydia now came to his aid.

'Antony and Cleopatra is one of Shakespeare's very best plays,' she announced. 'I've read them all, and there's nothing to touch Antony and Cleopatra, except King Lear, and Hamlet, and Othello. Romeo and Juliet is wonderful, and so is The Tempest, and of course Twelfth Night and Much Ado are stupendous. I always think Troilus and Cressida isn't properly appreciated. All that backchat of Cressida and Pandarus is absolutely like people to-day. It really is extraordinary how Shakespeare makes you feel you are the people. I felt I was Cressida all the time I was reading it. I wish I had a name out of Shakespeare. Of course Lydia comes in Horace, and I think Horace is perfectly splendid, but a Shakespeare name would be better. I'd like to be Lavinia – out of Titus Andronicus,' she added reflectively and in case no one knew.

'And very nice too,' said Noel.

'But Cassius isn't in Shakespeare,' said Rose, taking no notice of Lydia.

'He is in Antony and Cleopatra,' said Colin.

'But Noel said Shakespeare,' said Rose, perplexed.

'Which Shakespeare?' said Colin.

'Shakespeare of course. John Potter in Hamlet. I've seen Shakespeare fourteen times, so I ought to know,' said Rose, her lovely cheeks flushing with annoyance at other people's stupidity.

It had gradually become obvious to everyone that Rose

thought there was a play called alternatively Shakespeare and Hamlet. No one felt equal to explaining this.

'I know what's wrong with you,' said Lydia, gathering herself for the attack, 'you don't read enough. Shakespeare wrote more than thirty plays, besides the sonnets and some odds and ends, and even if Beaumont and Fletcher did write some of them, it all comes to the same thing. Seeing Hamlet fourteen times isn't Shakespeare, it's simply being potty about John Potter – shut up, Eric, it wasn't meant to be funny. I was a bit potty about him myself, but after all Shakespeare was not for an age but for all time, and being potty on one actor isn't Shakespeare, else when he was dead, where would you be? What you ought to do, Rose, is to read him all through. Miss Pettinger makes us paraphrase bits, but that's nonsense, because very often Shakespeare didn't exactly know what he meant himself, and anyway it spoils the verse to put it into prose, and alter the language. If Shakespeare had wanted it paraphrased he'd have done it himself.'

'I wish you had thought of that, sir,' said Morland to Philip, who looked so out of the conversation, 'when you made us put him into elegiacs in the Classical Fourth.'

'There's another thing about Shakespeare,' said Lydia, now well into her stride, 'the amount of Latin words he uses. It's not nearly as bad as Milton, but anyway Milton was only swank, but with Shakespeare it just shows you how much he knew. Some of his romantic plays are even more classical than his classical ones, if you know what I mean.'

'I think I do,' said Noel, 'and it's not a bad point.'

'Mr Lorimer has put The Phoenix and the Turtle into hendecasyllabics,' said Hacker, zealous for his teacher.

'Good old Mr Lorimer,' said Swan, 'sooner he than I.'

'I think Latin is sickening,' said Rose. 'I want Philip to stop teaching Latin and take a job.'

Everyone at the table disliked Rose a little more than they had yet done. Lydia glared and took a deep breath, but while she was preparing for the onslaught, Swan said carelessly:

'That would be a pity. If Mr Winter hadn't started Hacker on his classics he'd never have been top of Mr Lorimer's form,' and kicked Morland under the table.

'And then he'd never have got the scholarship, and Gibbon would have starved,' said Morland.

'And Hacker would have had to take a job,' said Lydia, advancing gladly to the fray. 'I think classics really matter almost more than anything. I mean look at Horace and that ode of his about the monument being more perennial than brass, or bronze or whatever it was he meant. It may sound like boasting, but after all just look at him. It isn't everyone that their books last about two thousand years. Of course there's the Bible, but people have to read that, but with Horace people needn't read him except at school, but they do, and heaps of him is quotations now. Like Shakespeare and Virgil and Caesar and Cicero and the rest. If people didn't read them they couldn't pass exams, and they'd get absolutely nowhere. Are you good at Horace, Mr Winter?'

'Mr Winter is writing a book about him,' said Morland.

'That's enough, Tony,' said Philip, embarrassed by his kind young friends, yet amused and a little touched by their and Lydia's championship of his cause. On hearing this Lydia gave Philip a *précis* of her views on classical literature, and Noel, always entertained by Lydia, joined the discussion. Matron then looked at her wrist-watch and said she had no idea and she must go at once. Philip had to return to his post, Swan and Hacker had reluctantly to leave the strawberries and cream to take part in the consolation race, and Morland accompanied them, carrying Gibbon in his cage so that he might enjoy

143

the fresh air and see his master run. Lydia and Geraldine went with them.

Rose's complacency had been shaken by this general defection. She looked round the party in search of entertainment. Kate and Noel were sitting in the deep window seat, looking at the sports and having pleasant conversation. Free as Rose was from any form of sensitiveness or tact, something told her that no third person was needed, and that, rather confusedly, she was the one. Colin, seeing her look low, took pity on her, and asked her to help him to tidy the tea-things away, and put glasses and bottles ready for more guests.

Kate and Noel were enjoying the view from the window. The long shadows from the elms lay peacefully across the playing fields and the sports were nearly over. White flannels, bright and in many cases hideous blazers, women's party frocks, made a pretty kaleidoscope of colour. The Birketts were conversing indefatigably with parents, known and unknown, with no daughter to help them. Mr Lorimer had raised a respectful cheer by appearing in knickerbockers that buttoned below the knee and a straw boater. The Dean and Mrs Crawley were talking to friends, among whom Noel recognized the Robert Keiths, who must have come over later. The sack race had just been won by a small boy who well deserved it, for he had practised with a pillow-case morning and evening all that term, without being discovered by matron. Matron herself, looking very attractive in her beige lace, was surrounded by a number of old boys, asking and answering twenty questions at once, and proudly introducing to them all her eldest nephew, the one who was her married sister's son and second wireless operator on an Atlantic liner. The consolation race was the last on the programme, and the audience was already making towards the cricket pavilion, where the Dean was to give the prizes.

Noel looked at the field, and looked at Kate, and thought, not for the first time, how very charming she looked, and how very kind and thoughtful she was. In fact the ideal wife, except that he didn't want a wife. He had also become aware, as his friendship with Kate had gently flowered, that except on domestic matters and books she seemed to have no conversation. Every time he met her he was struck afresh by her charming manners and unaffected interest in what he was doing, but he never got any further, and sometimes had a suspicion that her obvious interest in him dated from and was entirely nourished by the night she had so thoughtfully provided pyjamas, toothbrush, and other toilet accessories for him. Had he, so he was forced to admit, come to the house as an ordinary visitor with a well-stocked suitcase, it was probable that she would never have given him another thought. But one couldn't go through life without pyjamas and toothbrushes so that Kate might provide them and, providing them, smile on him. Kate, in fact, was a delightful friend and one in whose house when she married, for marry she must, it would be very pleasant to stay. Noel was ambitious, but marriage was not among his aims. Rather for him the life of the agreeable bachelor who is always in request as best man, trustee, valued guest, for whom good houses with well-bred host and fellow-guests, excellent food and wine, motors, yachts, will always be waiting. A life that cannot perhaps go on indefinitely, and sometimes Noel thought of Major Pendennis, but by that time he intended to be a wealthy man himself, and in his turn be host. Meanwhile it was pleasant to sit with Kate, and if he wanted to rouse her to animation, he only had to say some of the nice things that he honestly felt about Colin, or remark carelessly that his housekeeper had twice given him burnt toast for breakfast lately.

It was the easier just now to murmur something nice

about Colin, because he was being so excellent a host. He had given them a very good tea, and was now nobly sacrificing himself by entertaining that odious little beauty Rose Birkett. Ever since the day when Rose had taken two men's coats with hardly a thank you, and so heartlessly ignored that red-haired Winter, who was obviously quite devoted to her, Noel had felt it would be amusing to see exactly how far Rose's selfishness and love of admiration would lead her. Only for this had he allowed himself to be led by the hand to Colin's party and placed next to the enchantress. To see Philip's anxiety had made it all more amusing. Noel was not at heart unkind, but any man who let his naked emotion get beyond his control was, in Noel's view, fair play. If Mr Lorimer had known the havoc that Mr Merton was helping to make with his Junior Classical Master, he would have descended upon Noel, buttoned knicker-bockers, straw boater and all, and said exactly what he thought. But Mr Lorimer was arguing with Holinshed's father, now recovered from the heat, who had seven children, about the impropriety of married clergy, and would never know. Noel idly thought that to flirt a very little with Rose, and tease Winter, was a sport that might be repeated as occasion offered.

Kate, looking kindly at the playing fields, was thinking partly how nice Noel was, but even more whether any of Colin's socks needed darning, or his shirts new buttons. She had brought a small workcase with her, and was hoping very much that Colin wouldn't mind her using it. She also wondered if Rose would mind being told that she had a hole in her thin stocking, because a few stitches would put it right again, as it was only the seam.

Just as Colin, with Rose's very unhelpful assistance, which consisted chiefly in making up her face and breaking a saucer, had got things straight, Philip came back. Rose was so chastened by a little neglect that she greeted him with a relief which he mistook for affection. He looked so tremulously happy at her kindness that Kate quite forgave Rose her bad behaviour at tea, and Noel felt more strongly than ever that Winter was fair play. Rose so far unbent as to sit with Philip in the other window seat, and tell him how sickening school sports were, a statement with which Philip, who had sat for most of the afternoon at the secretary's table, in the burning sun, with just enough wind to send the scoring papers flying from time to time, heartily agreed.

Kate meanwhile had persuaded Colin to let her look at his wardrobe, and with moans of indignation had extracted two and a half pairs of socks, three shirts, and a waistcoat, all in need of darns or buttons, besides two collars she said he simply could not use again. With these she sat down at one end of the table and became happily absorbed. Colin talked to Noel about *Lemon* and other subjects, and all was delightful calm, which Philip, poised insecurely in his new-found happiness, felt could not last. Nor was he wrong.

A sound of applause from the pavilion indicated that the prizes had been given and the assembly was dispersing. Steps were heard on the landing and in came Lydia, bringing her brother Robert, his wife Edith, and Edith's brothers, formerly Fairweather Senior and Fairweather Junior, who had, as we know, been at the Southbridge preparatory school in their time. Colin and Kate were delighted to see their family. Rose was introduced and in two minutes had wrought such havoc in the breast of Fairweather Senior, home on leave from his regiment in Burma, and Fairweather Junior, fresh from his first cruise, that no one could hear themselves speak. The brothers, who were extremely devoted and always liked the same things, had bought a racing car between them to enliven their leave, and when they asked Rose to come out with them the following Saturday she accepted with enthusiasm. Philip, who had promised at her earnest entreaty to take her out himself, though what with exams coming on and papers to set, and a lot of special prize essays to read, he could but ill afford the time, groaned in spirit and fell back into misery.

Suddenly Geraldine appeared at the door, round-eyed, showing such symptoms of bringing news, good or bad, that even Rose and the Fairweathers stopped talking to look at her.

'What do you think?' said Geraldine, with a vivacity that surprised all who knew her. 'Hacker has won the Consolation Race!'

No one cared in the least, but some tribute was evidently fitting, so Kate said how very nice that was.

'He's just coming,' said Geraldine, holding the door open for Swan and Morland, who walked in looking extremely depressed, with Hacker between them carrying the chameleon.

'What do you think?' said Swan to the assembled company in a hushed, despairing voice. 'Hacker has won the Consolation Race.'

'Congratulations,' said Colin, rather tired of Hacker and his affairs.

'Sir!' said Morland reproachfully.

'Well, what about it?' said Colin, perplexed.

But before Morland could answer, Everard came in.

'Sorry I couldn't get up sooner, Colin,' he said. 'I had to do my duty by some parents.'

Colin introduced Everard to Robert and Edith and the Fairweathers, of whom Everard had a vague recollection as good football players in the preparatory school. Hacker slunk into a corner where his young friends moodily watched him, but Geraldine was not going to have Hacker slighted. She poked Lydia and said with unusual self-possession, 'I say, Hacker has won the Consolation Race!'

148

'Jolly good,' said Lydia approvingly. 'I bet the chameleon was pleased. I say, Mr Carter,' she added, in her turn poking Everard, 'did you know Hacker had won the Consolation Race?'

'What?' said Everard, and even Philip emerged from his gloom to say, 'Good God!'

'We didn't mean you to know till afterwards, sir,' said Swan, in an undertaker's low but penetrating voice, 'but she,' said Swan, with a cold look at Geraldine, 'gave the whole thing away. We told Hacker again and again, but he's quite dippy with his exams and must have lost his head.'

'But Eric came in twentieth, sir,' said Morland, anxious to restore in some degree the smirched honour of Mr Carter's house.

'I never meant to, sir,' said the wretched Hacker.

'Well, you have done it,' said Everard.

'It's the worst knock the House has ever had,' said Philip, forgetting his own troubles in those of the republic. 'The Consolation Race!'

Morland reminded Everard that a boy called Mowbray had once won the Sack Race, but Swan brushed aside such paltering with truth.

'Mowbray had a temperature and got pneumonia next day,' he said, 'so you can't count it. The whole school will be laughing at us. "Fancy Carter's winning the Consolation Race!" What made you do it, Hack?'

'I don't know,' said Hacker shamefacedly. 'I thought it would be something for Gibbon to remember.'

'If I had done my duty I'd have confiscated that chameleon weeks ago, when you let the bathroom flood,' said Everard. 'Well, it might have been worse. As Morland says, we did once win the Sack Race. And we've got thirteen out of twenty-four events.'

He turned from the guilty Hacker to talk to Kate.

'Oh, Philip,' said Rose loudly from the window seat

where she was holding court with the Fairweathers, 'you don't mind if we don't go out next Saturday, do you? They've got a racing car and we're going to the coast to bathe. Your car isn't much good for long runs, is she?'

The two Fairweathers hoped with one voice that they weren't butting in. Philip deprecated such an idea.

'Anyway,' continued Rose, 'I don't see why Hacker shouldn't win the Consolation Prize. I think, Philip, you are quite sickening about it. I think it's marvellous of Hacker.'

Hacker burst into a cold sweat of anguish, and hunted vainly for a handkerchief to mop his brow. Kate saw, understood, and thrust one of Colin's, on to which she had just sewn his name, into Hacker's clammy hand. Swan and Morland exchanged indignant glances. That Rose had done the dirty on Mr Winter again. Also she had publicly praised Hacker for his deed of shame, and though Hacker had most horribly let the House down by his misplaced exertions, to be pilloried by Rose was a punishment far beyond his deserts.

'Anyway, I expect Gibbon was jolly pleased,' said Swan to Morland, loud enough for anyone who was interested to hear.

'I say, Hack,' said Morland, in the same slightly artificial voice, 'we found who it was that put the red frock on your chameleon. It was Swan's fag.'

'I whanged him with my bedroom slipper,' said Swan. 'And I made him clean my corps uniform for it; buttons, green pipeclay, belt, boots and everything.'

'And I got Swan to lend him to me to do mine too,' said Morland, 'and that'll learn him to persecute saurians.'

'And to give cheek to his betters,' said Swan.

'Sir,' said Morland to Everard, 'wasn't there a boy in 1929 who got the Scripture Prize?'

'There was,' said Everard. 'Thanks, Morland, for the kind thought. That was a depth to which Hacker has not descended. Well, Hacker, you won't do it again here, and I daresay you'll never be tempted again. Colin, what about drinks?'

While conversation became general, and Robert and Edith were saying good-bye, Philip was again in torment. Damn it, those boys, well-meaning young asses, were being *kind* to him. He knew perfectly well, though no one else did, unless perhaps Everard, who knew too much about his house, that Swan's remark about punishing people who gave cheek meant that the senior boys had noticed and resented the impertinence of the boy, or boys, who had put the chameleon in its communist jacket into his desk. They couldn't openly defend him, or fight duels for him, but they had made it pretty clear that they felt for his position, and were not going to allow anyone else to pester him. And as for their encouraging remarks to Hacker about the race, they were obviously an indirect snub to Rose to comfort Hacker for her ill-judged congratulations. Blast their kindness! Blast himself for wearing his heart on his sleeve so that Fifth Form boys could peck at it. Blast everything! Perhaps it would be better to go to Russia, where things were ordered better, and stay there. Why hadn't he eloped with Rose as he at first intended. Why had he ever been born? He excused himself to Colin and went away.

Rose now said she must go home. The Fairweathers offered to drive her. Rose said it was only just across the quad, but it would be marvellous if they would, as it was perfectly sickening to have to walk, so with much hearty, meaningless laughter they went downstairs. Geraldine, who had gone back into her shell, said she supposed she had better go over and say good-bye to her parents before going back to school, where she boarded, so Lydia and the three boys said they would accompany her, Kate promising to pick her up in ten minutes at the head-master's house. Swan and Morland said good-bye and thanked Colin politely for the feast. Hacker was again stricken dumb, and Swan kindly said for him that his mother had told him to thank Mr Keith for the nice tea and say how much he had enjoyed himself and he hoped he had behaved well, which caused Hacker to scowl and go crimson. Then a message came from Mrs Crawley to summon Noel to the waiting car, so that Everard was left alone with Colin and Kate.

'I've just finished the mending, Colin,' said Kate, 'all except the waistcoat. I didn't bring any buttons with me. You haven't got one, have you?'

'If I had it wouldn't be off,' said Colin cryptically. 'I must take these glasses back to Philip's room. I borrowed them from him in case we hadn't enough. Back in a second.'

'Oh, Mr Carter,' said Kate, 'that spare button you asked for off that waistcoat of yours. You haven't got it, have you? I believe it would be just right for Colin's waistcoat.'

'I don't quite know,' said Everard, conscious that the button, relic once touched by Kate's fingers, had since Whitsun lived in a very safe inside pocket by day, and under his pillow by night.

'I *am* sorry,' said Kate, with genuine disappointment. 'It would just have done. Haven't you any idea if you kept it?'

'I might have it about me,' said Everard in an idiotic way, and feeling inside his waistcoat he produced a small, flat silver box.

'It is an old vinaigrette,' he said, opening it, as if this explained why he was keeping it on his person with a button in it.

'What a good idea to carry a button box about,' said

152

Kate approvingly, 'because you never know. Are you sure you don't need it? It will do perfectly.'

As Everard laid it reverently in Kate's hand, he reflected upon the mad thrill that a button, warm from the region of her heart, would be to him, and wondered if a similar button, tepid from incarceration in a vinai-grette in his waistcoat pocket, might be at all repellent to her.

He said he really didn't need it at all, and any button would do for him, and became aware that he was talking nonsense, and wished Kate would go before he turned into a raving lunatic under her eyes. When Colin came back he and Everard walked across the court with Kate to the headmaster's house to collect Lydia.

The Keiths' car was waiting, and Lydia, seated in it, was holding forth, as from a rostrum, to Swan, Morland and Hacker.

'I say, Kate,' she said loudly, 'couldn't we ask all these boys for the Bank Holiday week-end, when school breaks up? Tony and Eric and I could clean out the pond in the rose garden, and Hacker would like to come awfully. I say, Hacker, what's your name?'

Hacker looked hopelessly at his two friends and mumbled something.

'He means his name's really Percy,' said Morland, 'but he doesn't like it, and he wants you to call him Hack.'

'Right-oh,' said Lydia. 'I think Percy's pretty awful myself, but Hack's quite a decent sort of name. Could we, Kate, do you think?'

Kate looked perplexed.

'You do jump down people's throats, Lydia,' said Colin. 'Kate can't settle that sort of thing without asking the parents.'

'I was thinking,' said Kate, 'if mother doesn't mind we could easily have the three boys, if they don't mind sleeping in the gardener's cottage. The gardener's wife

153

has two very nice bedrooms,' said Kate, earnestly addressing the boys, 'with two beds in one and one in the other. We send over sheets and towels and things when she has our guests there, and I don't think she has let for Bank Holiday, and she washes beautifully and would mend anything for you. Of course you would come to us for all your meals and only go to the cottage at night. She hasn't a bathroom, but you can always have baths at the Manor, and if you wanted milk at night, or soup, or anything, she would love to get it. She used to be Robert's nurse. I think that's all, isn't it?' said Kate, getting into the car.

'One thing, Kate,' said Colin. 'Quite apart from the parents' views, we don't know whether the boys can come.'

'Of course they can,' said Lydia. 'We settled all that. I say, why not ask Everard too? He's awfully nice.'

Everard clutched at the sun-baked door of the car to steady himself.

'That would be very nice,' said Kate, eyeing Everard appraisingly, as if he were one of his own pupils. 'Robert and Edith and the children may be with us, and Noel Merton, but we could manage, I'm sure. If I speak to mother to-night, and then write to you, would that be all right, Mr Carter?'

Everard pushed aside with infinite labour several large Catherine wheels, two rockets, a noise like a Tube train, and a slight earthquake, and said how delightful it would be so long as Mrs Keith wouldn't think she saw too much of him, and wondered what he meant and why he had said it. Kate and Lydia with Geraldine were carried away in the motor, and darkness fell upon the world. From this darkness Everard spoke quite calmly and sanely to Colin about the sports, and would Colin go and ask matron how the senior boy with the sprained ankle and the junior boy with biliousness were getting on.

CHAPTER VII

The Last of School

TERM sweltered on towards the exams. The summer was the finest and warmest that anyone except Mr Lorimer remembered. The cricket-players became intoxicated by the succession of blazing afternoons and the number of matches they won, and their talk rose to such a pitch of dullness that Swan and Morland put a taboo on it in the prep room. In this they could hardly have succeeded, had they not been seconded by the Captain of Rowing, who was still dumbly in love with matron and trying to write an ode to her. Mr Carter, coming into the prep room after supper one evening, found all the senior boys sitting with what looked like turbans round their heads, and a large jug half full of dirty-looking water standing in a puddle in the middle of the table. Apart from the others, and turbanless, the Captain of Rowing sat hunched up over an exercise book.

'Is this Mahomet's Paradise?' asked Everard.

'Oh, no, sir,' said Swan, rather shocked, and rising as he spoke.

As all the other boys rose with him, the effect was very impressive.

'Then I suppose it's the Vehmgericht, or the Ku Klux Klan. Sit down, all of you. What is this tomfoolery, Swan?'

'Please, sir,' said Swan, 'we found it impossible to get any swotting done for the exams because the cricket people talked so much.'

'Well?'

'Swan and I thought we had better be Sydney Carton,' said Morland. 'He always worked best with a damp towel round his head, sir, and we let the cricket people be Sydney Carton too, if they swore to stop talking.'

'And what are you wearing on your heads?'

'Well, sir,' said Morland virtuously, 'we didn't think matron would like us to use our face towels.'

'I expect you were right. Well?'

'They are mostly running shorts, sir,' said Swan, 'or vests. We damp them in the jug when we need refreshing, and they get quite dry by next day. Anyone who talks cricket isn't allowed to be Sydney Carton, and Featherstonehaugh sees fair play,' he said, indicating the Captain of Rowing.

'It's the first time I've ever heard of fair play between Rowing and Cricket,' said Everard.

'We have punch, too, sir,' said Morland, 'to be more like. It was lemonade powder and Eno's, and we made it in the jug, but Eric put too much Eno's in, and it all fizzled over and got wasted, so we used it to damp the towels. I suppose, sir, you would rather we didn't be Sydney Carton.'

'Decidedly not,' said Everard. 'Take those things off your heads, and go on with your work. You don't seem to be getting on, Featherstonehaugh. Want any help?'

He looked over the Captain of Rowing's shoulder at a blank page, upon which that ardent lover had not yet succeeded in putting one of his thoughts.

'No, thank you, sir,' said Featherstonehaugh.

'Then you'd better do some work,' said Everard, and was going out when Swan asked if he could speak to him. Everard told him he could come to his study. 'Well, what is it?' he said.

'It's about Gibbon, sir.'

'Do you want to borrow him?' said Everard, going to a bookcase.

'No, sir. It's Hacker's chameleon, sir,' said Swan,

whose hair, since he had removed the damp running shorts, was standing on end in all directions.

'Am I never to hear the last of that loathsome reptile?' said Everard.

'That's just it, sir. You know Hacker is awfully pleased about the Montgomery, and no one grudges it him,' said Swan magnanimously, though he knew, and Everard knew, that no other boy in the house would have had the faintest chance, 'and he wanted to do something to thank Mr Lorimer and Mr Winter for helping him to get it, and he couldn't think of anything they'd like except the chameleon.'

'I always thought the Classical Sixth was a training ground for Colney Hatch,' said Everard.

'Yes, sir. The thing is that Hacker thinks he ought to give the chameleon to one of them, because he likes it better than anything. I call it silly, but I haven't a self-sacrificing nature.'

'You are a prig,' said Everard. 'Get on.'

'Well, sir, luckily Mr Lorimer simply can't abide animals of any kind, and he told Hacker the other day that if he ever saw that foul saurian again he'd put his foot on it. That was because Hacker let it go for a walk on that chapter in the *Decline and Fall* about the Byzantine games, because he thought it would be interesting to see if it would turn green or blue. We all thought it rather funny to make Greta Garbo Gibbon go for a walk on Edward Gibbon.'

'I sometimes find a certain comfort in your primitive sense of humour, Swan,' said Everard. 'It shows me that you are not twenty years older and wiser than I am, as you would like to make me believe. Do you think you could come to the point? I have to finish the General Knowledge paper for the Junior School before I go to bed.'

'Sorry, sir. That rules out Mr Lorimer, but Hacker still

feels he ought to sacrifice Gibbon, and if Mr Winter won't take it, he's going to give it to you.'

Everard exploded in a way that gave Swan deep satisfaction. Everard, though well aware that every word he said would be cherished by Swan and retailed in the prep room, allowed himself to get rid of his accumulated irritation, while Swan listened with growing respect for a master who could so heartily forget himself.

'Listen, Swan,' said Everard.

'I did, sir,' said Swan.

'I'll beat you if you are funny,' said Everard. 'Go and find Hacker and send him here, and then find Mr Winter, and ask him if he will come to my room. But get Hacker first.'

When Hacker arrived, Everard went straight to the point. A rumour had reached him, he said, that Hacker wished to express his gratitude to some of the staff by presenting a chameleon. It was, said Everard, a kind and thoughtful idea, but he could not encourage it. If the giving of live-stock became a precedent, goodness knew what the school would become. There was a Siamese prince in the Lower School, and an Indian in the cricket eleven whose father was Prime Minister of a native state and fabulously wealthy. If Hacker were allowed to present his chameleon, they might expect to have elephants, panthers, and peacocks showered on them. While very much appreciating Hacker's intentions, he could not take the gift. He saw, however, no reason why Mr Winter, who curiously enough came in at that moment, should not be told of Hacker's suggestion. If he refused the chameleon Hacker must understand that the incident was closed.

'Did you send for me?' said Philip.

Everard, ignoring the implication that he was a slave-driver, said that Hacker wanted to say something to him.

Hacker looked appealingly at Everard, but as his

housemaster turned his back and sat down at his desk, he was forced to take up his tale.

'Mr. Lorimer and you got me the scholarship, sir,' he said in a muffled, stammering way, 'and I wanted to give you something. Mr Lorimer doesn't like Gibbon, but if you'd like to have him, sir, I daresay he'd be quite happy with you.'

As he spoke he took Gibbon out of his pocket and held him lovingly in his hands.

'Thank you very much indeed, Hacker,' said Philip, touched and taken aback.

'Will you have him then, sir?' said Hacker, feeling nearer tears than was at all suitable for the boy who had just got the best open scholarship of the year.

Philip, struck by the change in Hacker's voice, looked at him. What he saw made him look away again at once. He pulled himself together quickly. This was one of his own boys in trouble, and his first duty was to get him out of it. The excess of sensitiveness which made him feel Rose's careless treatment so deeply, which made him suspect slights where none were intended, which spoilt so much of his life for him, suddenly showed him what Hacker might be feeling about an ugly lizard with a ridiculous name.

'I would very much appreciate having him, Hacker,' he said gravely, 'but I think he would miss you. I think the best thing for your chameleon, Hacker, would be to go to Oxford with you. If you liked, you might give him Philip for an extra name. Go along now.'

Not unkindly he pushed Hacker out of the room. Hacker looked in at the prep room and announced that the chameleon's name for the future would be Philip Gibbon. Swan and Morland shrugged their shoulders wearily. Featherstonehaugh, who but seldom saw a joke, laughed so much that he choked, and had to drink water out of the punch jug. The rest of the seniors took no notice. But Hacker, who had put Philip Gibbon into his cage for the night, would not have cared for the shrugs or laughter of the whole world. On a luggage label he was writing the words,

Philip Gibbon, Esq.,
c/o P. Hacker, Esq.,
Lazarus College,
Oxford.

He tied the label to the bars of the cage, and stood back to see the effect. The effect was excellent, and he took up his Sophocles and got to work again.

*

'Thank goodness you turned it down,' said Everard to Philip as soon as Hacker had gone. 'Hacker is a queer fish. His attachment to that chameleon is almost sublime.'

'You needn't laugh at him,' said Philip. 'You'd better laugh at me.'

'If it weren't for the General Knowledge paper, which has to be finished to-night,' said Everard, 'I might. Thank you for coming down. I don't suppose we'll hear any more of the chameleon now.'

'Does that mean you want to get rid of me?' asked Philip.

'It only means exactly what I said. I am glad you didn't take the chameleon, and now I've got to get this confounded paper done. Unless, of course, there's anything special you want to see me about,' he said, thinking as he looked at Philip's face that one assistant master could be more trouble than a houseful of boys.

'You don't mind if I have a talk with you, then?' said Philip.

Everard pushed away his papers without outward impatience and sat back. If Philip needed help, the General Knowledge papers could wait.

Philip stood staring out of the window at the head-master's house.

'I can't stand it, Everard,' he said. 'I'm going.'

'Have you told the Head yet? You can't suddenly rush off without notice.'

'No. But I shall. I don't want to upset the house, but it's unbearable. I'm simply a useless dead weight here now.'

'Not at all. Your work has been as good as ever this term, Philip, perhaps better. Try not to think about other things. No need to tell the world your affairs aren't going quite straight.'

'No need, indeed,' said Philip bitterly. 'The whole house, the whole school knows. The boys are kind to me, Everard, *kind* to me, because they see I'm a useless fool. Swan and Morland used to argue with me like anything in the history period. I thought I was helping them to see modern politics from a reasonable point of view.'

'Left, I gather.'

'Yes, left. Why not?'

'Well, there is right, and personally I think there is a great deal of middle.'

'Middle?' said Philip contemptuously. 'Our only salvation lies in the left. But anyway, those two used to get up the most fantastic arguments on the other side. I admit I lost my temper a bit sometimes if they were too clever, but we all enjoyed it and we got some really good talk. Now they say "Yes, sir" to whatever I say, as if I were a lunatic that had to be humoured. And Swan never puts on his spectacles except for his work. And now Hacker, comforting me with chameleons, for I am – oh, God, I can't stand it.'

'I'm sorry you feel it like that.'

'I don't mind you or Colin,' continued Philip, pursuing some apparently inconsequent train of thought. 'I've been pretty rotten to Colin and I've apologized.

It's that man Merton. He's going to be with the Keiths again, Colin tells me. He'll be at the Rectory all the time. What chance have I got? And she is so trusting and inexperienced.'

Everard, stifling a strong desire to say exactly what he thought of Rose's inexperience, said Philip was making mountains out of molehills.

'As far as I know,' he said slowly, as if he were choosing his words with great care and thought, 'Merton has no wish to be at the Rectory.'

'You mean –'

'Exactly what I say. And now, for God's sake try to be a little more reasonable, Philip. Don't think everyone is thinking of you, because they aren't. Don't think everyone wants to be your rival, because they certainly don't. And do go to bed, or write your book, and I must get on with this work.'

Just then a terrific clamour broke forth in the school quad. It was the Messrs Fairweather with their racing car, bringing Rose back from the cinema at Barchester. Hatless, flushed, alive, exquisite, she was standing on the steps of the headmaster's house, lit by the late daylight from the west and the bright light from the hall. For a few minutes she exchanged lively sallies with her escort, then kissed them both in a careless way and disappeared.

'There!' said Philip, and burst out again violently about his own misery, the inexperience of Rose, the black designs of the Fairweathers and Noel Merton. Everard, very tired, turned on him and told him in so many words not to be a damned fool and waste people's time.

Philip at once collapsed.

'I'm sorry,' he said. 'But if you only knew what being engaged –'

'Get out,' said Everard.

It was some time before he could compose himself enough to get on with the General Knowledge paper. To have put into words his conviction that Noel Merton would not wish to visit the Rectory had made him feel even more certain that Kate was only waiting for Noel to speak. He had deliberately said what he did, partly to comfort Philip, partly to have the bitter pleasure of telling himself what a fool he was. Not much better than Philip in fact, though one learnt, thank God, a little more self-control as one got older.

'To which University, or Universities, would you say the following belong, and how would you pronounce them?' he wrote. 'Caius, Trinity, Merton,' – on an impulse he ran his pen heavily through Merton, laughed at himself, and went on, 'Merton, Magdalene . . .'

*

Philip did not resign his post. He took some of Everard's advice and threw himself into his work for the last fortnight, coached the Classical Fourth and his own form to breaking-point, corrected examination papers with feverish energy, worked on his book till the small hours of the morning, harried the school orchestra, and put his own misfortunes in the background as much as he could; by which means life became much more agreeable for the other inmates of Mr Carter's house. Philip found that the less time he had to think of Rose, the happier he was, and blamed himself severely for this, without drawing any of the right conclusions. Mr Lorimer, thinking well of Philip's work, offered to submit his manuscript, with a strong personal recommendation, to the Oxbridge University Press before he went to Scotland for his holiday, an additional reason for getting it into final shape by the end of the term.

Colin found this chastened Philip a pleasant companion in his few spare moments, and when neither of them were correcting examination papers, or studying Horace, or the law, they dropped into each other's rooms for a good-night drink. Colin planned in his mind to get Philip over to Northbridge without Rose, where Lydia would supply a wholesome corrective to Rose's atmosphere.

Colin had an interview with Mr Birkett, in the course of which he learned, without much surprise, that he had given satisfaction in his temporary work, but would not be needed after that term.

'If you were really determined to make this your profession, I would do my best to find room for you,' said Mr Birkett, 'but I don't think your heart is in it. Harrison will be back next term, and unless there were some very strong reason, I wouldn't be justified in keeping you on.'

'It's awfully good of you, sir,' said Colin, 'and I've enjoyed the work most awfully, but I don't think I'd ever get quite used to boys.'

'You look well,' said Mr Birkett, eyeing Colin's neck absent-mindedly. 'Have you put on weight here?'

'I don't think so, sir,' said Colin, surprised at the Head's sudden interest in his physical welfare. The Head then said a few words about the pleasure of seeing the Keiths in the holidays, and the interview terminated.

Mr Birkett's next interview was with Everard, to discuss some school changes.

'I don't want to interfere, sir,' said Everard, 'but if you haven't decided about the Mixed Fifth yet, I hope you'll consider giving Winter a trial. He has come well on the whole through what has been a very trying term, and if other things go well I believe you'll find him a success. I don't think Harrison would mind going to the Classical Fourth for a bit. It has always been a subject of his.'

'I might try it,' said Mr Birkett, 'if you really recommend it, but only for a term, on approval. He must either settle down or go. I know the fault is largely in my own family, and heartily wish the situation had never arisen, but there it is. It couldn't be more awkward for everyone.

164

If it weren't for these domestic complications I like Winter very much, and I don't like the way he is treated here. "Our Polly is a sad slut, nor heeds what we have taught her." Well, next term will decide what I shall have to do. Now, about that boy in the Army Sixth –'

*

At last the exams sweltered to an end. Hacker got the Latin Prize, the Greek Prize, the Eleanor Cobbley Special Prize for Latin verse, the Featherstonehaugh Special Prize for Greek verse (given by an uncle of the Captain of Rowing, who became horribly embarrassed whenever he heard of it), and only missed the Lorimer Prize for Greek declamation because he found himself unable to speak until after the examiners' patience was exhausted. Young Holinshed got C minus in the General Knowledge paper, a mark richly deserved by one who had written that Caius and Magdalene were pronounced Cholmondeley and Marjoribanks. Swan and Morland came near the top of their form, and Swan disgraced the house by getting a reading prize given by the Chaplain.

'I only went in to please Holy Joe,' he complained to the prep room, 'and look what it's brought on me.'

He held up a copy of *Sartor Resartus*.

'Let's play football with it,' said Featherstonehaugh. 'Nobody'll mind on the last night.'

He gave the book a kick and it went right through the glass ventilator into the passage. Everyone was filled with pleasurable horror. Everard came in, holding the book.

'Any explanation?' he said.

'That's Swan's prize, sir,' said Morland.

'Well?'

'It's the reading prize, sir. He couldn't help it. Mr Smith made him go in for it. We were just looking at it and it got through the ventilator.'

'Four and six,' said Everard, who knew the price of every breakage in the house, 'settle it among you.'

Featherstonehaugh then did the one daring and romantic deed of a dull and blameless (except for inability to pass any examination) school career by asking Everard if he had change for ten shillings. Everard took the note and counted out five and sixpence.

'Here you are,' he said, 'and now the ventilator is broken, you might as well go on using it. What with Hacker winning the Consolation Race and Swan the Reading Prize, this house has come pretty low.'

This kind advice was acted upon with such spirit that *Sartor Resartus* came to pieces in ten minutes and was thrown into the waste-paper basket. Featherstonehaugh announced that Mr Carter was a sportsman, and in honour of this, and to celebrate the end of his career as Captain of Rowing, he was going to break training. He then went down to the village, out of bounds, drank a pint of beer, and was found by the school waterman, crying gently over the heavy punt used for rush cutting, under the impression that it was the first eight, and he had grown too old and weak to move it. He was got back into the house at a late hour by the fire escape, and though he went to bed in his trousers and shoes, no one in authority ever heard of it.

Hacker made everyone very uncomfortable by insisting on shaking hands and saying good-bye, but at this Swan and Morland protested.

'Hang it all, Hack, we're all going to the Keiths for Bank Holiday,' said Swan.

'It won't be the same,' said Hacker.

'If you think you're grown-up just because you've got a mouldy scholarship, you're wrong,' said Morland. 'You aren't at Oxford yet, and I bet you won't be able to pass the Thirty-nine Articles. Many a stronger faith than yours has split on that rock, my boy. Go away and say good-bye to matron. She's waiting.'

Hacker went off in offended dignity to matron, who said she would never forget the night he set the house on fire, adding that he had never given any trouble from the day he came into the House. She then, her custom with departing boarders, kissed him good-bye, thus causing him to leave school with even less regret than he would otherwise have felt.

Everard was doing reports in his study when Mr Lorimer, carrying an untidy brown-paper parcel with great care, dropped in to have a talk, or rather, as it soon appeared, to let off a grievance.

'I suppose you know what has happened, Carter,' he said. 'You housemasters always know these things first. The Head is thinking of trying Winter for the Mixed Fifth. The one good Junior Classical Master I've had since poor Turnbull was killed in 1915. If the Press don't take his Horace I'll have it published myself. I suppose that means I'll have Harrison, who has no imagination, or some new man with no background, which is worse. One of these confounded clever boys from a secondary school, who come up with State Aid to ruin our Universities. London or Leeds would be good enough for them,' said Mr Lorimer, to whom the word University had only two meanings in English, 'but they needs must come and ruin what is left of our civilization. Well, it may last my time, but no longer. I've brought you some good port.'

He undid the parcel, produced a bottle, demanded a corkscrew, and carefully uncorked it. Everard got two glasses out of his cupboard, when Colin came in.

'Oh, excuse me,' he said, 'I've brought the rest of those French marks.'

'Come and drink Lorimer's port,' said Everard. 'Get a glass for yourself.'

'So you're leaving us,' said Mr Lorimer.

'Yes, sir,' said Colin.

'Quite right. Better get out before you are caught in the machinery. Look at me. Thirty-five years I've been at this job, and no one has ever heard of me.'

'There is your Latin Grammar, sir, and that book of unseens. Heaps of schools use them,' said Colin.

'BAH!' said Mr Lorimer with extreme violence. 'Catchpennies. All classical masters write grammars, and exercise a sort of moral blackmail till the school makes it a standard book. Twelve first-class schools use my grammar and unseens. Do you know what that means?'

He put the question in so terrifying a manner that Everard and Colin judged, rightly, that he was prepared to supply the answer himself, and would indeed resent any effort on their part to do so.

'It means,' said Mr Lorimer, 'about five thousand boys, taking the very lowest figure, say between five and seven thousand boys per annum who loathe me, who wish I had never been born, who draw insulting pictures of me in the fly leaves of my books. And I get older and more stupid, and when I get a good classic like Winter, he goes to the Mixed Fifth, a bastard growth which tries to pander to the modern taste for learning a little ignorance of most subjects. And when I retire I shall be quite forgotten. I shall probably sign away my pension to a landlady, and live, a debauched, inebriate old man, on her charity, occasionally begging by letter from old boys who, for very shame, will have to help the master they once held in awe, if not in respect, God help me!'

'It sounds pretty awful, sir,' said Colin sympathetically, and noticing that Mr Lorimer was already well into his fourth glass of port, while he and Everard had not finished their first.

'Awful?' said Mr Lorimer angrily. 'You don't know what you are talking about! Obscure as the school-master's life may seem, depressed, degraded, we bear the torch for each new generation, we follow the gleam. Not all of us. I have followed, I have borne my light, nobly, for thirty-five years. Carter, though his whole span of life is no longer than my years of work, has the holy flame. You, young man, for I have no recollection of your name and very little of your face, have not the sacred fire.'

'That's what Mr Birkett said, sir,' said Colin, respectful to age and learning. 'He said he didn't think I was the sort and –'

'Lorimer has gone to sleep,' said Everard. 'He often does at the end of term. Well, Colin, we shall be meeting again at the week-end, I'm glad to say. I won't make a speech like poor Lorimer's, but I would like to say that you have been a real help, and I'll miss you.'

'Thanks awfully, sir,' said Colin. 'And I had a letter from Kate, and she said to give you her love and say they were all looking forward to seeing you.'

Everard fell into such a muse that Colin thought he was going to sleep too, and got up softly to go.

'All right, Colin,' said Everard, in a low voice. 'Don't turn the light on. I'll let Lorimer have his sleep out – and I rather want to think.'

'Can I do the reports for you then, sir?' said Colin, also hushing his voice.

'Oh, the reports,' said Everard. 'Yes. I had almost forgotten about them. No, I'll have to do them myself, thank you. You go to bed.'

Everard got up, went to his desk, turned his reading-lamp away from the sleeping Mr Lorimer, switched it on, and settled to his work.

CHAPTER VIII

A Glimpse of Freedom

ON the following day everyone went home. Mrs Keith sent the car to fetch Colin, asking him to pick Lydia up in Barchester, as she would have a good many books to bring back. Rose Birkett, who was exercising her dog in the school yard, or rather dragging it about on a lead to draw the attention of the junior masters to her fondness for animals, came up to look.

'Oh, Colin, you *have* got a car,' she said.

'It's not mine, it's my people's,' said Colin.

'Will they let you take me out in it?' said Rose, picking up her dog and holding it to her cheek.

'I shouldn't think so,' said Colin, unmoved by her charms. 'I can't drive it, and the chauffeur is usually doing odd jobs when he isn't driving the parents.'

'How sickening,' said Rose. 'Oh, Colin, will you write your name in my birthday book?'

She held up an oblong book bound in pink leather. Colin turned the pages to the third of November and wrote his name.

'Oh,' said Rose, 'that's only a month before mine!'

Simnet appeared to say good-bye in a respectful way.

'But I believe, sir, that we may have the honour of meeting in the near future,' said Simnet, 'as I understand that the Rectory where we propose to spend the Long Vacation – I beg pardon, sir, it is an old habit, the holidays I should say – is in the vicinity of Northbridge Manor.'

Colin said it was, and gave Simnet ten shillings.

'Thank you, sir. You can go on now,' Simnet said to

Sanders, the chauffeur, who at once hated him from the bottom of his heart.

Colin was driven off to Barchester, where Sanders was to fetch Lydia from school. As the car stopped before the large Georgian house where Miss Pettinger held sway, he was appalled to see what looked like hundreds of girls clustered on the steps in all stages of unattractiveness. All were carrying satchels, suitcases, cricket bats, pads, violin cases, or some form of luggage. A particularly loud hub-bub in the centre of the group directed Colin's attention to his sister Lydia, talking to her more intimate friends. She beckoned imperiously to Colin to come and speak to her. He shook his head, tried to make himself as incon-spicuous as possible, and hoped she wouldn't be long. Presently the crowd parted and Miss Pettinger herself came down the steps. She spoke to Lydia, who reluctantly led her towards the car.

'Miss Pettinger wants to speak to you,' said Lydia, making a hideous face at Colin, who half rose in his seat, nervously.

'Don't get up,' said Miss Pettinger to Colin, though that would have been impossible in the car, where he could only have crouched. 'This is Lydia Keith's brother, isn't it? So you have been at Southbridge. How do you like it?'

'Very much, thank you,' said Colin.

'That's right,' said Miss Pettinger, with the gracious smile that caused some of her pupils to become her slaves and the larger number to call her Old Kit Bag. 'I wish you every success in an honourable profession.'

'I've left the school,' said Colin rashly. 'I'm going to do law.'

'Oh,' said Miss Pettinger, in the voice with which she reduced girls to tears when they had stained the honour of the school by not hanging their coats on the right pegs in the cloak-room. 'Well, I only wanted to send a message to your mother, Mr Keith. Will you tell her that I hope very much to come over to tea on Sunday, as she suggests. I would have written, but I am very busy and she kindly added that a verbal message by you would be enough. Good-bye, Lydia.'

'Good-bye, Miss Pettinger,' said Lydia, bending her legs ungraciously.

'What on earth did you do that for?' said her brother as they drove away.

'What?'

'Well, what you did when you said good-bye to Miss Pettinger. I thought you were going to fall down.'

'She makes us curtsy,' said Lydia. 'Geraldine Birkett always says she won't, but she does. It's a kind of moral compulsion, if you get the idea. Why on earth does mother want to ask her to tea on Sunday when the boys will be here? They'll talk about people's first cousins once removed, and I shan't know which way to look I shall be so ashamed of them both. I shall clean the pond that day, and then the Pettinger won't be able to get at me.'

For the next few days Lydia was fully engaged in unpacking, getting her own room into the state of confusion that she preferred, and defeating Kate's efforts to tidy her person or belongings. Her mother took her into Barchester one day to replenish her wardrobe, but the only result was that Lydia forced her mother to buy her a red velvet evening dress, in which she looked so magnificent as to be almost improper. When Mr Keith saw it he said he forbade her to wear it again, but no one took any notice of him, owing to Mrs Keith telling a long story about a yellow shawl that her Uncle Oswald had once given to Lady Sibyl Carter, of which Lydia's dress had somehow reminded her.

On the Friday before Bank Holiday Noel Merton, now definitely established as a friend of the house, came down, and was at once annexed by Lydia, who wanted to bathe.

As Kate was out with her mother, Noel was perfectly ready to accompany Lydia, so long as he wasn't expected to bathe himself.

'All right,' said Lydia. 'You row the boat and I'll practise diving. There aren't many places where it's safe, but I know a good one, just below the Rectory.'

Accordingly Noel sculled up in a leisurely way to the diving pool, where Lydia practised her diving, taking off each time with a violence that made Noel afraid the boat would capsize. Old Bunce the ferryman came and stared at Lydia long and unwinkingly, after which he went back to his cottage and told his wife and three daughters that Miss Lydia was no better than the Babylonish woman, and if he caught any of them in such goings on he'd give them the stick. As the Bunce family were all celebrated for never taking off any of their clothes by day or by night, the warning was quite unnecessary. Mrs Bunce said, 'Don't be an old fool, Bunce,' and his daughters giggled and said Father was a one, so old Bunce went back to the river. But Lydia and Noel were on their way home, Lydia wrapped in a new bath-robe which she had taken from Colin's room without asking. On their way they passed a punt, on which Rose and Philip were seated side by side, gently paddling.

'Oh, Mr Merton,' said Rose, 'how marvellous to see you. Do come to tea to-morrow.'

'Thank you so much,' said Noel, 'but I am staying with Mrs Keith and don't know what her plans are. How are you, Winter?'

'How sickening,' said Rose, 'but you must come. Have you been bathing?' she added, looking coldly at Lydia, but somehow not directly addressing her. 'How ghastly!'

Lydia made no answer. Throwing off the bath-robe she dived from the boat straight under the punt, swam round it with a vigorous overarm stroke, turned over on her back and raised a small mill-race with her legs, threw up her arms, screamed, sank, and reappeared at the other side of the boat.

'That's the stuff to give 'em,' she said, as she scrambled on board and wrapped herself up again. 'Go on, Noel. Can you imagine anyone being dotty enough to like a girl like that Rose Birkett?'

'I can imagine it because I've seen it,' said Noel, hoping that his sculling had been strong enough to get them out of earshot of the punt, 'but heaven defend me from seeing more of her than civility demands.'

'She's a blight,' said Lydia. 'I say, what do you think about marriage?'

'Personally or in the abstract?' asked Noel, as he tied up in the boat-house and pulled Lydia out of the boat.

'Oh, any way. I mean when you look at those two it puts you off the whole idea, at least it does me, and I wondered what you thought. Come on, we'll be late for tea.'

'I think my feeling about it is,' said Noel, following her towards the house, 'that it is a very good thing for the right people, but not for everyone. I don't think of it for myself. Unless something very romantic happens to me, which I don't much want or expect, I shall be a kind of permanent uncle to everyone.'

'Quite right,' said Lydia approvingly. 'I expect I'll get married some day myself, because I'd feel an awful fool if I didn't, like Miss Pettinger, and Kate ought to get married, of course. I don't know about Colin, but I rather think he's an uncle, like you. I bet anything Rose won't marry Mr Winter. She'd never marry a person that looks unhappy when she speaks to anyone.'

'How did you think of all this?' asked Noel, amused.

'I didn't. You don't need to think about things like that. One just knows them. I *am* sorry for Geraldine Birkett, having a sister like Rose. Now Kate is a nice sort of sister. She may want to tidy one up a bit, but she's an angel about darning stockings and being decent if one's upset about anything. Who do you think she'll marry?'

Noel said he couldn't imagine, but hoped it would be someone very nice. Like Mr Carter, Lydia said. Yes, someone like Mr Carter would be splendid, Noel said, and then changed the subject, feeling that Lydia was alarmingly near the mark, for in his quality of universal uncle Everard's absorption in Kate had not passed unnoticed by him. They found that Mrs Keith and Kate had returned and were having tea in the library. Lydia went to change, and Noel talked to his hostesses. Then Colin came down.

'Hullo, Noel,' he said. 'I'm so glad you've come. I can't tell you how nice it is to be surrounded by human faces instead of thousands of boys.'

'Wasn't the experiment a success, then?' asked Noel.

'Oh, I liked the school very much and the staff were all right, but I never got used to the boys.'

'How can you say that, Colin,' said Lydia indignantly, as she came in, 'when Tony and Eric and Hack are coming to-morrow!'

'Sorry, Lydia. Those particular boys are almost human,' said Colin, 'at least Tony and Eric are. They are both more intelligent than I am in many ways, and you can meet Hacker, at any age from twenty-five to eighty, in almost every common-room in Oxford, I regret to say. But on the whole I'm glad to be free. I wish I were coming to you sooner, Noel. I'm reading like anything now.'

'Why don't you come abroad with me for a fortnight?' said Noel. 'I want to go to Austria, and I haven't made any plans. You must be rolling in money with your term's salary.'

'I wish I could,' said Colin longingly. 'Let's talk about it sometime,' he added, looking meaningly at his mother.

But Mrs Keith had heard, and wished to warn them against going to a certain hotel in Rome where one of her aunts had once been very ill owing to drinking unboiled water in August. As this had happened in 1887, and she could not remember the name of the hotel, no one could contradict her. Also, she said, did Colin remember that the Northbridge Flower Show was on the 14th, and she did hope he wasn't going to miss it. Lydia, stretching out a leg to hook a small table with cakes on it, distracted her mother's attention, who said that once for all Lydia must wear stockings in the house. Before this subject was fully thrashed out, Edith Keith with her two children came in, and Mrs Keith forgot Lydia in her grandmotherly joy. Henry and Catherine, aged respectively five and under two, were agreeable, well-behaved children, and were almost immediately whisked away by their nurse.

'You know Mr Merton, of course, Edith,' said Mrs Keith. 'We shall only be a small party for the week-end. Ourselves, Mr Merton, and Colin's friend Mr Carter, and three boys in the Twickers' cottage. But the Birketts will be at the Rectory, and the young man who is engaged to that pretty elder daughter of theirs, so I expect you'll get some good tennis. I asked them all over here to tea on Sunday, when Miss Pettinger is coming. The raspberries will be ready.'

Lydia remarked *sotto voce* that the raspberry was what Miss Pettinger needed, was told by her mother to speak distinctly, and overturning her chair as she got up, went out into the garden.

'Well, I've got something to cheer you up, mater,' said Edith, who was the only one of the family to use this hearty name for her mother-in-law. 'My brothers are staying with my people over at Plumstead, and they'll be looking us up. Geoff is on four months' leave from Burma, and John is at home while his ship refits. They want to see Rose Birkett again. They quite fell for her at the school sports. What a pretty kid she is, but the brains of a louse – sorry, mater, mouse I meant. Well, Mr Merton, and how has the great world been treating you?'

Mr Merton said he had no complaints to make of it, except that it kept him up rather late in the season. Then Mrs Keith and Edith went to see the children put to bed, so Noel and Kate went for a walk, while Colin returned to his books. Their talk was very restful and pleasant, being mostly about Kate's family. Kate said she was a little worried about Lydia, because she wouldn't trouble to conceal her feelings when she disliked people.

'Do you remember,' she said, 'how very rude she was to Mr Winter, the day of the picnic? And then at Colin's tea-party the other day she was so rude to Rose Birkett that I was quite alarmed. Rose is so stupid for such a pretty creature that I don't think she noticed, but the boys did; I saw them looking at each other. Mr Merton, why do you encourage her to be silly?'

'Do you think you need say Mr Merton?' said Noel.

'Certainly not, if you like,' said Kate calmly. 'We all say Noel behind your back, but with Lydia Christian-naming everyone at sight, someone has to hold back a bit. Noel, do you *have* to behave so badly with Rose, and make her worse? It makes poor Mr Winter wretched.'

Noel felt what he recognized as an unreasonable touch of annoyance that Winter's fate should interest Kate, and suppressed it, remarking that Rose simply asked for it.

'But Mr Winter doesn't,' said Kate. 'And it will be a very uncomfortable week-end if the party from the Rectory come over on Sunday, or we go to tennis there, and Mr Winter has the sulks on your account. Do you think, Noel, you could refrain from that form of amusement?'

'Do you want me to?'

'Please,' said Kate, stopping, laying a hand on his arm, and looking up at him.

'Did you ever look in the beginning of a little book of

177

Hardy's poems that I sent you by Lydia?' asked Noel, rather alarmed at himself, but unable to resist the lure of a mild situation.

'Oh, yes,' said Kate. 'It said "With your humble duty".'

Her voice was always sweet, and Noel couldn't say whether it sounded any sweeter than usual.

'Well, that holds good,' said Noel, in a low, thrilling voice, more alarmed than ever at the way he was behaving.

'You mean you won't encourage Rose to – well, flirt with you?' said Kate, wanting to be sure.

'Not if you don't like it.'

'Thank you so much,' said Kate, walking on. 'You can't think what a difference it will make.'

'Does it matter so much to you then if I flirt, as you call it, with Rose?' said Noel, adding to himself, 'Shut up, you blasted fool.'

'It matters frightfully,' said Kate in heartfelt accents.

Noel wondered if he was going to propose to her. He didn't want to in the least, and it was against his principles, but if his promising not to dally with Rose Birkett meant so much to Kate, he might find himself in honour bound. And then he suddenly remembered Everard Carter, for whom he had taken a great liking, and wished someone would come and rescue him.

'Because,' Kate went on, 'if Rose is silly, it makes Mr Winter so cross, and that is horrid for Colin.'

'Yes, I see,' said Noel.

Kate then related to Noel several delightful and, as it seemed to him, rather pointless anecdotes about her nephew and niece, and so talking of one thing and another they reached the house again. As they came in, the sudden gloom of the hall, with curtains drawn against the afternoon sun, made Noel feel half blind. From the gloom, Kate spoke.

'I wish you weren't going to Austria,' she said, in a voice like a prayer.

'Why?'

'Oh, a foolish reason,' said Kate seriously. 'So foolish, I can't tell you, Noel.'

She went upstairs to dress for dinner. As she dressed she considered her conversation with Noel. It had been very nice of him to promise not to bait Rose, but to her mind his profession of humble duty was a trifle overdone. She admitted that the inscription had appeared to her at the time excessively romantic. She could remember the actual thrill that the words, in Noel's queer, spiky, upright hand, had given her. It had been a weakening, but not disagreeable sensation, to feel a dithering feeling about where she should have liked to think her heart was placed, though it certainly felt much more like her stomach, whenever she thought of or re-read those remarkable words, but the sensation had not lasted long. After a week, in spite of valiant attempts at recapture, she had lost it entirely, and could only conclude that it was not true love. It was certainly always very pleasant to see Noel again, and nothing could have been nicer than his behaviour to her personally at Colin's party, but his thoughtless conduct with Rose had seemed to her rather selfish. If people did things that might lead to trouble for Colin, she could not like them quite so much as if they didn't, and she had gathered, though Colin hadn't actually complained, that Mr Winter's temper had been more difficult than usual after the sports. If only everyone could be nice and kind like Colin or Mr Carter. There was something particularly nice and friendly about a man who carried waistcoat buttons about with him in a vinaigrette in case of need, and he had been very kind to Colin. A man like Mr Carter, Everard as Colin called him, would not go to Austria when he might stay happily in London all through the

Long Vacation, helping Colin to read law. School-masters, she decided, were nicer than lawyers, because they thought more of others. She felt quite sure that if Colin or anyone needed help, Everard Carter would give it, at whatever inconvenience to himself. It was nice that he was coming for the week-end, and if Lydia were happily occupied with Noel and Colin and the three boys and the pond, perhaps there would be a chance for her to take Everard for a walk by themselves. With this thought she went down to dinner, and was able to give her undivided attention to the question of where they should have tea on Sunday. Mrs Keith was of opinion that if it were fine it would be nice to have it in the garden-room on the terrace, but if it were wet or cold, the drawing-room would be the best place. Everyone agreed, but no one could say what the weather would be at five o'clock the day after to-morrow, so no decision was reached.

Noel's dressing thoughts had been less pleasant. With all his perception he had not quite realized that Colin was, up to the present, the most important person in Kate's life. When she reproached him for misleading Rose, he had at first suspected her of a leaning towards Winter, and then decided he was mistaken. Still, some explanation there must be for her insistence, and without being fatuous he felt she might resent his attentions to Rose or feel them as a slight to herself. She had been so charming to him and then her voice had almost broken as she said she wished he weren't going to Austria, and wouldn't tell him why, and what on earth was a man to do? One didn't want to exaggerate one's own value or her feelings, but if she felt so strongly it might be kinder to go away, and certainly safer. He liked the Keith family, he liked Colin very much, he found Lydia a permanent source of amusement, but to fall in love with Kate, or be fallen in love with, would not be in the least what he meant. The universal uncle went down to dinner in doubt and discouragement, but as Kate seemed quite herself, and as friendly as ever, he tried to put the incident away. After dinner Kate went over to the Twickers' cottage to talk to the gardener's wife about the visitors, and as everyone went to bed early he did not see her again that night. At two in the morning he woke up and thought of Everard Carter, and the thought did not relieve his mind.

*

Neither had the Rectory had an altogether serene evening. After the meeting with Noel and Lydia on the river, Rose had chosen to consider her feelings insulted by Lydia, and was quite angry because Philip would not agree with her.

'But, Rose,' said Philip, as they walked up the garden to the Rectory, 'all Lydia did was to swim round the boat. She didn't mean to splash you, and after all she's only a kid, like Geraldine.'

Rose said it was Rudeness she couldn't bear.

'Well, if it comes to that, you were rather rude, too,' said Philip. 'You asked Merton to tea and never said a word to Lydia.'

Rose said Geraldine could ask Lydia if she wanted to, and anyway Lydia was only a kid, and Philip had said so himself, and wouldn't expect to be asked, and if Philip liked Lydia better than her he had better say so.

Philip said, almost roughly, that Rose was being silly, and things simply couldn't go on like this, upon which Rose burst into tears, and rushing upstairs to her room, yelled with such abandonment that the servants all said it was Miss Rose again.

Mrs Birkett, reading in the garden, heard her daughter's distress coming through the window. She hoped it would stop if she did nothing, but Rose was of sterner stuff, and went on sobbing, with an occasional tear-stained look out of the window to see if her mother had heard. It was no good knocking with so much noise going on, so Mrs Birkett went straight in.

'What is the matter, Rose?' she said.

'Boo-hoo,' said Rose.

'Now, try to stop crying and tell me what it is,' said Mrs Birkett. 'Everyone can hear you.'

Rose said she would like everyone to hear her, because it would show them how sickening Philip was.

'Well,' said her mother, 'what has he done?'

Rose said he liked Lydia Keith better than her, and that being so, why did he ever get engaged to her, and she wished she were dead.

'You must have made a mistake,' said Mrs Birkett. 'Lydia is only Geraldine's age. Philip couldn't have said a thing like that.'

'He did, he did,' bellowed Rose. 'Lydia came splashing round the boat, and he said I was rude to her.'

'I expect you were,' said Mrs Birkett. 'Rose, you can't go on like this. Daddy and I are not at all happy about you. You got engaged so very suddenly, and you and Philip don't seem to get on at all well now. If you feel unhappy about it, tell me, and I can talk to Philip, or daddy can, and no one will mind. It's no good being engaged if it only makes you miserable.'

At this Rose's sobs redoubled and she was heard to say in a thick voice that no one loved her, and she adored Philip, and why did mummy and daddy want to make her miserable.

Mrs Birkett would dearly have loved to hit her daughter.

'Drink some water,' she said, giving a glass to Rose, and trying to make her voice sound kind. 'We cannot have this going on all through the holidays – well, for as long as Philip stays here, and you will drive him away if you go on like this. Daddy and I do want you to be happy, but you must help. Do you really care for Philip enough to be nice to him, because if not it would be much better to stop being engaged and you and Philip can just be friends.'

On hearing this Rose said no one should come between her and Philip, and she would go and tell him at once. She then threw her bath sponge across the room with great vehemence, so that it went out of the window, made up her face, and banged out of the room and downstairs. Mrs Birkett felt almost sick with worry and the noise Rose had made. She heard Rose burst into the study, and the sound of voices. Trying to calm herself she tidied the room a little, went downstairs and aimlessly into the garden. Under Rose's window Geraldine was reading Woodstock, which was her holiday task, with Rose's bath sponge by her side.

'Have you been sitting there long, Geraldine?' said Mrs Birkett.

'Yes, mummy,' said Geraldine simply. 'Rose made such a noise that I couldn't help hearing. I wish Miss Pettinger could have heard her. She'd have passed out, and a good thing too.'

Mrs. Birkett chid her younger daughter for eaves-dropping and for speaking unbecomingly of her head-mistress and went slowly indoors.

'Poor mummy,' said Geraldine to herself, as she resumed her reading, 'she hasn't much grip.'

When Rose left him, Philip stood irresolute for a moment, and then went indoors. With the sound of his affianced's ringing shrieks in his ears, he knocked at Mr Birkett's study door. Philip's real efforts to control him-self and be less difficult with his colleagues had not escaped Mr Birkett's notice, and what Everard had said had confirmed his opinion. Although he was very fond of his Rose, her alienating ways of late had made him feel more and more sorry for Philip. A good classical master was not to be easily found, nor lightly thrown away, but for the peace of his house and school he might have to make the sacrifice. When he had unwillingly given his consent to Philip's spending the beginning of the holidays with them, he had anticipated an uncomfortable time for everyone, but with Philip in this better frame of mind, his fears were slightly dissipated. Perhaps Rose would settle down, perhaps all would yet be well when the lovers could meet peacefully every day. And he must speak to Philip about the Mixed Fifth. All these confusing threads were hindering him in the composition of a speech to be given in September at a conference of headmasters, and his pen traced circles and crosses and spirals on the blotting paper, while his thoughts wandered.

A loud shriek from above his head, followed by a sound of determined crying, recalled him to the present. Rose again! His sympathy for Philip increased, and he hoped he would begin their married life by beating her, and wished they could get married at once and let him write his address in peace. A minute later Philip knocked at the door and came in. Their eyes met, and a faint gleam of amusement flashed between them, which both men instantly suppressed.

'Well,' said Mr Birkett, 'I suppose your visit is not unconnected with that devilish noise upstairs.'

'I'm afraid it's my fault,' said Philip conscientiously. 'I said something to Rose that hurt her.'

'Hurt! No one makes a noise like that about being hurt. Sheer temper. Philip, I'd give a year's pension if you would marry that daughter of mine out of hand and thrash her.'

'There was nothing I would have liked more,' said Philip. 'To marry her, I mean. I think, sir, if you'll forgive my talking shop in the holidays, I had better give you my resignation now, and leave the Rectory to-night. Have you a few moments?'

The eternal question from boys to form masters, from boys to housemasters, from boys and junior masters to housemasters, from boys, junior masters and house-masters to headmasters. People needing help all the time and mostly getting it. Mr Birkett put his speech into a drawer.

'Have you any reason for those decisions?' he asked.

'Yes, sir. I think I'm a nuisance here, and I'm afraid I've been a nuisance at school this term. I'd better go.'

'You'll be a nuisance if you do,' said Mr Birkett. 'Will you young men *never* learn any consideration?'

'What do you mean, sir? I've behaved rottenly all this term, and the least I can do –'

'Is to allow me to judge. I don't want to know how you behaved. I don't care. If you want to come clean – excuse the revolting phrase from Hollywood – go to the Chaplain. You have done very good work this term and your conscience is your own affair, not mine. I am going to suggest that you should try the Mixed Fifth next term. Your private affairs must not interfere with the school. We will discuss Rose in a minute. Are you resigning?'

'The Mixed Fifth, sir?' said Philip. 'Of course, sir, if it's for the sake of the school – oh, damn it, excuse me, sir, I'm being heroic – I mean, I believe I could make a do of it.'

'I shouldn't have asked you if I'd thought you couldn't,' said Mr Birkett. 'Very well. Now, what about you and Rose? This can't go on,' he said, looking at the ceiling, which was almost quivering under Rose's outburst. 'Have you and Rose broken off the engagement?'

'No, sir.'

'Then, do you want to marry Rose, and does she want to marry you?'

Philip said nothing.

'I haven't much time to spare,' said Mr Birkett in his firmest headmaster's voice.

'Rose must say,' said Philip.

'That isn't an answer.'

'As far as I am concerned, Rose could be free, with my love and gratitude,' said Philip, looking at the floor, 'but as long as she wants me, I am here. I don't mean to be heroic again,' he added anxiously.

'You're not heroic, you are very silly,' said Mr Birkett, 'though not half so silly as Rose. If Rose doesn't behave better to you, I shall break off the engagement myself.'

Philip's heart leapt, but he said, 'I don't think you could, sir.'

'Perhaps not,' said Mr Birkett ruefully. 'I don't know at what point we, I mean my generation, lost control of our children, but there it is. They have the whip hand of us all the time, just because they don't care. We brought them up to be independent and they are. Where did they get their strange inhumanity, their want of consideration, even of ordinary good breeding?'

'Rose isn't like that, sir,' said Philip, again approaching the heroic.

An even louder shriek came from above, and a sponge hurtled through the air into the garden.

'You win, sir,' said Philip, laughing in spite of himself. 'I can't decently give up Rose, sir, you do see that. But if she wants me to –'

The door was flung open and Rose burst in, her lovely locks in slight disorder, her face flushed. Crying, 'Oh, Philip, I'll never, never leave you,' she threw herself into his arms. Mr Birkett, who hardly ever lost his temper, went out of the room and banged the door as hard as he could to relieve his irritation. In the hall he met his wife, looking quite distraught.

'You needn't say anything, Amy,' he said. 'I heard the noise. It's my belief that Philip would be thankful to get

186

out of his engagement at once and go, but he feels it must come from Rose. I wonder if you took her up to London for the autumn – it would be awkward, but I'd manage without you. I will not have a good master spoiled for all the daughters in Christendom.'

They sat for some time in depressed silence, trying to guess from the voices what was happening between Philip and Rose. Simnet came through from the kitchen quarters and approached them.

'Excuse me, madam, but the dressing bell went some time ago, though doubtless you was prevented from hearing it, and cook is wondering about dinner. Shall I request her to postpone it?' he said, looking significantly towards the study door.

'No,' said Mr Birkett sharply. 'We'll have it at once.'

'Without dressing, sir?'

'I said, at once.'

'Very good, sir,' said Simnet and retired.

Rose and Philip emerged from the study. Rose sparkling, refreshed and triumphant, clinging to her lover's arm, Philip looking haggard and exhausted.

'It's all right, mummy,' she said. 'I've forgiven Philip and it's absolutely all right. Oh, and Geoff and John are coming over to-morrow with the car and we're going to the Barchester cinema. You won't mind, darling, will you?' she added to Philip.

'Do you want your sponge?' asked Geraldine, coming in from the garden.

'Oh, there it is,' said Rose. 'I wondered where it went. Put it in my room when you go up, Geraldine, like an angel.'

At dinner Philip behaved as well as anyone can behave who has seen a glimpse of freedom and then had his fetters more firmly riveted. So well indeed did he bear himself that Simnet had nothing more to report to the

187

servants' hall than that Miss Rose and Mr Winter seemed to be as taken with each other as ever.

By tacit consent the whole party kept together all evening, so that no private speech was possible. Rose amused herself but no one else on her piano-accordion, while Geraldine told the others how old Pettinger had had the meanness to refuse swimming colours to Amber Dandridge, simply because she had cheeked Miss Moore in the bookroom. Only as they separated for the night did Mr Birkett say to Philip, 'Promise you won't do anything without letting me know.'

'All right, sir,' said Philip, and Mr Birkett thought he had seldom seen a more hopeless face.

CHAPTER IX

Croquet at the Rectory

By lunch-time on Saturday Swan, Morland and Hacker were blissfully installed in the gardener's cottage, with Lydia to assist. Mrs Twicker had the old Nanny's passion for gentry children, and welcomed them with as much joy as if they had once been babies in her charge. Of her own children, who were all out in the world, she never had thought much, owing to their parentage, though she had treated them with the impartial kindness due from the upper classes to the lower. To her Robert was still 'Master Robert', though she had married when he was only four; and none of the other Keith children could hold the same place in her estimation.

When the boys arrived, having been met by Sanders and Lydia at Northbridge Halt, she at once provided thick cocoa and bread-and-dripping which the boys, though it was twelve o'clock on a blazing hot day, and they had all had good breakfasts before starting, fell upon with avidity. Mrs Twicker was a farmer's daughter from Westmorland, and though she had been a nurse until she married, her housekeeping was that of the north, and it was her boast that her husband had never eaten baker's bread except for a week at the birth of their various children. Her kitchen with a large open range, her little dairy with bowls of cream on stone shelves, her wash-house and copper, her mangle, were all the subject of enthusiastic praise.

'I say, Mrs Twicker,' said Morland, after mangling Hacker's blazer and breaking two buttons, 'I wish I could help you with the washing. I'd love to see the water swishing off the sheets and things in the mangle.'

'Oh, no, Mr Tony,' said Mrs Twicker, who had immediately inquired and adopted the names of all three,
'that's not young gentlemen's work.'

'Oh, do let me, Mrs Twicker. We'd all turn the
mangle. Oh, Mrs Twicker, Hack's buttons off his blazer
got broken in the mangle.

'Of course they did, Mr Tony. You don't ought to go
putting blazers through the mangle. Now come along in
the kitchen and we'll see if Nanny has some buttons in
her work-basket that will match.'

They followed her to the kitchen, where Lydia was still
eating bread-and-dripping. From a chest of drawers Mrs
Twicker got a large basket, once lined with quilted blue
satin, and full of all sorts of enchanting odds and ends,
such as strawberry emery cushions and ivory stilettoes,
among them a shell box containing apparently one of
each kind of button in the world. Mrs Twicker, putting
on a much worn thimble, with an agate top, sewed them
on, while the boys looked at the dough that was rising in
a big earthenware bowl before the fire, and the chickens
that were being reared by hand in warm flannel in a
basket, with a cat taking care of them.

When Mrs Twicker had finished the jacket she took the
dough out of the bowl and shaped it into loaves for bak-
ing. Each visitor was allowed to prick his initials on the
top of a loaf, and Mrs Twicker promised them that each
should have some of his own loaf next morning, before
they went up to the Manor for breakfast. It was at this
point that Swan said he would like to live there for ever.

'I wish you could, Mr Eric,' said Mrs Twicker. 'I do
miss having young gentlemen about the place. Where I
was in service before I came to Mrs Keith there were five
young gentlemen, and they all came to Nanny for everything, some of them quite big young gentlemen, from
school, like you.'

'I say, Mrs Twicker,' said Morland, 'if we are going to

stay till Tuesday, do you think we could call you Nanny, like Lydia does? It would feel friendlier.'

'Of course you can, Mr Tony, it will be quite like old times. And here's a bit of dough left over, and I'll give you some currants for a bun man.'

By the united efforts of the visitors two shapeless, grey masses, studded with currants, called by courtesy bun men, were made, and Nanny put them into the oven with the loaves.

'You'd better hurry up,' said Lydia, eating a few fragments of dough to round off her repast. 'It's quarter-past one, and lunch is at half-past.'

'O.K.' said Swan. 'What about Gibbon?'

'Is that Mr Percy's rat, sir?' said Nanny. 'Isn't that a funny pet for a young gentleman to have? Master Robert used to have white mice, but rats are nasty, dirty, vicious animals.'

'It's not a rat, Nanny, it's a chameleon,' said Lydia.

'If you leave your rat with me, Mr Percy,' said Nanny, taking no notice of Lydia, 'he'll be quite safe. Pussy wouldn't touch him. I always looked after Master Robert's mice.'

Accordingly Gibbon's cage was hung on a nail by the kitchen window, and the party set off to the Manor.

*

During lunch Mrs Keith announced that anyone who liked was invited to tea and tennis at the Rectory. She and Mr Keith would not be going. Edith was delighted at the idea of tennis, for the Rectory court was better than the Manor court. So was Robert, who had driven out from Barchester with his father and was staying for the week-end. Noel, Colin and Kate said they would go. Lydia wanted to start cleaning the pond, but her mother said they could do that another day. After lunch Edith's children were brought down for a short visit, and

Hacker suddenly came into prominence as an enter-
tainer of the young, telling a long story of aeroplanes and
battles which enchanted Henry, and inventing a game
of pretending to lose his handkerchief and finding it up
his sleeve, which exactly suited Catherine's style of
humour.

'I'll tell you what,' said Lydia to Swan and Morland,
'we've got to see about the pond. To-morrow's Sunday,
and mother will want us all to go to church, but if we
empty the pond before breakfast we can get too dirty to
go.'

This delightful plan met with the full approval of the
boys, who had each brought specially dirty clothes for the
job at Lydia's request, and it was decided that they
should all be up early next day and get things in order.

When the Manor party arrived at the Rectory Mrs
Birkett apologized for Rose's absence.

'She had promised to go to the Barchester cinema with
your brothers, Edith,' she said to Mrs Robert, who
replied complacently that Geoff and John were quick
workers. 'But they'll be back for tea,' continued Mrs
Birkett, 'so we might get some tennis first.'

Edith and Robert, both very good players, went off to
the tennis court with Mrs Birkett and Noel, while Mr
Birkett and Kate said they would watch them and cut in.
The others adjourned to the croquet ground, where
Lydia suggested they should play a seven-ball game, but
no one wanted to, and luckily there were not seven balls,
so this plan fell through. Geraldine, however, had plans
of her own and took Hacker off to play clock golf on an
adjoining lawn, which they did in complete silence, but
apparently with satisfaction. So the others tossed for
partners, and Lydia and Morland played against Philip
and Swan.

'I'm going to umpire,' said Colin, when they suddenly
discovered that he was left out, 'and talk to you all and

put you off your strokes. Everyone should know that the third hoop isn't straight. It never has been since Lydia balanced on one foot on it in 1936 and drove it right into the ground. The blue mallet has a large chip out of it, which happened when the Rector nailed up a branch of the wistaria against the wall last summer, using the mallet as a hammer. There is a hump between hoops three and four attributed locally to moles, and a depression round the first stick where the Rectory dog dug for a rabbit. Otherwise the court is in perfect condition.'

'What does it feel like not to be a schoolmaster?' asked Philip, who was yellow, while the others drove off.

'Very nice,' said Colin. 'No, Lydia, that ball does *not* count as through. How are you all going to get on without me, and who will smoke my meerschaum pipe when I am far away?'

'The Head is in despair,' said Philip, 'but I may tell you in confidence –'

'Here, your turn,' interrupted Colin. 'Knock blue sharply on the left, and watch her lose her temper.'

Philip neatly hit Lydia's ball as he was told and Lydia accused Colin of favouritism. Swan, who was using his mallet as a crutch, and speeding, in the character of Long John Silver, across the lawn in pursuit of seaman Tom, a character ably sustained by Morland, A., hurled his mallet at the unfortunate sailor, who fell dead on the ground with a blood-curdling yell.

'That's just like the noise Rose was making yesterday before dinner,' said Geraldine from the neighbouring clock golf course.

'Why did she make that noise?' said Morland, getting up.

'I don't know,' said Geraldine. 'One of her usual tempers. She's always having rows with –'

'Here, Eric, your turn,' called Philip sharply.

Geraldine returned to her game.

'What were you about to remark in confidence?' asked Colin, when he caught Philip up, just beyond the third hoop, where the jump was.

'Blast,' said Philip, as the hump deflected his ball, which ran away sideways. 'Confidentially, as you have no further interest in the school, the Head thinks I might make a do of the Mixed Fifth.'

'Oh, *good*!' said Colin. 'I always felt I owed you a kind of apology about that, though I was but an instrument in the hands of Mr Birkett. Tony! up the middle now!'

'Rubbish,' said Philip, 'I ought to apologize if anyone ought. Watch me hit Tony to blazes.'

He carefully eyed his ball, swung his mallet backwards, and hit hard. A piece of turf flew up and landed a few feet away, and Morland's ball remained where it was. With a yell of joy Swan seized Morland's mallet and whirled it and his own mallet round his head like Indian clubs. Lydia at once mounted her mallet as if it were a hobby horse and galloped at him in a threatening way. Morland, forgetting the sacred character of games, said 'Bang!' in a very loud voice, and bowled a red cannon ball at them. Swan shouted the Valkyrie theme at the top of his voice as an accompaniment to Lydia's ride and the whole game came to confusion. The younger members lost interest and strolled over to interfere with the clock golf.

'I haven't laughed so much,' said Philip to Colin, 'since Rose and I –' he checked for a moment, then continued in a level tone, 'since we went to the cinema the day we got engaged. How we laughed.'

He became so silent that Colin, guessing not inaccurately that Rose had been up to some of her tricks again, looked at him sympathetically and strolled off to the tennis court, where he found Robert and Mr Birkett sitting together while the others played.

'How are you enjoying your freedom?' said Mr Birkett.

'That's almost exactly what Philip has just said to me, sir. With all due respect to you I'm enjoying it excessively.'

'Merton tells me he is going to Austria and thought you might join him,' said Robert.

'I'd love to,' said Colin, 'but I think I ought to work. You see, I've wasted –'

He stopped, confused.

'– a whole term,' Mr Birkett placidly finished his sentence for him. 'Not so much waste as you think, though.'

'No waste at all,' said Robert. 'A very good bit of experience. You'd much better go with Merton, Colin. It's only for a fortnight, and then you can start reading in good earnest.'

Robert enjoyed being the Good Elder Brother so much that Colin sometimes wondered what he would have done as the junior member of a large family. From an early age he had taken Colin under his protection, proudly guided his first tottering footsteps across the lawn, held him on the garden pony, kept an aloof but vigilant eye on him at prep and public school, during the brief periods that their careers had overlapped, tipped him in a lordly way out of his own pocket money, and always given him good advice. Though Colin had outgrown the stage at which an older brother is a divine being, when not a diabolical one, he still respected Robert's solid common sense and was very fond of him, and would not have been in the least surprised if Robert had still tipped him half a crown from time to time. Robert, who had a great belief in Colin's ability, had always been strongly in favour of his reading law, and though he found the term school-mastering a suitable way for his brother to fill in time, was thoroughly satisfied that Colin should now turn seriously towards Merton's chambers.

Colin was very glad that Robert approved of his going to Austria, and then he fell into school shop with Mr Birkett. Presently the tea-bell rang.

'I can see that your time has not been wasted,' said Mr Birkett, getting up. 'You will be able to talk master's common-room for the rest of your life, and take it from me, though you mayn't believe it now, that will make you free of the company of some men worth knowing. Come along, they are just finishing their set.'

The three men moved towards the house, Robert privately thinking that though Birkett and Carter were excellent fellows, Colin would hear better talk and meet men more worth knowing in the Inner Temple, where Merton's chambers were. A conversation on that subject between Mr Birkett and Robert Keith would be interesting, but we shall never hear it.

Tea was at a large round table in the hall. Simnet, who was putting the finishing touches to the table, waylaid Colin near the door.

'We are very glad to see you here, sir, in your unofficial capacity,' he said. 'I understand from very good quarters, sir, that your departure will be felt as a Distinct Loss.'

Colin thanked him.

'I daresay you will be interested in a small item of news, sir. I heard from the Honourable Mr Norris's man, with whom I occasionally correspond, that Mr Norris may be shortly to appear in the Court Circular under the heading of Forthcoming Marriages.'

'Well done, Norris,' said Colin. 'Who is it?'

'I fear you would not know her, sir,' said Simnet pityingly. 'It is the Honourable Eleanor Purvis.'

'Of course I know her,' said Colin; 'she is one of my mother's half great nieces or something of the sort.'

'Indeed, sir, I was not aware,' said Simnet, almost cringing.

'That's all right,' said Colin.

Just as they had settled themselves for tea Everard Carter walked in. He begged Mrs Birkett to excuse his unceremonious arrival. He said he had just come from the station, and hearing at the Manor that his host and hostess were out and the rest of the party at the Rectory, had walked over. Everyone was delighted to see him and a place was found for him by Mrs Birkett, from which he could feast his eyes upon Kate and Noel opposite.

'Well, Colin,' he said, 'is it fun being loose again?'

'All right,' said Colin. 'That's the third time this afternoon and if anyone asks me that question again I'll shoot him. I am enjoying it very much indeed, thank you, and don't do it again, that's all.'

'I heard from Lorimer yesterday,' said Everard to Mrs Birkett. 'He seemed very glad to be back in Scotland. I think he has been feeling the heat and the strain of exams a good deal this term, and he isn't having any boys to stay with him till later. He asked me to tell you, Philip, that he had heard unofficially that the Oxbridge Press thought very highly of your manuscript.'

Philip looked almost happy as he thanked Everard for the message.

'The Press are delightful people to deal with,' said Mr Birkett. 'You have to sell entirely on your own merits, which is so flattering.'

'What he means,' said Mrs Birkett, 'is that the books he does for them are so dull that no one would buy them unless they have to.'

'I thought Mr Birkett's *Determination of Logical Causality* was very interesting,' said Morland. 'I read it in the school library, and I used a bit in an essay for Mr Winter, but he spotted it, and told me to remember that there were some very useful little signs called notes of quotation.'

'I didn't know you were interested in that kind of thing, Philip,' said Mr Birkett kindly.

197

Philip was just going to answer when a loud roaring noise was heard outside, drowning all conversation. This was the Fairweathers and their racing car, bringing Rose back from the cinema. Their arrival caused considerable disturbance, as an atmosphere of everyone talking at once and paying no attention to what anyone else is saying is very catching. Rose, partly from absent-mindedness, partly from a wish to exhibit her devotion to Philip to the Fairweathers, and thus inflame their jealousy, sat down affectionately near Philip and insisted on drinking the rest of his cold tea till such time as fresh supplies arrived.

'It was a good thing you didn't come, darling,' she said. 'It was only a silly film. You wouldn't have enjoyed it a bit, but we laughed till we were nearly sick, didn't we, darlings?'

The Fairweathers said they had, and laughed again a great deal in support of the statement. Colin remembered how Philip had said that he and Rose laughed at a film when they were first engaged, and how suddenly he had fallen silent. He was silent enough now.

Lydia, having eaten as much as she felt necessary for the moment, cast a challenging eye on the younger Fairweather, and asked him if he could punt. He said he could.

'All right,' said Lydia. 'I'll tell you what. We can each have a punt pole and stand one at each end of the Rectory punt, and see who can make the other go in the other direction from the other one.'

Fairweather Junior saw what she meant almost at once, and was enthusiastic over this form of sport: Rose, not approving of Lydia's attitude to one of her admirers, interrupted to say to Fairweather Junior:

'Oh, John, darling, do tell them what we saw at Barchester. It was too marvellously funny.'

'The film?' said Fairweather Junior. 'I don't remember

the name. Something about pyjamas or something like it, but it was awfully funny, all about a girl and she gets married after a bit of a binge and the fellow doesn't know who either of them are, and there are some awfully good wisecracks, and an awfully good bit where they do a fox-trot up and down a fire escape. Do you remember that bit, Geoff?'

'No, I don't mean that,' said Rose. 'Don't be so sicken-ing, John. I mean what we saw outside the cinema, you know, that man.'

'Oh yes, that was awfully funny,' said Fairweather Junior. 'It was a man selling little books. One of those blackshirt fellows, you know, like Puss in Boots in a polo jersey. I don't know why, but it was awfully funny. Lord! It was funny!' he added, breaking into laughter again.

'I'll tell you another funny thing about those black-shirts,' said Lydia. 'No one knows who they are, or where they go. I mean, have you ever seen one, except standing on the pavement in waders, looking a bit seedy? You meet quite a lot of Communists and things in people's houses, like Philip,' she said, pointing at him, but quite kindly, 'he's a Communist. But you never go to tea with someone and find them sitting there in their boots.'

'I expect they have a secret cupboard in the hall of their houses,' said Swan, 'and the minute they come in they take off their boots in a jiffy and chuck them into a sliding panel and they go down to a hiding-place in the cellar, and then they take off their detachable polo collars and look just like us, only nastier.'

'That's a jolly good idea,' said Fairweather Senior, 'but you don't get long boots off in a jiffy like that. It needs a batman, or anyway a strong bootjack.'

'The Black Batman would be a good name for a film,' said Morland. 'Or else they have boots that zip all the way up. I think if you must sow wild oats, red ones are better than black ones, but I'm an individualist, so I shall sow mine by myself, not in gangs.'

'Are you really a Communist, sir?' said Fairweather Senior respectfully to Philip.

'Oh, don't be sickening, Geoff,' said Rose, 'I want to play tennis.'

'All right, Rose, hang on a moment. We discuss it a bit in the regiment, sir, but we don't see much sense in it. The government is doing every blessed thing they can for the lower classes, and nationalizing one thing after another, and taking most of our money to do it with, and what more do you want?'

'Freedom,' said Philip.

'Excuse me, sir, but all this nationalizing doesn't seem to make one very free, does it?' said Fairweather Senior.

Philip, which shows how misfortune had improved his character, instead of making a contemptuous noise and walking out of the room, tried to explain quite carefully to Fairweather Senior what he meant. Noel and Everard, both rather middle, both interested intellectually in any discussion, joined in the talk, and Fairweather Senior, to his everlasting surprise, found himself talking away to three very brainy chaps, quite as an equal. In this intoxication he quite forgot Rose. She turned for help to Fairweather Junior, but he was so happy with her mother, talking over his early days at the prep school, under Mr Birkett, that he took no notice of her at all. Robert Keith and Mr Birkett were discussing the Dean of Barchester from various aspects, and Rose was reduced to reading a book, by which, in common with many of her contemporaries, she meant an illustrated weekly.

Swan and Morland had been standing by, ready to encourage Mr Winter's progress by throwing in bits of anti-red propaganda, but to their surprise and pleasure he was arguing away like anything, just like before Rose came bothering. At last Lydia, who without listening had rapidly formed her own conclusions, broke in.

'You're all right and all wrong,' she announced in a ringing voice. 'Noel and Everard are the rightest, because they don't exaggerate so much. Royalty is good enough for anyone, and whenever I think of the Royal Family it makes me cry, because that is real loyalty. If everyone was English there wouldn't be half so much bother. The minute you encourage foreigners they go uppish, like Mademoiselle Duval at school. She kept Geraldine in two days running, just because she hadn't done her prep, and the Pettinger encouraged her. The Pettinger is coming to tea to-morrow because mother asked her, but I think it's to meet you, Everard –'

'Oh, Lord!' said Everard.

'– and I think it's jolly unfair of mother, as if we didn't see enough of her in term time. Come on,' she said, addressing Fairweather Junior, 'and we'll have our punting race.'

The punting race, if a stationary event may be so called, took place before a large and enthusiastic audience, neither opponent gaining a foot over the other till Lydia fell into the river. As Mrs Keith was not there, and the river at that point was only four feet deep, no one minded. Lydia, after shaking herself all over everyone like a large dog, went off to Geraldine's room to dry herself and borrow some clothes.

'I say,' said Lydia, when she was dry, forcing herself into one of Geraldine's frocks, 'what was Rose making the noise about that you were saying about when Tony pretended he was the murdered seaman?'

'About Philip as usual,' said Geraldine. 'I wish you'd split that frock for me. I loathe it.'

'All right, I'll do my best,' said Lydia. 'What about Philip?'

'I don't know,' said Geraldine. 'She just enjoys having

rows. She used to have awful rows at Miss Pettinger's. Philip used to argue back at her, but now he never does. I think she's broken his spirit.'

'I think it's gone a bit round the armhole,' said Lydia, twisting herself, and inspecting with satisfaction her back view in Geraldine's looking-glass. 'I'm awfully sorry for Philip. He's a bit young, but a lot better than I thought. Why doesn't he chuck Rose?'

'I expect he'd like to,' said Geraldine, 'but when you're a man you can't. That's a splendid tear across the shoulder, Lydia. Thanks awfully.'

'I daresay I can manage a bit more,' said Lydia. 'Come and help us to clean the pond to-morrow before breakfast.'

'Right-oh. I'll wear your frock, and you wear mine, and then we can change.'

Everard and Kate, who had been playing a final set against the Birketts, were the last to leave the Rectory. Old Bunce ferried them across and they went through the water meadows towards the house. Everard looked at Kate as she walked before him on the narrow, rush-bordered path, and thought not for the first time how lovely she looked, how exquisitely she had danced with Noel, how well she played tennis, and how very kind and thoughtful she was. In fact, the ideal wife, and one whom he desperately wanted. As his friendship with Kate had gently flowered, he had become increasingly aware of the charm of her conversation. Her good manners, her unaffected interest in what he was doing, struck him afresh each time he met her, and her conversation was the sweetest and wittiest he had ever heard. Matron, by her status and environment suspicious of mothers and sisters, had taken to her completely, and had several times asked Mr Carter about that delightful sister of Mr Keith's and expressed a hope that she would visit the school again. Everard's answers, though carefully calculated to put matron off the scent, failed entirely in the desired effect, and matron was able to write to her married sister whose son had now joined his ship with promotion, that Mr Carter was a Case.

Everard decided that as Kate was as good as engaged to Noel Merton, he could safely treat her with the friendly familiarity suitable to the promised bride of another. He liked Noel Merton, in fact if it hadn't been for a ridiculous and unreasonable something which he would not encourage by calling jealousy, he would like him very much indeed, and he felt a remark to this effect would be appreciated by Kate.

'I'm so glad Merton is down here again,' he said.

'The rushes swish so much that I didn't hear what you said. I wish they'd hurry up and cut them,' said Kate.

The words were not so easy to repeat, but Everard repeated them.

'Yes, isn't it nice?' said Kate.

Everard's spirits sank.

'He is so very nice to Colin,' said Kate.

Everard's spirits rose a little.

'So are you,' said Kate. 'Colin says you were so nice to him all last term that he will miss you dreadfully, though he is glad to be doing law.'

Everard tried to think of a remark which would imply that he hoped Kate would miss him dreadfully too, but it sounded so fatuous and presumptuous that he gave it up. Kate enlarged upon his kindness and the pleasure her visit to the school had given her, and inquired after matron. There were, she said, a lot of interesting things that she would have liked to ask matron about, only there wasn't time, as, for instance, how the cook's and housemaid's times off were arranged, and if she had much difficulty in getting servants. She thought a job like matron's must be one of the most interesting things one could do.

'What did you say?' said Kate.

Everard had actually said nothing, but he had made a noise which was the beginning of a wild suggestion that if she thought she could care for him, he could offer her the job she liked. But he had to stifle it, for it was ungentlemanly to offer your heart where it wasn't wanted, and in any case he didn't want a matron, he wanted a wife, so he made a kind of clucking noise instead, and had to say it was a cough.

'I'll tell Palmer to bring you some lozenges,' said Kate. 'Suck one before dinner and one when you go to bed. When Colin had a cough at Easter they did him a lot of good. But I do wish,' she added, thinking as usual of Colin's career and happiness, 'that Noel weren't going to Austria.'

'Is he?' asked Everard hopefully.

'Yes,' sighed Kate. 'And if only he would have stayed in England – but that is silly of me,' she finished, with a note of forced gaiety that wrung Everard's heart and did not deceive him for an instant. In his anxiety to feel as well as do the right thing, he found her confidence in him a very beautiful and touching thing. If she cared for him enough to tell him her secret sorrow, that ought to be enough for him, though he strongly felt that it wasn't. He couldn't ask if Noel were trifling with her affection, he couldn't reasonably ask Noel whether he knew what he was doing. He must content himself with a silent worship, a chivalry that could never be expressed except in thought, a sword which could never be drawn in her defence, though what exactly the sword was he wasn't sure. It made him think of German poems where people become monks and nuns because they haven't the wits to speak out on the one side and are so pure on the other, and the landscape seemed a little obscured.

As they passed through the wicket gate into the garden, Kate plucked a piece of honeysuckle and offered it to him. He took Kate's hand and looked at it. It appeared to exercise a strong and irresistible magnetic attraction upon his head, for try as he might he simply could not help stooping lower and lower till he could lay his cheek against it. At the same time Kate felt an inclination to stroke the top of his head which positively alarmed her by its intensity. After faintly struggling with her better self, she shut her eyes so that she should not see what she was doing, and touched his hair with her free hand. There they would probably have stayed till midnight, mute, adoring, extremely cramped and uncomfortable, had not Noel come down the grass alley. Even tennis shoes on grass are heard by lovers' ears. Everard grabbed the honeysuckle and stood up, carelessly looking at his wrist to see what time it was.

'Hullo,' said Noel, 'what's the matter. Bee stung your hand?'

'No,' said Everard lightly. 'Oh, no. I just wondered what time it was.'

'I see you haven't a watch,' said Noel. 'It's about half-past seven.'

Everard, remembering that he had left his wrist-watch on his dressing-table because he was going to play tennis, said, 'Well, I'll leave you to look after Kate,' and walked quickly away.

'I was giving Everard some honeysuckle,' said Kate, as if in a trance. She was standing in the full evening sun and Noel was not sure how much the flame in her face and neck came from without, how much from within, but thought he could guess. She made the words sound very loving.

'Would you care for some?' said Kate, pulling the branch towards her and plucking another bloom.

'Do you know,' said Noel, 'I think honeysuckle is more suitable for Everard. I shall pillage the conservatory for a red carnation. Do you think it will be open still?'

'Oh, yes,' said Kate.

They found the door still unlocked and got the carnation. As they came out onto the terrace, Noel paused.

'Do you think you could look upon me as an uncle, Kate?' he asked. 'A nice uncle I mean, not a wicked one.'

'Yes, darling,' said Kate.

Something in her voice that he had never heard before made him look at her. Her eyes were looking into some imagining of her own and her thoughts were beyond her eyes. Noel knew that the caressing word had been thrown to the air, to be carried where her eyes and thoughts were musing, and he felt an absurd compassion and affection for her.

'Well, remember that uncles have their uses,' he said. 'You can tell them anything.' And putting an arm round her in an avuncular way, he gave her a reassuring hug and went indoors.

Kate, who had hardly heard what he said, or noticed what he did, stood in the sunlight, honeysuckle in her hand. Everard, looking out of his bedroom window, saw Noel detaching himself from Kate's waist, and thought if it weren't for the bitter pleasure of seeing her again he might as well send a telegram to himself and leave next day.

Swan and Morland, going back to the cottage that night from the Manor, made a detour by the river, just to get wet and dirty. While they were doing so, and despising Hacker who had gone straight back to reassure himself about Gibbon, they became aware on the opposite bank of a solitary figure, moonlit against the dark trees.

'It's Mr Winter,' said Swan. 'Hullo, sir, isn't it a lovely night?'

Mr Winter stopped and looked across.

'Hullo, Swan,' he said. 'Yes, lovely.'

He strolled onto the little wooden footbridge and looked into the water.

'That was a very interesting talk you had at tea, sir,' said Morland. 'Eric and I were listening.'

'Why didn't you join us?'

'We didn't think you needed us, sir.'

'Why should I need you?'

'Well, sir,' said Swan, emboldened by the night and the holidays, 'sometimes if people are feeling a bit down, it is rather a help to be contradicted. It peps them up.'

'So you think I need pepping?'

'Oh no, sir,' said both boys together.

'Well, heaven knows what you think,' said Philip, 'and heaven knows what I think. One just has to go on. Thank God I'm off to Russia next week. If I had some stones I'd throw them in the water.'

'It's mostly mud here, sir, but we'll see what we can do,' said Swan obligingly. He looked along the bank, assisted by Morland, and found a little patch of pebbles. They each chose a handful of the best and went onto the bridge.

'Thanks,' said Philip, as he dropped the biggest into the river. 'That was a most satisfactory plop. It did me a lot of good. So did that. Well, thank you very much. Good night.'

He walked away up-stream towards the Rectory. Confound it, he thought, if those boys weren't being kind again! Getting stones for me to throw into the water as if I were a baby. He thought of all these queer, agreeable animals called Boys, hiding their eagerness under an air of ancient wisdom, critically kind, agreeably aloof, living private lives in the public eye, exploring every wilderness of the mind, yet concerned with a tie or a scarf. Then without a word of warning this pleasing anxious being vanished, leaving behind it undergraduates, subalterns, civil servants, bank clerks, airmen. Perhaps, thought

Philip, one's real death is at about seventeen, and I have been dead for eight years. What happened to me at seventeen? Where did I go? But such thoughts were too difficult, too much like thinking of infinity and eternity. He quickened his pace and walked back to a silent house. Rose and her cavaliers had gone to dance at a roadhouse on the other side of Barchester and the Birketts were in bed. At least, thought Philip, there will be next term, and somehow the thought of being back among his inscrutable pupils was comforting.

Swan and Morland, having exhausted the pleasures of wet mud, went back to the cottage where Mrs Twicker, who had sat up for them, regaled them rapturously on cold duck and her own dandelion wine, and anecdotes of all her former charges and the prizes Twicker had won at the Flower Show.

CHAPTER X

Cleaning the Pond

On Sunday morning the early sunlight illuminated the heavily sleeping forms of Swan and Morland in one room, Hacker in the other. As for Gibbon, no one had yet discovered whether he ever went to sleep or not, for at whatever hour his master looked at him, he had the same cold, unwinking stare. Swan and Morland, in a spirit of scientific discovery, had once decided to keep awake all night to make observations, but after midnight their minds had become a total blank, and they knew no more till the school bell rang. This Swan attributed to the peculiar soporific effect of Hacker's snoring, for at that time they all slept in the dormitory and Hacker refused to help Swan with his Latin Unseens for two days.

Mrs Twicker, who rose early, came upstairs in her bedroom slippers. She had been asked the night before to awaken them without fail by half-past six, but when she saw Swan sprawled starfish-like across his bed, and Morland looking like a cherub, as she said to herself, her heart failed, and she went downstairs thinking of all her former charges.

Lydia, barefoot, in Geraldine's frock with one sleeve half out, came over the dewy grass and up Twicker's path, between his brilliant flower borders. She was carrying a large glass bowl and a landing net.

'Hullo, Nanny,' she said to Mrs Twicker, who was getting an early breakfast ready. 'Aren't the boys up?'

'No, Miss Lydia,' said Mrs Twicker. 'They looked so peaceful I couldn't bear to wake them. Would you like some breakfast? There's new bread.'

'Love it,' said Lydia. 'I couldn't find anything to eat

except pickles in the dining-room. They'd finished the biscuits last night. But I must get those boys up. We've got to clean the pond.'

She went towards the staircase.

'No, Miss Lydia, you don't,' said Mrs Twicker. 'None of my young ladies goes into my young gentlemen's rooms. I don't know what their mothers would say. I'll go up myself.'

Lydia looked pityingly after Nanny and began to cut the best pieces of crust off the loaf and anoint them liberally with butter. Sounds overhead announced that the boys were getting up at a hand gallop, and in a few moments they were down, in old shorts and coloured sweat shirts, as they were elegantly known at school.

'I hope you don't mind we haven't washed,' said Morland, 'but as we were going to get dirty in the pond, it seemed rather waste.'

'I say, Lydia, you are mean, taking all the crust,' said Swan. 'Nanny promised me the crustiest bit.'

'I'm ashamed of you, Miss Lydia,' said Nanny, taking the rest of the crusts off Lydia's plate. 'Here you are, Mr Eric, and here's some for you, Mr Tony and Mr Percy.'

'Hurry up,' said Lydia. 'The great thing is to let the water out soon, because once it's out they can't stop us cleaning the pond, because it'll stink like fun. Twicker won't interfere, will he, Nanny?'

'No, miss,' said Nanny. 'He's laying in this morning, and I've got him something nice for his breakfast.'

'Not washing is one thing, but you might wipe your face a bit, Hack,' said Lydia. 'It looks filthy.'

Swan and Morland burst into ribald laughter.

'He has to shave twice a week,' said Swan, 'and it's Tuesday and Saturday, and yesterday he forgot, and this morning he hadn't time. He's going to train Gibbon to shave him when he goes to Oxford. He really ought to do it every day, but he's lazy.'

'How often do you shave?' asked Lydia, helping herself to jam.

'According. Once a week for ordinary, twice for special. Tony only needs once yet, because he's fair, but I'm going to be one of those fine, black-a-vised men who have to shave twice a day if they are taking the girl friend out.'

'And have great hideous hairy chests like the Chaplain's,' said Morland, beating upon his breast after the manner of a gorilla.

'And what do you know about the Chaplain's chest, my boy?' asked Swan, shocked.

'Not what you think, my lad,' said Morland.

Lydia then regaled the party, amid vain hushes from Nanny, with an account of a mistress at school who had a moustache, and the party went off in high good humour, with Nanny waving from the porch.

The pond was supplied by a little stream, tributary to the river. Lydia first shut the little sluice by which the pond was filled and then opened the lower sluice, standing knee-deep in the water with the landing net, to catch the three goldfish popularly supposed to live there. No goldfish appeared, but Hacket caught with his hands a large frog, which was sitting on a damp stone, and put it in the bowl, stating that frogs made good barometers.

'That's true,' said Swan. 'Because Dumas knew a frog called Mademoiselle Camargo, and she went up and down a ladder to show what the weather would be. Let's make a ladder.'

'Not now,' said Lydia. 'We must start cleaning the pond first. If we get some of the muck and squelch out on the lawn, they'll have to let us miss church to get it all tidied up.'

The muck and squelch proved to be of a thoroughly agreeable nature, being partly green and all slimy. Hacker sat a little apart, cross-legged on the grass, talking to the frog, while the others worked in fits and starts. They were presently joined by Geraldine, who was wearing the frock in which Lydia had fallen into the river. As it had spent the night lying in a heap in Geraldine's shoe cupboard in case anyone came prying it looked extremely crumpled and disreputable.

'Hullo,' said Lydia, 'we'd better change. Come into the rhododendrons. I've split another bit of your frock for you, where it does up down the side.'

'Thanks awfully,' said Geraldine, looking complacently at the frock, which now hung almost in rags about her.

About nine o'clock Nanny came to warn them that it was nearly breakfast-time. She found the lawn round the pond strewn with smelly green weed and mud, and all the workers in the pond, through which Lydia had allowed a little trickle to run, cleaning the concrete bottom and sides with brooms and scrubbing brushes.

'Wherever did you get those brooms and things, Miss Lydia?' asked Nanny, recognizing some of Twicker's cherished twig besoms.

'The tool-house window was open,' said Lydia. 'Tell Twicker the catch wants seeing to. I got the scrubbing brushes out of the housemaids' cupboard. We're making an awfully good job of it.'

'Whatever will your mother say?' said Nanny. 'And it's nearly breakfast-time. You young gentlemen had better come back and get yourselves nice for breakfast, and your mother will be looking for you, Miss Geraldine.'

Such is the power of Nannies, even when out of office, that Geraldine went home without a murmur, while the three boys went back to the cottage to wash and change, the frog in his bowl being left in a shady spot to wait for them.

Mrs Keith came down to breakfast with a letter that Lydia at once recognized as her school report, which must have come by the previous night's post. Mrs Keith, who never took any particular interest in her children's education in term time, considering it the affair of their teachers, always fell into a paroxysm of flurry and worry when the reports arrived. Robert and Colin had always done brilliantly, so that she had a very high standard. Kate had not been very clever at school, but so sweet-tempered and obliging that her mistresses had filled up her reports with such remarks as, 'Kate has a very good influence in the Lower Fifth', 'Science not very good, but Kate is a conscientious worker.'

But Lydia, a frank rebel, was apt to earn such unfavourable commentary as, 'Could do far better if she tried or paid attention,' 'I would like to see Lydia show a more constructive spirit of leadership', remarks which made Mrs Keith feel that Lydia would never get married, though on what grounds she based this argument, no one knew.

'Your report came last night, Lydia,' said her mother, next to whom Lydia was unluckily sitting. 'Father and I are really worried about it. You must do better.'

'Can I see it?' said Lydia.

'I think better not,' said Mrs Keith, who believed, in common with many parents, that reports are not only true, but sacred.

'Mother,' said Colin, 'did you know that Cousin Eleanor is engaged?'

This red herring was perfectly successful for a time, leading Mrs Keith into an elaborate analysis of the Purvis family, into which her Aunt Marian, the third daughter of her grandfather's second marriage, had married. Colin also bore with excellent good-humour his mother's searching inquisition into the family and personal characteristics of Mr Norris, whom Colin had known fairly well for two terms at Oxford, and never seen again. But like many rather rambling people, she had a way of disconcerting her hearers by suddenly pouncing back upon the subject she had originally started.

'Well, I suppose we'll have to send Eleanor a present,' she said. 'Something out of the silver chest that we don't want would do nicely. But, Lydia, I cannot see why you only do well in Literature. It seems to be the only subject you got more than sixty marks for. You really must make a great effort next year,' said Mrs Keith, looking distractedly round the room as if an effort might suddenly materialize before her eyes.

Before Lydia could speak her father came in from the garden in a state of explosion, to ask who had put all that mess on the lawn. Whoever it was, he said, must tidy it away and get the pond properly cleaned and refilled before they did anything else; did they hear, *anything*. Mrs Keith asked, 'What mess?'

'It's only the pond, Mrs Keith,' said Morland, who was on her other side. 'We got most of the weeds out before breakfast, and we shall have it clean by the afternoon.'

Mr Keith could not scold his guests, for that was against his nature, but he spoke so sharply to Lydia that everyone knew exactly whom he meant, and Noel said in a low voice to Everard that this was one of those conversations so much more embarrassing to the guest than the host. Mrs Keith, while agreeing in principle with her husband, raised the question of church. Mr Keith said church was all very well, and if he didn't read the lessons there was no one else to do it at this time of year, but the lawn was like a pigsty, and had they heard what he said about tidying it up. Lydia said she had, and suggested to her fellow-workers that they should at once resume their labours. Accordingly the four pond-cleaners went back to their brooms and brushes, with the pleasant certainty that church was now entirely out of the question.

The rest of the party went suitably to church, some walking, some in the car. After a good deal of shuffling, due to Mrs Keith wishing to sit next to three people at once, Everard and Kate, who had hardly spoken that morning, found themselves side by side, and, what was worse, obliged to share, owing to a shortage of prayer books. Each, of course, knew the routine part of the service by heart, and luckily most of the hymns were trusted Ancient and Modern friends, but the psalms they could not pretend to know. Kate, gloved, had great difficulty in turning over the India paper pages of the book, all sticky with gold along the edges, and was already two verses late. Everard felt it his duty as a gentleman to help her, but if he took the book he would have to touch her, and he didn't know whether she would like it or not. Also, if he did touch her he thought he might go mad, and as he was right at the end of the pew farthest from the door, that would have been uncomfortable for everyone. Kate had by now found the page and held half the book at him, which he gingerly took, but, paper being notoriously unconductive, was able to survive. Neither of them had any singing voice, and each was ashamed of making before the other the humble noise which represented their usual attempt at worshipping with song. Also, no one knows how many words of any given verse of a psalm are to be gobbled together onto one or two notes, and whatever one does is wrong. Kate listened enviously to Edith's clear, assured voice on her other side, and took refuge in moving her lip to the words. Everard made some ill-advised attempts to follow the choir, lost heart, and knew Kate must be despising him. As the psalms finished they both let go of the book, which balanced for a second on the edge of the empty pew in front, and fell over onto the floor. During the sermon both had ample leisure to reflect upon the astounding beauty of emotion as roused by the

relish, he put the honeysuckle back into his pocket and went in to lunch.

As the afternoon was so hot, Mrs Keith finally decided on tea in the garden room. This pleasant room had been added to the house in about 1820 and was approached by a glass door from the library. Its walls were white, with columns painted on them, and it was lighted by an immense French window opening on to the terrace, and an equally large sash window which looked over the lawn. Palmer resented it so much, considering that a room onto the garden was not a parlourmaid's legitimate province, that Mrs Keith had put a service hatch from the kitchen passage, but she might as well have spent her money on something else, as Palmer preferred to carry trays through the library with a sense of injury. Mrs Keith had then bought an excellent tea-trolley with rubber wheels and ball bearings. This Palmer occasionally consented to push before her as if it were a dust-cart that she unfortunately found herself obliged to drive. However, with nine in the house, apart from Robert's children, and a party coming from the Rectory, and Miss Pettinger, Mrs Keith felt that an informal tea with tennis players coming and going would best meet the case, and Palmer said, 'Very well, if you wish, madam,' in a voice of ice.

Lydia, Swan and Morland, after snatching a hasty lunch of salmon mayonnaise, roast beef, potatoes, peas, French beans, salad, chocolate soufflé, charlotte russe, cream cheese, Bath Oliver biscuits, raspberries and cream, begged to be excused coffee and returned to the scene of their labours, promising that the pond would be ready by tea-time. Hacker basely deserted them to spend his afternoon with Henry and Catherine pretending to fish for whales with bulrushes in the rain-water tank in the kitchen garden, with the frog in his bowl to keep them company.

217

Soon after three Edith's brothers roared up in the sports car, prepared for tennis, and were warmly greeted by Mrs Keith who hadn't seen them since their return to England, and loved to have young people about. Edith was just going to take them off to the tennis court when the Rectory party arrived. Geraldine, much to her annoyance, had been forced by her mother to put on a fresh afternoon frock and accompany her elders. However, Mrs Birkett had accepted Geraldine's quite truthful statement that the frock she had worn that morning had got torn and had pronounced it only fit for the rag-bag, so Geraldine was not altogether ill-content.

Rose, in white muslin with a blue sash that matched her blue eyes, at once claimed the Fairweathers as her own, and said they could take her on the river.

'Not on your sweet life, my girl,' said Fairweather Senior, with great want of gallantry. 'Tennis for us. The muscles are getting flabby with evil living. You're coming out with us to-night. Come on, John.'

'Oughtn't one of you to stay with Rose?' asked Edith, as she walked with her brothers to the court.

'Why?' said Fairweather Junior. 'We took her out last night, and we're taking her out to-night. Besides, it's time she paid a little attention to Winter. After all, the chap's engaged to her and he doesn't seem to get much of a show. Gosh, if the girl I was engaged to went off with two handsome young fellows like me and Geoff, I'd have a word to say. But I suppose schoolmasters are hardly human, poor fish. Who is playing?'

'Robert and me to start with,' said Edith. 'Mr Merton and Kate as extras. We can get more if we want them. Mr Carter is good, so is Colin.'

Rose was for once utterly disconcerted when her devoted cavaliers left her without even a backward glance, and got rid of some of her mortification by snubbing Philip severely. Everard, who was not intending to play till after tea, tried to intervene but did more harm than good. He wished he could get Noel to come, whose pleasant, easy way of talking might placate Rose and draw the lightning from the unfortunate Philip. But Noel was playing tennis, and in any case it would be another act of caddish bounderism to get the man that the girl one worshipped was very fond of to break her heart by paying attention to a flibbertigibbet. So he did nothing, and Rose relapsed into sulky silence. To the Keiths and the Birketts sitting under a shady tulip tree on the lawn, with Palmer bringing tea into the garden room and happy sounds coming from the tennis court, everything seemed very delightful. Little did they think that to the three people sitting with them the sky was black, the earth a desert. Everard admired Philip's restraint under Rose's pinpricks and wondered how long he would remain patient under such treatment. Philip was wondering exactly the same thing. He felt that as long as he stayed at the Rectory he must repay the Birkett's hospitality and forbearance by courtesy to Rose, and at least the show of a fidelity which, he could not but admit, his heart no longer felt. To his unhappy situation he saw no outlet which honour could allow, and hoped vaguely that on his Russian visit he might somehow turn into someone else, or even get sent to Siberia by mistake.

Palmer now came across the lawn, followed by Miss Pettinger, and handed her over to Mrs Keith as one who renounced all responsibility for misfortune. Miss Pettinger, who held the mistaken belief that when off duty she was almost as others, though better educated and more important, was in dark blue flowered chiffon with a large hat, and many of her pupils would have agreed that she had overdone it a bit.

But nothing could surpass her graciousness to Mr Birkett as a Fellow Worker and almost an equal, or the nicely graded difference in her greeting to Everard, whose position as a housemaster gave him a status that she could not deny. To Philip, though but an assistant master, she bowed, for one owes a duty to oneself, and *noblesse oblige*. Rose, who was lolling in a deck chair, suddenly had an extraordinary experience. Her year of freedom, her four engagements, were annihilated. She suddenly felt, and much resented the feeling, that she was Rose Birkett of the Fifth Form, and that she had again failed in her Matric. Unwillingly she rose to her feet, unwillingly she came forward. Miss Pettinger disentangled her pince-nez from her scarf, adjusted it, and looked at her ex-pupil.

'Oh, it's Rose Birkett,' she said. 'How are you, dear?'

To Rose's horror and everlasting shame, an unseen power caused her to take Miss Pettinger's proffered hand and drop a slight curtsy as she said, 'Quite well, thank you, Miss Pettinger.'

Miss Pettinger said graciously that she was glad Rose had not forgotten the rule of courtesy inculcated at the High School. Mrs Birkett silently thanked heaven that Rose was behaving nicely, and Rose retired to her seat, her bosom torn with rage and mortification. Presently Palmer announced tea. Mrs Keith asked her to ring the outside bell so that the tennis players could hear, which she did with resentment in every line of her body. Mrs Keith and her guests went up to the garden room and the tennis players came dropping in by ones and twos till the whole party was assembled except Hacker and the pond-cleaners.

Mr and Mrs Birkett could not think why the afternoon was so unexpectedly pleasant, and if the thought occurred to them separately that they rarely attended a social gathering with their elder daughter at which she did not monopolize the attention of the whole company, and through sheer want of personality bring the talk to her own level, the thought was loyally suppressed. What increased Rose's indignation was that Edith Keith, whom she had dismissed in her mind as a negligible grown-up, was the heroine of the moment. With her two brothers, to whom she was devoted, as they to her, she made the centre of a group of cheerful if not very intellectual talk. Miss Pettinger, though she had regretted Edith Fairweather's lack of ambition for a university career, now looked benignly on her former Captain of Hockey, Captain of Cricket and, for Miss Pettinger disapproved of a too slavish adherence to the methods of the Public Schools and liked to invent some of her own titles, her former Girl of Honour, for such was Miss Pettinger's beautiful interpretation of the more prosaic Captain of the School. Edith had then made a very suitable marriage and produced two well-behaved children, a career which Miss Pettinger, no bigot though herself a virgin, found worthy of her approval. To Edith she unbent and condescended to remember how the School had beaten the Hosiers' Girls' Foundation School by one run, Edith carrying her bat. To her Edith showed the sprightly reverence which Miss Pettinger found so sadly lacking in the modern girl. Miss Pettinger then broke in upon a quiet talk that Everard was having with Mr Birkett about the Lower Fourth, and drew them both into the conversation with the easy tact of a university woman.

Presently Edith's children came into view on the lawn, still accompanied by Hacker and the frog. Edith called her offspring and asked Hacker what they were going to do with the frog. Henry, who had taken Hacker under his protection, answered for him that Aunt Lydia was going to fill the pond and they were going to put froggie in the water. Mr Keith, roused by the mention of the pond, said Twicker had no business to let Lydia make all that mess, and he must speak to him.

It was just about at this moment that Lydia came in. She had changed her pond clothes for more civilized attire, and seemed in excellent spirits.

'Hullo, Miss Pettinger,' she said, shaking hands with the warmth of a generous and forgiving nature, and quite forgetting to curtsy. 'I say, we've got the pond clean. We're going to have a Grand Opening and turn the water on. You can all come as soon as you've had your tea. The goldfish were there all the time. I mean Twicker had taken them out because he thought we might hurt them, and he's got them in a bucket and we're going to put them back as soon as the water's in. I say, Geoff, what about you and John giving me a hand with the top sluice? It's got stuck a bit, and Tony and Eric can't move it. They've gone to clean up for the Opening, and Geraldine's keeping guard.'

The Fairweathers rose as one man.

'You can come, too, Philip,' said Lydia. 'It'll cheer you up. Come on. We'll get the gong out of the hall and take it down with us. You can all come down as soon as you hear it.'

Swept away by her enthusiasm, the three young men followed in her tempestuous wake through the library to the hall, where they collected the gong, and so on to the pond. John had the good idea of taking the extra horn off his car and bringing it too, a suggestion that met with Lydia's full approval.

Rose, deprived of three admirers at once, by a schoolgirl whom she despised, made a last bid for attention by going and sitting by Noel, but he was amusing himself with Miss Pettinger, and when Rose broke in with a request to be taken on the river, Noel said, 'Presently, Rose,' and Miss Pettinger said, 'Don't interrupt, Rose,' just as if one were still at school. Before Rose had sulked for long the air was rent by the gong and the motor-horn. Mr Keith said he supposed they had better go, or Lydia would never stop that noise, so the whole party moved towards the pond.

Here a scene of unparalleled splendour met their eyes. Lydia, Swan, Morland and Geraldine, all spotlessly clean, were lined up on the opposite side of the pond, which was now as clean as Mrs Twicker's kitchen table. At the upper sluice, in which a Union Jack was stuck, stood Philip and the Fairweathers. Mr Twicker in his Sunday clothes holding a bucket, Hacker with the frog in its bowl, Henry and Catherine and Mrs Twicker, stood in respectful attendance.

'Look here, Twicker,' said Mr Keith, whose respect for the Sunday rest of his gardener had forbidden him to look for him and complain, but who wasn't going to miss this chance, 'I can't have this sort of thing again. Mess all over the lawn. You shouldn't let Miss Lydia do it.'

Twicker said it wasn't no good speaking to Miss Lydia, and so long as she didn't cut her initials on the marrow he was saving up for the Flower Show, the way she done last year, he didn't hold with interfering, and Miss Lydia and the young gentlemen had cleaned the pond up a treat, and did Mr Keith know that the catch of the tool house needed repairing and how he was to do it with the Flower Show coming on and all the young vegetables, he didn't know.

'All right, Twicker, all right,' said Mr Keith.

'Ready?' said Lydia, who had been champing and chafing while this conversation went on. 'All right. Go!'

At this word Philip pulled up the sluice gate, the Fairweathers cheered loudly. Swan and Morland beat the gong and blew the horn, the children shrieked with joy, and water came gushing into the pond. Twicker then emptied the goldfish into their home and went off with his wife. Hacker carefully decanted the frog onto the grass. The frog, who had not at all enjoyed his Sunday outing, looked at his surroundings, disliked them, and leapt away into the bushes. Edith's nurse descended on the children and removed them, followed by Hacker, who had promised to tell them a story while they had their supper.

'That's all,' said Lydia.

'Well, that has been most amusing,' said Miss Pettinger, 'and I must really be going now. Good-bye, Lydia. We shall meet again next term. Good-bye, Rose. You ought to keep up your physical exercises, dear; you are getting quite a slouch. I can always arrange for her to have special gym at the school if you like, Mrs Birkett.'

Mrs Birkett thanked her and said she must think of it. Rose felt that she was now a new girl in the Lower Second, and wished she could hurt someone.

'Can we send you home, Miss Pettinger?' asked Mrs Keith.

'Oh, no, thanks. I have my little car,' said Miss Pettinger. 'I drive myself everywhere. I went to Dalmatia in the holidays with my secretary. It was most interesting.'

As no one wanted to hear about Dalmatia, Mrs Keith made a move towards the house with her guest. Some of the tennis players drifted back to the court. Everard, Colin and Philip lingered, somehow back in school shop again, and Rose nursed her growing wrath and mortification. Lydia, with Swan and Morland, was absorbed in watching the water rise, and waiting till it had reached its usual level before opening the lower sluice gate.

'Oh, Philip,' said Rose, 'let's go on the river. It's sickening to do nothing but talk all the time.'

'I'm afraid I can't just this moment,' said Philip. 'I promised to have a single with Everard as soon as this set is over. But we shan't be very long, and then I'd love to.'

'I'll ask Noel then. He *can* punt,' said Rose.

'Yes, do,' said Philip. 'He's playing now, but he'll have finished soon.'

'But I do think it's sickening of you,' said Rose. 'You never do anything I ask you to. You won't even get a new car.'

Philip said nothing. Colin and Everard felt acutely uncomfortable and didn't know if it would be kinder to move away, or to pretend everything was normal.

'Well, you might answer me,' said Rose, working herself up for a good scene. 'Of course if you like letting water into a pond with Lydia better than being with me, that just shows.'

'I'm sorry, Rose,' said Philip. 'If I could please you by talking I would, but if I can't it isn't much good.'

'Well, if I'm not fit to talk to, we'd better not be engaged any more,' said Rose. 'Here is your horrid old ring, and I hope you'll be very happy and all that, and it's all perfectly sickening.'

As she spoke she pulled off her ring, threw it at Philip and walked away. The ring fell short of Philip and lay on the grass. No one liked to speak. Colin cast an anxious glance at the other end of the pond, but Lydia and the boys were intent on the sluice and their own conversation.

'She's full enough now,' said Lydia. 'I'll open the sluice a bit. That's it. Now we'll go and bathe. You boys go and get your things. I'll wait here for you.'

Philip stooped, picked up the ring and walked towards the end of the pond where Lydia was standing.

'Do you think he's going to drown himself?' Colin asked Everard, awe-struck at his first experience of real life.

'No,' said Everard, 'but it would be a very good thing if he could get drunk. Mind, Colin, you and I are witnesses that Rose broke off the engagement. Nothing is to get Philip back into that mess – nothing. Look here, don't tell anyone yet. Go back to the tennis court. I'll be along soon.'

Everard went over to Philip. Lydia had pulled up the

225

gate, and the little stream was pursuing its way. Just below the sluice it widened into a deep pool fringed with wild mint and grasses. In the clear water above the muddy bottom some minnows were flirting about. Philip was standing by Lydia, looking into the water.

'What's that you've got?' asked Lydia.

'A ring,' said Philip.

'Whose?'

'It was Rose's,' said Philip. 'I gave it to her. She has given it back to me.'

He dropped it into the pool. It sank down into the mud. A little swirl of clouded water rose from the bottom and settled again. In the clear water above the minnows wove their ceaseless pattern.

'I'll see that no one clears out the pool,' said Lydia.

'Thanks awfully, Lydia,' said Philip.

'If you and the boys took Philip bathing it wouldn't be a bad idea,' said Everard.

'Rather,' said Lydia, with a sudden sense of responsibility that she felt but could not have expressed. 'I'll get Colin's bathing things for him. I say, Philip, stay to dinner. We shan't be changing much, what with Sunday and playing tennis late and all that.'

Philip looked undecided.

'I'll tell the Birketts you are staying, if you like,' said Everard.

'Thanks. You might tell them everything,' said Philip. 'God! I could do with a drink.'

'Come on then,' said Lydia. 'I'll get you a whisky and soda. Would that be the right thing?' she asked anxiously.

'Quite right,' said Philip gravely.

'Hi, Tony!' shouted Lydia, as the boys appeared. 'Philip is coming with us and I'm going to get him some things. You go on down to the boat-house and we'll come.'

In the dining-room Lydia gave Everard and Philip whisky and soda, contenting herself with grape-fruit squash.

'Many happy returns of the day,' said Lydia, looking at Philip.

'Thank you,' said Philip. 'I don't suppose it will last but I didn't know one could feel so happy.'

He went off with Lydia, while Everard, a considerable weight off his mind, went in search of the Birketts. Mrs Birkett had gone home, taking Rose and Geraldine to evening service, but by great luck Mr Birkett was watching the tennis by himself. Everard sat down beside him.

'I was looking for you,' he said.

'When will you young men learn that the phrase, "I am looking for you", at once conveys to the sensitive ear that there is trouble about, trouble which you are too cowardly to approach by direct methods,' said Mr Birkett. 'Out with it.'

Everard laughed.

'It isn't exactly trouble,' he said. 'Rose's engagement is broken off.'

'It may mean trouble, but it's certainly good news,' said Mr Birkett. 'How do you know?'

'I was there. Rose was annoyed with Philip because he wouldn't take her on the river at once. He had promised to play a single with me, as a matter of fact. So she said the engagement was off and threw her ring at him – but it didn't get anywhere near him,' he added reflectively.

'No girls can throw,' said Mr Birkett. 'You don't think Philip will ask her to think it over?'

'Philip dropped the ring ceremoniously into the pool below the pond,' said Everard.

'A little on the heroic side,' said Mr Birkett, thinking of his last interview with Philip, 'but a good move. This is going to simplify next term, Everard. If Philip takes the Mixed Fifth and gives his whole mind to his work, he may make a success of it for us.'

'Lydia asked him to stay here to dinner to-night,' said Everard. 'It may save some awkwardness, and I said I'd tell you.'

'Good girl, Lydia,' said Mr Birkett, secretly thinking that, much as he disliked his Rose in many of her aspects, he was heartily glad that his daughter was so pretty and attractive, not a loud-voiced Amazon like Lydia Keith. 'But about the Lower Fourth, Everard. If Harrison takes the Junior Classics, we might get Prothero to change with Smith. Did I mention, by the way, that we are getting Prothero back next term? He writes to me that he enjoyed his year at that Canadian school very much and hopes he'll never see the place again. They might make a good team for the Lower School . . .'

The talk became wholly technical.

*

Dinner at the Manor had an atmosphere of discreet hilarity that Mr and Mrs Keith and their eldest son and his wife could not quite understand, though they enjoyed it very much. Colin had told the good news to Noel and Kate, Lydia had told Swan and Morland. No one thought it necessary to tell Hacker. Colin persuaded his father to have champagne, nominally to celebrate the clearing of the pond, and what with the fizzy taste to which they were unaccustomed, and their excitement over the news, Lydia, Swan and Morland all choked. It was not till after eleven that Philip got back to the Rectory. Seeing a light in the library he thought he had better get it over, and went in.

'Don't say a word about Rose, because I'm sick of the subject,' said her father.

Philip shook hands, feeling extremely happy and a little ashamed.

'I've got to apologize, sir, for all the trouble I've given you. If you don't mind I'll go home to-morrow till I go to Russia. It will be more comfortable for everyone.'

'Perhaps it will,' said Mr Birkett. 'But make it Tuesday if you can. I want to talk over one or two things with you and Everard. You know I'm hoping to get Prothero back next term from Canada, and we'll have Harrison, so –'

*

Philip settled down to a really interesting talk with his headmaster, no longer, thank heaven, though with all due respect, his future father-in-law. So absorbing did they find their talk that Rose's return, her whispered giggles of farewell to the Fairweathers, her going upstairs to bed, passed entirely unnoticed by them.

CHAPTER XI

Bank Holiday Excursions

On Monday morning Philip woke up in a confused state of mind. For weeks he had been used to waking with a sense of oppression, which, when examined, turned out to be a deep apprehension for the future, that had to be resolutely pushed away into the dark places of his mind, from loyalty to Rose. To-day he woke as usual with a feeling of impending doom. Heavy black clouds obscured the horizon, a dead, terrifying waste of land lay ahead. It was impossible to retreat. One could only walk forward by the path on which one had wilfully set one's feet, a beautiful encumbrance at one's side, making every step more difficult, bringing no help, no companionship, uttering loud complaints. But as the exquisite face and form of Rose drifted querulously across his inner vision, light began to break. The clouds lifted, the land ahead began to blossom, the lovely phantom threw something at him and disappeared. Philip suddenly sat bolt upright in bed, with the glorious certainly that his Rose was his no longer. This thought made him jump out of bed, do a little shadow boxing, sing, whistle, cut himself while shaving, and carry on a lively conversation with himself in Russian. Not till he was half-way downstairs did it occur to him that he still had to meet Mrs Birkett and Rose under these new conditions. About Mrs Birkett he felt no particular anxiety, but Rose might do anything. She might say she wished to be engaged again, and though Philip was determined to resist to the death, jumping into the river and drowning himself if the worst came to the worst, he felt that he might have a very uncomfortable time before him. Rose never fought under

Queensberry rules, and would be quite capable of metaphorically tripping him up and hitting below the belt.

To his mingled relief and terror Mrs Birkett was alone in the breakfast-room when he came in. Before he could begin any apology she had spoken to him very kindly about the engagement, saying that she and her husband were both relieved that it was over, that it had all been largely Rose's fault, and that they both blamed themselves for having allowed the engagement in the first place. Philip said, as he had previously said to Mr Birkett, that he didn't think they could have prevented it.

'Perhaps not,' said Mrs Birkett, 'but we do feel to blame all the same, especially as this is driving you away earlier than you would have gone. Rose told me about it last night on our way to evening service, and she would like to have a talk with you before you go. Not to ask you to be engaged again,' she said hastily, seeing a look of panic come into Philip's expression, 'only to thank you, I believe, for having been considerate about it, and to say good-bye to you on friendly terms.'

'It's very nice of Rose,' said Philip nervously, 'but need we really have a talk do you think?'

'I do think so,' said Mrs Birkett firmly. 'It isn't as if you were going off this very moment, and it will be better to clear the air. From what she said I gather that she didn't behave very well last night, and she wants to apologize. Then you will be able to meet at school next term as if nothing had happened. It needn't last long. Will you ask Rose to walk round the garden with you after breakfast?'

Philip, feeling that one could escape more easily in the garden than in the house, said he would. Mr Birkett, Rose and Geraldine then came in and conversation became unnaturally general. Rose, who was full of the cinema she and the Fairweathers had seen at Barchester the night before, seemed to Philip to be exactly as usual. Any embarrassment that was felt was felt by him and in a lesser degree by the Birketts, but Rose appeared to be entirely unconscious of any tension in the atmosphere. Geraldine, who had been up to Mrs Twicker's cottage before breakfast, reported that the chameleon had escaped while having its supper the night before and been lost for two hours, at the end of which time it had been found in the basket with the chickens, the cat benevolently watching the whole brood. And so they managed to get through breakfast, by the end of which meal, the post and newspapers not having yet arrived and Mr Birkett being a little peevish in consequence, Rose, Geraldine and Philip were glad to escape into the garden. Philip and Rose walked up and down the flagged path with Geraldine in close attendance.

'Do you very much mind not coming with us, Geraldine?' said Philip. 'I want to talk to Rose rather privately.'

Geraldine said she didn't see what they had to say to each other, but in any case she had to finish the fourth chapter of Woodstock, a book which she freely characterized as mouldy, and intimated that they could say anything they had to say while she did her reading, after which she thought they might pick raspberries. She then sat herself with her book on a seat which commanded most of the little garden and the tennis court, so that Rose and Philip had to go away into the vegetable garden, where a gardener was occupied among the pea-sticks, which forced them to betake themselves to a rather drab corner by the rainwater butt to get a little privacy. Here Philip found that he had nothing to say. As Rose also appeared to be incapable of speech, they walked slowly towards the incinerator, where Rose stopped.

What Rose's thoughts for the last eighteen hours had been, or indeed what they were at any time, we shall never know, owing to their complete vacancy. Vague ideas may have floated like thistledown in and out of her so-called mind, but she could have formulated none of them. On the way to church on Sunday evening she had told her mother, with some indignation, that Philip had been sickening, and she had thrown his old ring at him, and never wanted to see him again, and being engaged was horrid. At first her mother had taken no notice, but as Rose went on talking about it, boring Mrs Birkett and Geraldine dreadfully, Mrs Birkett had gathered that the engagement was really over for good, and was extremely thankful. After the service Rose had apparently forgotten her wrongs and talked about nothing but the Fair-weathers, who came to dinner and took her to the cinema. When she got home she had slept comfortably for eight hours, but between getting up and coming down to breakfast she had put what mind she had seriously to work.

There had been, she felt, something a little undignified in throwing a ring at a person, especially when it didn't hit him, and although the episode itself had given her a very dashing feeling at the time, she was a little ashamed on looking back, and decided that she must redeem her character in Philip's eyes. Thank goodness she wasn't engaged to him any more, but he might as well have a good opinion of her, because that made one feel better.

Thinking of a precedent to follow, the name of Ophelia naturally suggested itself. It was true that Ophelia had an unsympathetic father who ordered her to give up Hamlet, and that she was in any case on the verge of going mad, but Ophelia was a heroine and everyone was sorry for her, and this Rose thought a pleasant combination. She could not quite persuade herself that her father and mother had persecuted her, and she didn't feel at all mad, but one thing she could do was to give Philip back the letters he had written to her while she was on the Algerian cruise, letters into which poor

233

Philip had poured everything that would least interest his beloved.

She now therefore from the bosom of her dress, thus explaining a rather lumpy appearance for which Philip had been unable to account, pulled a small packet which she handed to her former lover. It was tied up with a piece of blue ribbon stamped at intervals with the name of a well-known chocolate shop, and endorsed: Phillips letters.

'I thought you'd better have them back,' said Rose.

These were not exactly Ophelia's words, but beautiful as Rose felt these words to be, she could never quite memorize them and this was after all their sense.

Philip, uncomfortably conscious that he had not kept the three postcards she had sent him from the cruise, and so had nothing to give her in exchange, thanked her.

'You could burn them now,' said Rose, who had in some ways a practical outlook.

Philip thought the advice good. As he dropped the letters one by one into the smouldering garden stuff in the incinerator, he thought of the mixture of love and politics he had inflicted on Rose, the contented egoism which had thought the highest compliment he could pay was to write at great length about himself. The more he considered this, the more he realized that his feeling for her had not been the pure and unselfish passion he had imagined. He had treated her too much as an audience, had not made enough allowance for her extreme youth and her childish mind. It seemed to him in this access of self-examination that Rose might have found her bonds as galling as he found his. If so, she had had courage for them both when she broke the engagement, a step he would not himself have had the courage to take, or even to suggest.

'I can't tell you how nice it is not being engaged,' said Rose with deep satisfaction.

The words so chimed with what Philip had been thinking that he felt a pang of remorse for the inexplicable puzzle that her engagement to him must have been to her.

'I don't know how it is,' Rose continued, wrinkling her forehead in the effort to reduce her rambling thoughts to some kind of order and explain them to Philip, 'but I always seem to get engaged. People will ask one. It isn't that I mind being *engaged*,' she said, evidently feeling that this made everything clear, 'but being engaged seems to make people so dull. Mr Smalley at Miss Pettinger's was so dull, talking about old masters and things and Herr Lob at Munich got awfully dull when he had proposed, and talked about nothing but orchestras, and as for Lieutenant von Storck, he talked so much about what he was going to do when he retired from the army and went to live on his father's estate somewhere or other, that I was awfully glad when mummy sent for me to come home.'

This, the longest consecutive sentence that Philip had ever heard Rose utter, made him feel even more guilty than before. He could hardly fathom the depths of boredom that this pretty creature, who lived entirely on pleasure and was so suited for it, must have experienced with her various admirers. How much more fitting it was that she should racket with the Fairweathers.

'I suppose I was dull, too,' he said.

'Ghastly,' said Rose. 'It isn't because I don't like you, Philip. I think you're marvellous, but being engaged was so awful that I think this is much better. If only you could have got a job, but being a master in daddy's school and all about Greek and Latin is too sickening.'

'Yes, I was dull,' said Philip, 'and I hope you'll forgive me. And I'd like to say thank you very much for having been engaged to me, and for being brave enough to stop being engaged. I couldn't have done it. And now, don't get engaged to anyone else for a bit unless you are really sure he isn't dull.'

'I'll say No, whoever it is,' said Rose emphatically. 'It'll be marvellous practice, and if he is really keen he can always ask me again. If it was anyone as dull as Mr Merton I'd say No at once. He thinks he's amusing, but he hasn't seen anything, not even *Passion in the Purple*, that one about Cardinals that we saw last night, and if a film gets to Barchester it means it's been released for simply months. Let's see if the paper has come.'

As he accompanied her back to the house, Philip wondered how he could ever have been so silly as to think he was jealous of Noel Merton.

The post had arrived when they got back. Philip saw one rather dull-looking letter for him with a typewritten address and opened it without enthusiasm, thinking it was a bill or a receipt. He read it once, looked perplexed, and read it again.

'Excuse me, sir,' he said to Mr Birkett, who was opening his letters at a tremendous rate and tossing them into piles, saying as he did so, 'Parent, Governor, bill, Governor, staff, parent, female parent blast her, guardian, bill . . .'

'Stop playing tinker, tailor, for a moment, dear,' said Mrs Birkett, 'Philip wants to speak to you.'

'Well?' said Mr Birkett. 'I do wish, Amy, that Holinshed's father would keep his advice for his own parish. The mere fact of his having taken orders at an unusually late period of his life does *not* make him an authority on the running of a large school. What is it, Philip?'

'Would you mind reading this letter, sir?' said Philip. Mr Birkett glanced through it.

'Very satisfactory,' he said. 'I didn't think they'd offer you anything myself. I thought they'd want you to pay. Ten pounds in advance on royalties is a nice little sum. Congratulations.'

'Is it true?' asked Philip, his eyes sparkling.

'Well, I should think so,' said Mr Birkett. 'It's the Oxbridge Press notepaper. I don't suppose anyone would go to the trouble of forging it. Now, where did I put Gibbs and Hudson's letter about the boiler?'

'But do they really mean they'll publish it?' said Philip, sticking to his point.

'Nothing less,' said Mr. Birkett. 'You'll never make another penny out of it, of course. It's a pity you didn't make it a bit less scholarly; we might have got it onto the school book list then. Never mind, it will be quite a good advertisement if you want a job in another school. Amy, I'm going to write letters in the study. I won't see anyone before lunch.'

He collected his correspondence and went off. Mrs Birkett asked what it all was, and when Philip showed her the letter in which the Oxbridge University Press announced their pleasure in accepting a book of 50,000 words on the Epistles of Horace by Philip Winter, with an advance on royalties of ten pounds, and no mention of American rights, she was as pleased and enthusiastic as even Philip could have wished. Rose, grasping the fact that something marvellous had happened, almost as good as a job, was also loud in congratulation, and flinging her arms round Philip's neck, kissed him with delightful want of affection and a general desire to be agreeable.

The Messrs Fairweather, arriving at this moment, were suitably shocked.

'I say, I say,' said Fairweather Senior, 'this is a bit hard on us poor bachelors.'

'Don't be sickening, Geoff,' said Rose. 'Philip and I got unengaged yesterday, didn't I tell you? And he's an author.'

'Oh, I say!' said the Fairweathers, in tones expressing sympathy about the engagement and respectful admiration of an author.

237

'It is really the greatest relief to us both,' said Philip, 'and no one need be sorry. Rose was simply splendid about it, and we were just saying good-bye.'

Fairweather Junior remarked gallantly that he wished Rose would say good-bye like that to him, and did she want to see the otter hunt at Plumstead. With shrieks of joy Rose said she did, and even the inclusion of Geraldine in the party did not dim the pleasure. As they crowded out to the racing car, Rose turned back and caught at Philip's hand.

'You've been really marvellous,' she said, and fled from the room. Philip felt that he cared more truly for her as she left him than he had ever done before, and that the joy of losing her and having his book accepted was almost more than he could bear.

Fairweather Senior came back into the room holding a telegram.

'So sorry, I forgot this, Mrs Birkett,' he said. 'We met the post-woman with this telegram for Mr Birkett, so we took it to save her walking. She said it seemed important, so she hadn't telephoned it in case there was any mistake.'

'Thank you, Geoff,' said Mrs Birkett. 'I'll take it to him now.'

'Oh, Mrs Birkett,' said Philip, 'could you wait one moment. Do you think the proofs will come soon?'

Mrs Birkett looked kindly at him, thinking, as she sometimes did, what fun it would have been to have a son, and how one could guide and help him; a sentiment of whose underlying fallacy she was quite unconscious.

'Not for quite a long time, probably,' she said. 'They are very busy, and you have to take your turn.'

'Oh, of course,' said Philip, 'but I thought it would be a pity if I went to Russia and the proofs came while I was away.'

'You can be quite certain they won't do that,' said Mrs Birkett, and went into the study. Philip was, on the whole, disappointed, but bore it bravely. And after all Mrs Birkett had never had a book accepted and published by a University Press, and couldn't understand. Pleasant if vague visions of printers' devils waiting day and night outside his door, glowing notices in *The Times* and the *Classical Review*, money pouring into his account, these were filling his mind when Mrs Birkett came in, looking perturbed, and said her husband wanted to see him at once in the study.

*

On Monday morning Mrs Twicker, who never let public holidays interfere with her pleasures, had the washing in soak by six o'clock. By half-past six her three lodgers were down, anxious to be allowed to get in her way. Though Mrs Twicker still held to it that the wash-house was no place for young gentlemen, she could not resist the thought of having the boys all to herself for a whole morning, and gave in. Twicker undertook to leave a message at the kitchen door that they were breakfasting at the cottage, and the boys then chopped wood for the copper fire, and lighted it with a ruinous expenditure of matches and paper which shocked and yet pleased Mrs Twicker, as showing that the gentry still possessed the combined incompetence and wastefulness which she so much admired.

'If you had joined the School Scouts, as Holy Joe asked you to,' said Swan to Morland, 'this wouldn't have happened.'

'I'll tell you what would have happened,' said Morland, 'we wouldn't have had a fire at all. Do you remember the time Holy Joe tried to light a camp fire with three matches, and they were the three that some fool had used and put back in the box, and what the troop told us about his Biblical language? What do we do now, Nanny?'

'Breakfast, sir,' said Mrs Twicker. 'It's fried eggs and bacon, and some of my bread you like, and my new strawberry jam.'

'Lydia'll be sorry she's missing this,' said Swan with his mouth full.

Mrs Twicker said cryptically that Miss Lydia wasn't behind the door when teeth were given out, and she'd manage all right.

'Nanny,' said Morland, 'there was a boy at my prep school called Donk, and he used to eat eggs like this: watch!'

He carefully sliced the white off his egg and lifted the untouched yolk on his fork. Just as he opened his mouth, the yolk slipped sideways off the fork and fell onto the table-cloth.

'Letting down the Honour of the School,' said Swan indignantly.

'Never mind, Mr Tony,' said Mrs Twicker. 'I'll fry you another, and we'll pop the table-cloth in the wash-tub and then give it a nice boil, and it'll come up as white as snow.'

Then Twicker came in for his breakfast, bringing with him three peaches, warm from the glass-house, for his guests. He had been a little shy of them at first, but after a hunt by candle-light in his little garden, in which the boys had found a hundred and thirty-five snails and forty-one large slugs and put them all into a basin of brine 'to make snail soup', Swan said, amid horrified exclamations from Mrs Twicker, the gardener had accepted them as friends, and even allowed them to carve their initials on the next largest marrow that he wasn't keeping for the Flower Show.

After an uproarious breakfast, during which Mr Twicker, undeterred by his wife's remonstrances, convulsed his audience by imitating the village drunkard at closing time, he went back to his work and the boys to theirs. Never had Mrs Twicker enjoyed a morning's washing so much. All three boys became clowns for her benefit, and not till Morland, turning the mangle wildly, had caught the short-sighted Hacker on the elbow with the handle, did they stop laughing. So what with this and the hearty meal of tea and jam tarts they had at eleven, the morning passed like lightning, and as Mr Twicker was going to turn a pig he had put in brine after his dinner, they sent up their excuses to the Manor, and so missed most of the interesting things that happened that day.

Lydia got the boys' message before breakfast, but decided not to join them. Her interests were literary rather than domestic, and though she wanted to talk to someone, to almost anyone in fact, about Browning, she felt the boys would not understand, though here she was wrong, for Swan rather specialized on the Victorian poets. Browning had suddenly come into her life the night before, because the literature mistress had set a holiday essay on 'My favourite Browning poem, and my reasons for preferring it'. Lydia, to whom the poet was unknown, had contemptuously taken the volume of Dramatic Lyrics to bed with her, and fallen head over heels into it. Seeing Everard, Noel and Kate sitting under the tulip tree after breakfast, this seemed a good opportunity for a symposium on the subject that was filling her mind.

'I think,' she announced loudly, as she sat down on the swing chair and began to rock herself to and fro, 'everyone ought to read Browning.'

'Quite a lot of them do,' said Noel.

'Oh, well, of course they read him in English literature,' said Lydia, 'but I mean really reading him. I think his understanding of human nature is wonderful. It's just like Shakespeare and Horace, you feel you are everyone in his poems.'

'I hope you don't,' said Noel.

'Well, anyway all the beautiful ones and the noble ones,' said Lydia truthfully.

She then, having an excellent verbal memory, quoted from the poet's works at such length that her hearers could hardly bear it.

'Need you rock all the time, Lydia?' said Kate. 'It makes me feel so sick.'

'Did you say you'd play a single with me, Kate?' said Noel, getting up.

Kate knew she hadn't, but sensing an appeal for help, she got up too and went away with him to the tennis court.

'And what was marvellous,' continued Lydia, fixing Everard with her eye and taking no notice of the others' departure, 'was his own life. Do you know he ran away with his wife when she was an invalid, and never stopped adoring her his whole life. There is something,' said Lydia, gazing into the distance, 'about happy married life that is even more beautiful than being in love with people. What do you think about it?'

'Well, I'm not married,' said Everard, 'so I can't very well judge.'

'Of course you're not,' said Lydia, 'but you must have some ideas. Don't you ever think about things?'

Everard said he sometimes did.

'Noel does,' said Lydia. 'I had a very interesting conversation with him on Saturday about marriage.'

Everard said nothing, feeling that Noel's views on marriage, presumably to Kate, would be highly distasteful to him.

'He said,' Lydia went on, giving Everard the feeling that he was at a lecture by a very competent female don, 'that he thought marriage was very good for people it was good for, but not for the others.'

'That seems reasonable,' said Everard.

'I said I'd probably get married,' Lydia went on, 'and I still intend to, but Noel said he didn't think it would suit him at all. He said he would be a kind of uncle to people instead. And we both thought Kate ought to marry someone very nice. Someone like you or Colin, I thought, and so did Noel. I'd like to marry someone like Hamlet and Richard the Second and Richard Hannay and Browning.'

'Well, I hope you will, Lydia,' said Everard, getting up. 'You deserve them all. There's Colin. Let's see if he will play squash, and you can score.'

But Colin had not come for pleasure. He looked anxious as he said to Everard:

'Simnet has just rung up from the Rectory to ask if we can go and see Mr Birkett, Everard. He says Mr Birkett seems quite upset. I expect that is only his literary way of putting it, but I'm going over at once if you will come too.'

The two men hurried down to the footbridge, not trusting Bunce to be at the ferry.

'You don't think it's Philip,' said Colin. 'He wouldn't have – done anything?'

'Of course not,' said Everard, but a cold fear assailed him. His relief at hearing Lydia's account of her talk with Noel had been so great that he had hardly heard what Colin was saying. If Noel was not a marrying man, if Kate had not been attracted by his charming manners and were heartwhole, then there was still a chance for him. He made a vow to give Lydia a complete Browning gorgeously bound, if what she had said were true. Gradually the sense of Colin's question came through the golden cloud of his thoughts, and he pulled himself together. His common sense told him that Philip wasn't likely to have done anything, as Colin delicately put it, just when he was free from an irksome entanglement, but he didn't know what might have happened last night. Rose might have regretted her outburst and bullied

243

Philip into renewing their engagement. Philip might have had a nervous breakdown, or lost his memory, or gone too near the weir. In imagination he reconstructed the whole scene, travelled to Philip's home to break the news to his father, dealt with his belongings, edited his literary remains and by the time they had got to the Rectory had rearranged the whole school time-table to suit altered conditions.

When he came into Mr Birkett's study with Colin and saw Philip sitting there quite well and normal, he was so much relieved that he did not grudge the waste of his mental efforts.

'Good morning, Everard,' said Mr Birkett, who certainly looked what Simnet had called quite upset. 'Good morning, Keith. I'm sorry to disturb your holiday, but I've just had a wire from Lorimer's sister in Perthshire. It's about Lorimer.'

Everard looked at Philip, who nodded. There was no need for Mr Birkett to say what had happened. There was a moment's silence.

'Heart, I suppose,' said Everard.

Mr Birkett said yes.

'He sounded tired in his last letter,' said Everard. 'You remember, Philip, the letter about your book.'

'I do remember,' said Philip, whose joy and excitement about his book had been honestly wiped out by his sorrow at the death of his old master.

'Here is the wire,' said Mr Birkett, pushing it over to Everard. 'It just says that he died peacefully, and the funeral will be to-morrow, for members of the family only. We must have a Memorial Service in the School Chapel, of course, at the beginning of next term. I'll have to write to Smith about it.'

'He had extraordinarily good sherry,' said Everard, thinking of a day when he had gone to complain about Hacker.

'And very good port,' said Colin, thinking of his last evening at school, and how Mr Lorimer had preached against the Vanity of Human Wishes.

'Not a bad epitaph,' said Mr Birkett, and there was silence again till the headmaster broke it, coughing before he spoke.

'This will mean·some changes in the school,' he said, 'and as we are all here, we might as well discuss them. The best we can do for Lorimer is to see that his work is carried on as he would have wished. Do you think you could take the Classical Sixth, Philip?'

'Sir!' said Philip, and fell dumb.

'You needn't make up your mind immediately,' said Mr Birkett. 'I shan't suggest anyone else till you decide, only it must be before you go to Russia.'

'Do you mind if I don't stay, sir?' asked Philip, and without waiting for an answer blundered out of the room.

'He'll take it,' said Everard, as the door closed behind Philip, 'and he'll do it well. And he'll be too busy to think so much about politics. I hope you don't want to move him out of my house, sir. We got on quite nicely.'

'No, no,' said the Head. 'I'm not going to interfere. But I want to have a talk with you, Everard. You needn't stay, Keith, if this bores you.'

Colin, interpreting this rightly as a suggestion that he was not wanted, rose to his feet, and then did a really heroic deed.

'If Mr Lorimer's death is going to give you trouble, sir,' he said to his late headmaster, 'I mean, if you'll be shorthanded or anything, I'd be very glad to come back for a term or two if I'd be any help.'

As he said this his heart sank as he knew how he would loathe to turn his back on the calm of Noel's chambers and plunge once more into the seething cauldron of school life. But some kind of loyalty, some real liking and respect for the two men under whom he had served, forced him to say the words.

'Thank you very much,' said Mr Birkett, 'but Harrison will be back next term, and Prothero, a man you don't know, is coming back from a year in Canada, so we shan't have any difficulty about staff. I very much appreciate your offer all the same.'

With deep thankfulness Colin escaped.

'Nice of young Keith to suggest that,' said Mr Birkett, 'but I want a real master. Now, Everard, if you can spare the time I'd like to run through the time-table with you and make a tentative programme for Philip and Harrison and Prothero. I shan't put another resident master in your house next term, so you'll have Keith's room free. Do you think Philip will really take the Classical Sixth?'

Everard said he was certain there was no doubt about it. Then they worked together till nearly lunch-time, when Mr Birkett put down his pen.

'That about settles it,' he said. 'Now let's forget it till next term. How much longer are you here?'

'Only till to-morrow. And next week I'm taking those History Sixth boys to Hungary, you remember.'

'Oh, yes, of course. And Philip is off to Russia. Well, I'll say good-bye till next term. We'll miss Lorimer.'

'We shall, sir,' said Everard.

*

There was only a small lunch-party at the Manor. Mr and Mrs Keith with Robert and Edith had gone to a political garden party at Courcy Castle, and were not expected back till dinner. The boys were having their midday meal at the gardener's cottage, Everard and Colin were sobered by Mr Lorimer's death, and the others were sympathetically subdued. After lunch Everard asked Kate to come for a walk with him. Leaving Noel, Colin and Lydia sitting on the lawn, they went across the river and up onto the downs. They said very little; Everard had no mind to break the happy calm of this afternoon's companionship, and not till they were at the honeysuckle gate did he speak to her of what was in his heart. He spoke of the school, of the advantages to a house master of being married, of the help a wife could be with the boys, of the unlimited opportunities for mending, darning, and sewing on buttons. He said he was not well off and so far had not been ambitious, but that with Kate's help he might get a good headmastership in time. He also mentioned, though with such delicacy that Kate could not understand what he was talking about, that owing to Colin's departure he would have an extra bedroom in his house.

Kate listened, standing by the gate, and became paler and more pale.

'Is that all?' she asked, when he had finished.

'I am offering you everything I have to give,' said Everard, very seriously.

'It isn't enough,' said Kate, and turned away.

Everard begged to know in what he had fallen short, whether she cared for anyone else, only just stopping himself from saying Another.

Kate, her face averted, made no reply.

'May I ask you again?' said Everard.

'Oh, yes, when you know what to say,' was Kate's answer, and she went into the house, leaving Everard ill at ease. He took from his pocket a piece of tissue paper containing the spray of honeysuckle, now looking nastier than ever, gazed nostalgically upon it, made as if to throw it away, and put it back in his pocket.

Tea was even quieter than lunch. Swan and Morland, though it was happily not yet in their nature to feel grief for long, had been genuinely shocked by the news, obligingly and without very much tact communicated to them by Lydia. They said Hacker was composing

247

valedictory verses in Greek and had some secret about Gibbon which he would not tell them. Philip, roaming about the neighbourhood in a state of personal grief and literary dementia, dropped in to tea, and added to their gloom by talking about Russia, for which country he seemed suddenly to have developed an inexplicable distaste.

'I always thought it sounded a horrid place,' said Colin. 'Why don't you come to Austria with Noel and me?'

'How long do the posts take?' asked Philip.

'Oh, I don't know. A couple of days at the outside. Much less by air-mail.'

'I was thinking,' said Philip, 'that if my proofs did come, they would take ages to be forwarded to Russia.'

'And when they did get there they'd probably be confiscated,' said Noel.

'Good God! so they might,' said Philip. 'That settles it, I shall cancel my Russian trip.'

'And come to Austria?' said Colin.

'I'd love to if no one minds.'

'I think it would be great fun,' said Noel. 'And perhaps we'll go and meet Carter in Hungary with his young charges.'

Kate looked up, startled, but said nothing.

Colin got an atlas, and the four men gathered about it, pushing aside cakes and fruit, elbows on the table, discussing, arguing, laughing.

'Come on, Tony and Eric,' said Lydia, 'let's take the boat up the backwater. Last time we went there it stuck, and we had to get out and push, and I got up to my knees in black mud, and Colin pulled up a stick that was marking a wasps' nest in the bank, and we had to run as fast as we could, and got into the field where Farmer Brown keeps his mad bull, and didn't get back for ages.'

On hearing of this attractive programme, Swan and Morland said they would get their bathing things and be back in a moment. Kate, entirely neglected, could bear it no longer, and went out onto the terrace. That Everard thought of her as a kind of superior matron she had long suspected, and now it was only too plain. When he had showed her the honeysuckle he had kept, she had dreamed of romantic love, but all he asked was someone to mend and sew. And then, without a word, he was going to Hungary. Tears sprang to her eyes. As fast as she angrily wiped them away, so fast they welled up again, till she had no self-control left, and shaking with sobs went wildly down the garden towards the pond.

Lydia, whom Kate had not noticed, stood staring after her. For Kate, the sister upon whom everyone relied, to be in such a state was to Lydia a reversal of all natural laws. She ran back to the drawing-room and burst in, wild-eyed, upon the map-readers.

'Look here,' she said. 'Kate is crying like anything. Will you come and see what the matter is, Colin? She's down by the pond.'

'I'll go,' said Everard, and before anyone else could move he was out of the room and hastening down the garden.

Colin and Philip looked surprised.

'Hadn't we better all go?' asked Colin.

'No,' said Noel. 'Haven't you any sense? This is Carter's job. Lydia, don't leave this room till I tell you, or I'll burn all the Brownings in the house. You are now seeing romance. Mr Browning was all very well when alive, but he has been dead for a long time, and Mr Carter has taken his place. If you go down to the pond in about ten minutes I daresay you'll find him kneeling at her feet.'

Lydia drew a deep breath.

> Gosh, he will but say what mere friends say,
>> Or only a thought stronger;
> He will hold her hand but as long as all may,
>> Or so very little longer,

she said.

'A fair comment,' said Noel, legally, 'but that's quite enough, Lydia. Bless your heart, my girl, how I do like you. Mr Silas Wegg isn't in it. Put the atlas away, Colin, and after a short but decent interval we'll stroll in the direction of the pond.'

Lydia, pleased with Noel's praise and her own apt quotation, sat down, counting the minutes till the decent interval should have elapsed.

*

Meanwhile Kate, sobbing with more and more abandon by the pond, was nerving herself to face a life of stern renouncement. Never would she marry a man who wanted a matron rather than a wife. Though it broke both their hearts, as it undoubtedly would, she would never change. With low voice and hushed footsteps she would move about her daily tasks, cheering her parents in their declining years. She would be the beloved aunt of Robert's children and Colin's and Lydia's, if they married as they assuredly must, besides any more of Robert's if he and Edith happened to have any. Aunt Kate's room would be the shrine to which all the young would bring their griefs, telling her the secrets which they could never tell to their own parents. And this all seemed so awfully dull and depressing, as indeed it would truly have been, that she cried more than before. But before her long life of self-sacrifice had lasted more than a few moments it was nipped in the bud by Everard coming up, out of breath, and taking her in his arms so tightly that she could do nothing but go on crying, though in a quite different and wholly pleasant way.

'I thought,' she said presently, 'that you only loved me because I could do housekeeping.'

'I was afraid,' said Everard, 'that you couldn't possibly care for me, but I thought if you liked running a house you might get used to me in time.'

'Would you love me just as much if I couldn't do anything sensible?' said Kate.

'I'd adore you if you were as silly as Rose,' said Everard.

'I'd adore you if you were as silly as yourself,' said Kate, giggling feebly from sheer joy, and stroking his coat sleeve in a way which nearly destroyed Everard's reason, so tender it was. 'Darling,' she went on, 'your shirt cuff is frayed. I must turn it for you. Are you really going to Hungary?'

'Yes, confound those boys, I must. But I'll be back at the beginning of September. Oh, Kate!'

'Oh, Everard!' said Kate, and sat down on the stone balustrade at the end of the pond through sheer weakness.

'Angel,' said Everard. He took out of his pocket a small parcel, the worse for wear, opened it and laid reverently in Kate's hands a wilted, battered, almost unrecognizable spray of honeysuckle.

'Everard!' she breathed, holding the precious relic as if it were a living thing. Everard went down on his knees and kissed both her hands.

This rapturous sight was seen by Noel, Colin, Philip and Lydia as they came carelessly walking in the direction of the pond.

'Gosh!' said Lydia.

'Yes, that's the real thing,' said Noel. 'And I am sure you will vote with me, Lydia, by common consent, that it is no more than his due who brought good news from Ghent.'

'Browning understood everything,' murmured Lydia, fascinated by the group.

At this moment Hacker came up from the cottage, carrying Gibbon's cage.

'Please, sir,' he said to Everard, apparently not noticing his housemaster's unusual position, or not finding it worthy of his notice.

'Well,' said Everard, responding automatically to the familiar appeal, as he got up and dusted the knees of his trousers.

'Please, sir,' said Hacker, producing a sheet of foolscap, 'I've done a set of verses on Mr Lorimer. I'd like you to look at them, sir. I don't think he'd have found any false quantities.'

'That's very nice of you, Hacker,' said Everard. 'Later on I'd like to read them, but just now I'm engaged to Miss Keith.'

Hacker looked at Kate with a marked want of interest.

'Hymen O hymenaee,' he said tolerantly, but without enthusiasm. 'And please, sir, I've got something that I think would please Mr Lorimer very much. I got some black stuff from Nanny and she lined Gibbon's cage with it for mourning, and I think, sir, he's really turning black.'